A TASTE TO DIE FOR

Recent Titles by J G Goodhind from Severn House

The Honey Driver Mysteries

SOMETHING IN THE BLOOD
A TASTE TO DIE FOR

A TASTE TO DIE FOR

J.G. Goodhind

This first world edition published in Great Britain 2007 by
SEVERN HOUSE PUBLISHERS LTD of
9–15 High Street, Sutton, Surrey SM1 1DF.
This first world edition published in the USA 2008 by
SEVERN HOUSE PUBLISHERS INC of
595 Madison Avenue, New York, N.Y. 10022.

British Library Cataloguing in Publication Data

Goodhind, J. G.
  A taste to die for. - (Honey Driver mystery series ; 2)
  1. Murder - Investigation - England - Bath - Fiction
  2. Male cooks - Fiction 3. Detective and mystery stories
  I. Title
  823.9'2[F]

  ISBN-13: 978-0-7278-6577-9   (cased)
  ISBN-13: 978-1-84751-043-3   (trade paper)

All Severn House titles are printed on acid-free paper.

Typeset by Palimpsest Book Production Ltd.,
Grangemouth, Stirlingshire, Scotland.
Printed and bound in Great Britain by
MPG Books Ltd., Bodmin, Cornwall.

One

A cooking competition between quality chefs was bound to be murder. Honey Driver was sure of it.

The event was part of the Bath International Taste Extravaganza – BITE for short. Following a process of elimination the six finalists were now coming together in one place to compete for a £5,000 prize. The money was just reward, but chefs were like stags. When stags come together in the mating season they stick their antlers into each other. Chefs were worse than that; they had knives; worse again it wasn't something as trivial as sex that wound them up. It was all about cooking and no other kind of rivalry compared to that!

The day had started in the quirky kind of way days in the hospitality industry sometimes had a way of starting.

Despite the hammering of the chambermaid on the bedroom door, the occupant of room twenty had failed to rise and shine, appear at breakfast or pay his bill.

'Perhaps he's dead,' said Honey's daughter, Lindsey.

Honey was pragmatic. 'No worries as long as it's not food poisoning. It's bad for business. We'll soon find out one way or another.'

She punched in the night porter's number on her speed-dial facility. He answered groggily, not surprising for a man who hadn't long clambered into bed.

'Reg, did you see Mr Slade in number twenty come in late last night?'

'Yes. Him and his wife came back at about one in the morning.'

'I guessed that.' Honey snapped the phone shut. 'Give me your keys,' she said to the maid.

'Did he come in late?' asked Lindsey, matching her mother's marching pace up the stairs and along the landing.

'Yes. With his wife.'

Lindsey giggled. The maid looked puzzled until the penny dropped. Mr Slade, a sales manager for an IT software company, had booked into a single room. He had had no wife with him.

'What's the betting he's severely indisposed,' remarked Lindsey.

Her mother smiled wryly. 'Where did I get such a worldly wise child?'

Lindsey, just a shade closer to nineteen than eighteen, grinned wryly back. 'Under the gooseberry bush?'

'Poor Mr Slade. If my instinct serves me correctly, we'll have to do a check of the left luggage in the storeroom and find him something to wear,' said Honey as she opened the door.

Just as she had expected, the overnight occupant of room twenty was laid out on the bed stark naked. He was also bound and gagged and wearing a leather harness with little bells that jingled between his legs.

Following a swift assessment of the circumstances, she turned to Lindsey. 'How's our petty cash?'

The sales manager's clothes were gone. So were his brief-case and whatever else he was carrying. The high-class tart he'd picked up had pickled him right and proper.

'I refreshed it yesterday afternoon. I've only bought postage stamps since.'

As the maid threw a crumpled towel over the poor man's credentials, Honey checked the state of his bill from the dossier Lindsey had brought with her.

She then peered down at the bondage addict. 'We've got your name and address, Mr Slade, and we've taken an imprint of your credit card. We'll give you enough petty cash to get home and we'll find you some clothes.'

He looked up at her bug-eyed.

'Do you understand?' she asked.

He nodded and mumbled.

'That's good. So you won't be offended when we charge you the price of a double room instead of a single?'

More mumbling came from behind his gag, accompanied by a frenzied jerking of his bound hands. In consequence the towel covering his meat and two veg slipped.

Honey readjusted it, then glanced at her watch. 'Things to

do, places to go, and an impatient chef waiting. Lindsey will take care of you.'

Lindsey pulled a face. 'Thanks a bundle.'

Honey checked the storeroom halfway along the landing, a place of forgotten candlewick dressing gowns and assorted garments. Unfortunately for Mr Slade, most were women's except for a few old chefs' outfits of varying sizes. The choice was obvious; a pink candlewick dressing gown or chef's white jacket, blue checked trousers and tired white clogs.

She lay the chef's outfit outside the door. Lindsey would have to deal with the rest.

Smudger Smith, her head chef, was waiting for her at the bottom of the stairs hopping impatiently from one foot to the other. She explained what had happened. He was unimpressed.

'Silly sod! Can we get going? The kitchen's taken care of . . .'

He listed all that had been done to ensure a smoothly running kitchen in his absence. Not that it could run as well as when he was there. No chef would countenance otherwise. Like a lord of the manor, they were kings of all they surveyed. It was the cooking that counted; always the cooking.

The final cook-off was being held at an afternoon 'do' in the Pump Rooms, that epitome of Regency elegance. Everything they needed had been transported in the hotel van and installed in fridges adjacent to the competition area. Things were already buzzing by the time they got there. The atmosphere was electric.

Stainless-steel work tables had been set up on either side of the room. Only six chefs had reached the finals. Those already there eyed the new arrival with barely veiled hostility. If looks were knives they would have been throwing them.

Honey's ample chest expanded further with pride that her own chef, Mark 'Smudger' Smith, bless his cotton socks, was one of them. And he was keen. Keen as mustard. Especially when he'd heard there'd been a change of judges.

He'd arrived at the hotel early that morning and before everyone else was up and about he'd been whizzing around the kitchen like lightning, gathering pots, pans and ingredients. He'd whipped one straight out of the kitchen porter's hand, hot, straight from the dishwasher.

'Have you heard the news?' His voice and demeanour had crackled with excitement.

Honey had made a wild stab at an answer. 'All the other chefs have withdrawn because they heard you were entering.'

He'd grinned, his eyes shining. 'That's possible. OK, so what's the second best thing?'

'You've bribed the judges?'

'Getting warm.' He'd paused, enjoying the moment of keeping her in suspense. 'Casper has been asked to step in as chairman of the judging panel. Now there's a man who knows a classic when he tastes it.'

Her dear, slightly volatile – well, very volatile – chef wasn't far wrong. When it came to fastidious tastes, Casper St John Gervais came top of the tree. He adored quality and no amount of money or persuasion was likely to colour his judgement.

However, it wasn't likely to be *that* easy. 'You're up against stiff competition,' she reminded him.

Smudger Smith jerked his head in a so-so fashion. 'At least there's a chance the judging will be fair.' For no apparent reason, his expression suddenly darkened. 'As long as everyone plays fair,' he added.

That was the point when she began to get *really* apprehensive.

Her misgivings were swiftly justified the moment she saw Smudger's reaction to Oliver Stafford, head chef at the Beau Brummell Hotel. There were some people Smudger liked, some he tolerated and some he hated on sight. Most chefs and catering suppliers fitted into the second bracket; Oliver Stafford fitted into the third.

She might have been able to keep the lid on things if it hadn't been for the chicken breasts.

'Someone's been in my fridge,' said Smudger, his evil look swivelling in Oliver Stafford's direction. 'These aren't my breasts. See? They're not properly defrosted. Mine were totally defrosted. And anyway, I looked in his fridge. He had boxed stuff. Already ground-up chicken. No need to pinch mine!'

Honey grabbed his arm before he had a chance to swing over and get himself in position to slug Stafford on the chin.

'Don't! Do you want to get disqualified or do you want to win?' Swallowing her misgivings, she kept her voice even and appealed to him with her eyes.

She felt his arm relax. The anger remained, boiling in the pinkness of his face. He began cracking eggs.

'I could kill 'im,' he said, clutching his egg whisk with a murderous look in his eyes.

'With an egg whisk?' Her mind boggled.

'There are ways,' he muttered, his eyes narrowing to needle-fine slits.

Unfortunately, the object of his criminal intent was working alongside them at the next table.

Honey, not only by name, used sweet words to keep things on track. 'The dish, Smudger. Concentrate on the dish.'

'He nicked my breasts.'

Other ears might have misinterpreted quite where Smudger was coming from, but luckily no one heard.

'He just took yours by mistake.'

Smudger scowled. 'I don't believe that.'

'Lucky that we brought some spare ones.' She said it gaily in an effort to jolly him along.

The sound of meat being minced could be heard from Oliver Stafford's station. Smudger glared. Oliver smirked. He also had the effrontery to wink at her. She had no problem with that. She liked having youngish men wink at her. Cheeky. Sweet really. But the look in his eyes was bolder. My, but he was sexy. And knew it! That much was obvious.

A bell sounded.

'Let the contest commence,' proclaimed the master of cere-monies, a professional man of ample proportions, his face as red as his jacket.

The judges swept forward. There were four of them: a food writer, a television chef, an official from the tourist board and Casper.

Resplendent in a lavender jacket and crisp white cravat, Casper St John Gervais, chair of Bath Hotels' Association, was the most highly visible judge the contest had ever had. He looked absolutely wonderful. But that was Casper; always rising far above the occasion.

He slid past Honey, smelling of lavender.

'Wonderful attendance,' he murmured with a sideways shift of his mouth. 'People from all over the world.'

'They must have heard you'd be here.'

'Sweet,' he said, and glided on.

She wondered if his aftershave had been chosen to match his jacket.

Judging that the worse part of the crisis was over and that Smudger was as self-controlled as he was capable of being, she joined the gathering who'd come to watch rather than to participate. En route she bumped into Stella Broadbent, owner of the Beau Brummell Hotel. Oliver Stafford was her head chef.

When they spotted each other, smiles froze on each of their faces.

'Hannah!'

She spoke Honey's real name sharply and quickly, as though she wanted it out of the way.

Honey reciprocated. 'Stella!'

Friends would have air-kissed. They didn't. Their teeth remained bared like vampires competing to take the first bite.

As usual Stella Broadbent was wearing enough gold jewellery to sink the *Titanic*. It gleamed, it dazzled and was too over the top for the outfit she was wearing. The gold was the reason for her nickname. Bling. It suited.

Stella's smile was red and hard. 'Everything going well with your chef?'

She means I hope he drops dead.

'I think there was a mix-up with chicken breasts. I think your chef picked ours up by mistake,' Honey said to her.

The wide mouth stalled into a rictus smile. 'If he did, I'm sure it was a genuine mistake. But I doubt it. We only use ingredients of the highest quality.'

'Frozen ingredients?'

Stella was one of the early birds who'd navigated their way to the drinks table. Judging by the colour of her cheeks, she'd found it long before anyone else.

'Such accusations! I assume this means you're going to be a bad loser!' Her manner was haughty, her tone belligerent.

'I'll send you a bill.'

Stella burst out laughing. 'You'll do . . . what?'

Honey waited for her to stop laughing. Punch lines only achieved their full impact when someone was paying full attention.

'Unless you can't afford to pay for a few measly chicken breasts?'

Stella's mouth froze open. The liquid in her wine glass slopped from side to side.

'I'll send it to you.' Honey turned her back abruptly.

She could do with a drink herself after that. She was no coward, but Stella made her toes curl. That yellow and black outfit made her want to swat her with a fly whisk. And all that bloody gold. How did she afford it?

What was even worse, the Beau Brummell was one of the few privately owned hotels in Bath with its own car park. Nothing could take the beauty away from the compact city that had its finest flowering in the days of sedan chairs and carriages pulled by matching bays. But this was the age of convenience travellers. Despite all the urging to use public transport, people did not easily give up their cars. To be able to park them and wander off into the city centre was a rarity in a place like Bath. Honey told herself she wasn't jealous. Nevertheless she seethed all the way to the drinks table.

Liquid refreshments to suit most tastes were on offer. Those in the audience of a health-conscious nature could sip the iron-rich water distilled from a Georgian fountain. The Celts had worshipped the hot spring, the Romans had splashed about in it naked, the Georgians had 'taken the waters' fully clothed, and modern-day tourists drank little glasses of it. Some swore by its health-giving properties. Others just spat it out and sought more palatable alternatives.

Wine could be purchased by the glass or the bottle. Bottles went very quickly. Honey restricted herself to one glass. This was going to be a long day. That evening, stalls would be set out all around Abbey Square, and the public would be invited to sample food cooked by chefs from the city's top-class hotels. The money collected would go to charity.

Honey had promised herself that she'd keep a clear head. If Smudger won this competition he'd want to get drunk and if he lost he'd want to get drunk. She was there to channel his energies to the outdoor event, impressing on him it was the good causes that would win the day – that's if he didn't win the competition. Either way he'd be unbearable to live with. With that thought uppermost in her mind, she reached for a second glass, had second thoughts and resolved to remain sober.

Her phone rang just as the final judging was about to commence. It was her mother.

'Has he won?'

'They're just doing the final judging now.'

'Have you told Casper he should win?'

Honey closed her eyes and counted to ten. Her mother had no scruples when it came to being successful; a reason why she'd accumulated only rich husbands.

'Of course not.'

'You should. Tell him you won't do that police liaison thingy any more if he doesn't give him top marks.'

'Bye, Mother.'

She flipped her phone shut. Her mother believed you could achieve anything if you bullied hard enough. She was like a dog you couldn't have put down. Well, not without feeling guilty about it.

Casper St John Gervais was hobnobbing with the other judges. Heads together, pens poised over clipboards, they were muttering to each other, eyes sliding sidelong, rechecking their notes, everything and anything to make it look as though they really knew what they were doing. This competition was a shop window for the high-class cuisine on offer. Bath depended heavily on foreign tourists visiting the Roman Baths, the Georgian Pump Rooms and the elegant crescents and squares. Businesses, especially those in the hospitality trade, knew the power of bad press on visitor numbers.

If a show had to be put on, Casper was the one to do it. It was Casper who instigated the police 'thingy' her mother referred to, which had turned out to be more than just liaison. She'd actually got involved in a murder case and been instrumental in solving it. Most of the liaison side of things happened between her and Detective Inspector Steve Doherty, and it wasn't entirely professional. There was an undercurrent burning between them. It was just a matter of time before they lit the fuse.

It was good to have a day out. Running a hotel was not the glamorous job it was cracked up to be; all grateful clients and huge tips, celebrity guests and the champagne lifestyle. Routine was the best way to describe it. Order meat on a Monday, vegetables on a Tuesday, see the wine rep on a Wednesday, and in between lay tables, fold napkins and deal with guests who'd sampled too much Highland malt.

She'd been hankering after a second career for a while. Her

duties as Crime Liaison Officer helped alleviate her humdrum existence. So did Steve Doherty.

The four judges stopped at each table, tasted, tittered amongst themselves, nodding like donkeys dining from the same manger. Coming to an agreement, they then jotted down their deliberations.

Not once did their gaze drift from the food, their clipboards or each other to look at the chefs. All the dishes were based on chicken; the rest of the ingredients were up to each individual chef. All that mattered to the judges was the taste and presentation of the dish. Eyes, nose and mouth; sight, smell and taste. The judges nibbled, poked and prodded the meat; dismembered the dishes; sipped at the sauces using nothing bigger than a teaspoon.

At last the decision was made. Filing one after the other through the crowd of hotel owners, freelance food journalists and hungry hordes from the outside world, they made their way to a raised platform. On normal weekdays this was where a string trio played Handel for the benefit of cream-bun diners. Today there was not a cream bun in sight – perish the thought.

Honey said a silent prayer and crossed her fingers. She glanced over to a smirking Stella Broadbent and crossed her legs too. Something bad was about to happen. She could feel it in the pit of her stomach.

Casper was the judges' spokesman. Craning his long neck to reach the microphone, he bore a striking resemblance to a giraffe about to devour a large, black plum.

'Ladies and gentlemen.' His voice was crystal clear, ringing to the rococo ceiling, ricocheting off the high-arched windows. His piercing eyes swept the gathering to attention. 'The best chefs in Bath were given the task of producing a dish using chicken as its main component. They were allowed to choose the rest of the ingredients themselves . . .'

Honey looked at Smudger. His eyes were fixed on Casper, almost daring him not to pick him. Usually his complexion was pale pink; but it was presently paler than super-refined white flour.

Setting down her wine glass, Honey stuffed her fingers in her ears and closed her eyes. *What would it be? Celebration or commiseration?*

Applause filtered through her fingers. She opened her eyes

to see the top of a white toque bobbing up to the platform. Her heart sank.

Not Smudger. Smudger was about five feet ten. If he'd won she would have seen his blushing complexion and his corn-coloured hair – almost the whites of his eyes.

A beaming Oliver Stafford, five feet seven, possibly eight in his white kitchen clogs, stepped up on to the stage, accepted his prize and blew kisses at the audience.

'The best man won,' he shouted.

Applause erupted. Oliver Stafford played to the crowd, shaking men's hands, kissing those of women he didn't know, the cheeks of those he did. His eyes seemed to be everywhere. They settled on her. Again that wink, the obvious appraisal and the salacious smile. The meaning was obvious. *I'm game if you are.*

Honey looked away to where Smudger was standing clapping disconsolately, a blue, second-prize rosette pinned to his chest. If looks could have killed and cooked the corpse, Oliver Stafford would have been stewed steak.

There was no time to lose.

Turning her back on events, she pushed her way through the crowd. 'Congratulations. You did very well.'

God, that sounds lame! She rethought her strategy. 'I think you're due a bonus.'

Smudger's scowl returned with a vengeance. 'I think that bugger's due a kick in the—'

'Quick,' she interrupted, as though she hadn't heard. 'We've got to get to Abbey Green and get the best spot.'

'Clint said he'd do that.'

His voice lacked interest. His eyes were still fixed on Oliver.

Clint, whose real name was Rodney Eastwood, worked as their casual washer-upper, odd jobber and general kitchen help. He had indeed promised to grab a pitch and start setting things up, but Smudger needed to occupy himself with something other than stamping on Oliver Stafford's head.

'But you need to be there to oversee things.' An even lamer excuse.

Smudger didn't budge.

Honey looked to where he was looking. A beaming Oliver Stafford was taking a photo call, holding his silver cup above his head whilst wedged between two scantily clad blondes.

'Come on. No time to lose.'

Honey began packing things up. The knives first; they were the most dangerous. A vision of Smudger and the egg whisk flashed into her mind. She found room for that in with the knives.

'Over here, over here.'

Oliver, the blondes and a bevy of photographers and other interested parties, barged over to the row of steel tables.

'Behind the table, please, chef,' ordered one of the photographers.

Before taking up his position, Oliver kissed one blonde then the other and gave each a quick squeeze. 'Won't be long, darlings. Keep it all hot for me, won't you?'

Honey grabbed Smudger's arm. Too late. Stafford was shorter than Smudger. Smudger had hold of him by the ears.

'Let go of me.'

Some of the photographers carried on clicking.

Casper pushed through the crowd. 'Please control your chef, madam! How dare he grasp that man's extremities?'

'Smudger. Let go of his ears.'

Smudger growled. 'He should thank his lucky stars it's only his ears!'

There was uproar all round and through it all the paparazzi kept snapping. Muttering various reasons why he shouldn't disconnect Stafford's ears from his head, Honey tugged at Smudger's arm. Angry eyes glared above strawberry-pink cheeks – though they weren't nearly as red as the other chef's ears. There were only inches between their faces.

'I know what you did, Stafford, and I'll get you for it. Hear what I say, I'll get you for it,' Smudger shouted.

Finally he let go.

'He's bloody mad,' said Stafford, vigorously rubbing at his bright red ears. 'You're mad, Smith. Right bloody mad!'

Up until Stafford had opened his cake hole, Smudger had been responding to her urgings to get out.

Now he lunged again, fists ready to deal damage to the other chef's face.

Honey flung herself forward, arms out in a rugby tackle – it was not graceful – hanging on to a bloke's waist, cheek resting against a male buttock. She lost her shoes, her legs splayed out. Elegant it was not, though she must have shown some skill judging by the applause from the crowd. Banoffee Pie had a lot to do with her carrying enough weight to pull it off – quite a few pounds were down to that. Legs dragging behind her, she clung on for all she was worth.

'Come on, Smudge,' she muttered against a mouthful of starched cotton chef's jacket.

He looked down over his shoulder at her and frowned. 'Blimey, it's like being tackled by a sack of potatoes.'

'Charmed I'm sure.'

Still, she didn't let go. She daren't.

'What about our pots and stuff?' he said, his eyes still following Oliver Stafford whose overinflated ego was being smoothed by his boss. 'Bling' Broadbent's peachy complexion glowed with inner light as she tossed a contemptuous sneer in Honey's direction.

'My, my, taking defeat lying down and with your legs open. Well, that's par for the course from what I hear.'

Honey struggled to her feet. Now it was her turn to lunge. 'You bitch . . .' It was Smudger's turn to hold *her* back.

Stafford made a flamboyant gesture of dismissal. 'Bad chefs make bad losers!'

Honey felt her skin tightening. She looked hastily around her. She'd put the knives away, but what about the steak mallet? A whack in the middle of the forehead and hey presto – no more pesto from that chef!

Smudger was frighteningly calm, the kind of silent calmness that happens before a storm. She had to get him outside before the storm broke and he flattened Stafford's nose.

'Come on, Smudge. Let's get going.'

She tried pushing him. He was like a rock, totally immovable. He pointed an accusing finger at the other chef. His voice was steady. 'That prize was mine. You robbed me, Stafford. I know bloody well you did. But I'll get you; mark my words if I don't!'

Two

Emma Pearce stifled a yawn. She'd been on reception duty at the Beau Brummell Hotel since three that afternoon. It was now close to eleven p.m.; tonight she'd had to stay late.

Oliver Stafford, the hotel's head chef, had emerged victorious over a number of other excellent chefs in today's competition and the celebrations were still going on.

The sound of laughter, popping champagne corks and the reassuring clink of numerous toasts to the chef filtered through to the Reception. If past performance was anything to go by, they'd still be at it until the early hours.

Sighing and stifling another yawn, she eased her right foot out of her sensible shoe and rubbed it against her ankle. Her feet were killing her. The night porter was late but would be here soon. There was no point in asking Mrs Broadbent if someone could stand in for her. Mrs Broadbent expected her staff to stay until relieved – like tired, loyal troops holding an important bridgehead.

A blast of air came in as the main reception doors swished open.

Emma prepared to plaster on a smile before raising her head and welcoming the late-returning guest. Instead her jaw dropped.

The black man towered over her. The way he was dressed made her jaw drop.

'Good evening, miss. I have come to see my wife and claim my half of this hotel.' Grinning, he tilted back his head and looked around. 'It is very nice, yes?'

Emma tried to retrieve her jaw. She couldn't possibly say a single word until she did. Was she dreaming? She blinked hoping that if she was she'd wake up at home in bed and quickly fall asleep again. It wasn't just that the man was tall.

It was the way he was dressed – similar to that American actor who'd played an African chief searching for a bride in New York. What was his name? She couldn't think of it. She was too busy taking in the animal skin clothes and the myriad coral, white and yellow beads contained in the huge collar he wore around his neck.

He clocked her interest. 'I see you like my tribal outfit. It is Masai. Do you like my spear too?'

Emma gave the spear a brief glance as she tried to regain her voice. 'I . . .'

Her tongue stuck to the roof of her mouth.

'So where is she?' asked the man, his dreadlocks whipping around his head as he looked this way and that. 'Where is my bride, Stella Broadbent Jones? My name is Obediah Jones. We met on safari in the Masai Mara last summer on her holiday and we married there. My wife should take my name. Names times two are good, yes?'

Emma presumed he was referring to the amalgamation of Mrs Broadbent's name with his own. 'Uh . . . yes.'

A sudden explosion of laughter came from the bar. The man turned his head in that direction. 'She is there, yes?' he asked.

Emma nodded, her throat too constricted by surprise to say anything. If this was a wind-up, it was a good one. She giggled. If it was real – well, how embarrassing a situation for Stella Broadbent could you get?

He strode across to the wide double doors leading into the bar. At the same time a Japanese couple came through the front door. They'd been chattering about the play they'd just seen at the Theatre Royal. Their progress to the reception desk came to an abrupt end. Emma didn't even flash them her welcoming smile. Mrs Broadbent was not the best boss she'd ever had. Fuelled with half a dozen pink gins, she could be downright nasty or totally oblivious to what she was doing. The possibility that she'd got so tanked up that she'd married an African warrior would certainly dent her awesome arrogance.

Ignoring the gob-smacked Japanese guests, she half skipped, half ran to keep up with him.

The moment he entered the bar all sound ceased. All eyes turned in his direction.

Stella Broadbent took another swift gulp before focusing her attention. At first she looked puzzled, and then she began to laugh. 'OK, who booked the stripper? Come on. Was it you, Oliver?'

Though a smile played around his lips, Oliver Stafford's eyes narrowed. He wasn't one for making snap appraisals. 'Not me,' he said and took the cork out of another bottle.

The tall warrior strode up to Stella.

'My,' she said, looking him up and down and playfully stroking his arm. 'You're a bit skinny, but the muscles are in the right place.'

Titters of amusement ran through the onlookers.

'Wives should not talk to their master like that,' he said with a grim expression as he looked down into Stella's face. He held his arms wide and addressed the onlookers. 'We met on safari last year and married at a very pretty watering hole. I now claim my wife and half of this very nice hotel.'

There was still some laughter, but not everyone. Stella was livid.

'I know your game! You've been put up to this by the same person who daubed graffiti on the front wall and damaged our guests' cars. Who put you up to it? Go on! Tell me!'

Obediah looked hurt. He shook his head dolefully. 'I should have known when you drank from many bottles that you would deny me what is mine. But I will not argue. I do not want a woman who lies with me then drinks and forgets me. It is not good.'

The tittering of amusement ground into disbelief. Was this an entertaining moment or was this man for real? The latter view seemed to be gaining ground.

Stella Broadbent seemed to grow; all head and high-heeled shoes, face puce and eyes saucers. She inflated and then *exploded.*

'Get out! Get out! Get out!'

There was pandemonium. People shouting, laughing; some demanding that the police be called, others laughing and ordering more drinks.

The burly security man employed to deter graffiti artists came rushing in.

'That man,' Stella shouted, by now surrounded by friends and guests. 'Get him out!'

Shouted at and jostled from all sides, the security man lost his cap. In his quest to retrieve it from the floor before it was squashed flatter, his hand was trodden on. By the time he was upright, the gangly man he'd been called to throw out was gone.

'This way.' Feeling somehow responsible for the tall man, Emma got him outside.

The sound of a police siren panicked them both.

'In here,' said one of the Japanese tourists, opening the door of his car.

The police car cruised on by. The tourist, now satisfied with the evening's entertainment, left him in the car.

Snuggled down out of sight on the back seat, the tall man fell asleep equally satisfied with a job well done.

He didn't know what time it was when he awoke, only that his limbs were stiff from being folded up like a seaside deckchair.

Stretching his long legs through the open door, he peered cautiously around him. Nothing. Only a few lights were burning in the hotel.

Everything was in order, he decided as he rubbed his aching back, except . . .

His right hand was empty.

'Shit! Where's the bloody spear?' He also decided he needed the bathroom. Presuming the door to Reception was now locked and bolted, he made his way round the back and tried that one. It opened.

The smell of cooking had permeated the very fabric of the building. The tall man wrinkled his nose and hoped this passageway led into the main building.

He would have gone on through but heard voices. He pressed his ear against the kitchen door. Someone was arguing; a man and a woman.

He backed out. They might hear him. He turned and left. Outside he skirted the building heading for the front doors. On his way he saw the spear lying on the ground and picked it up. Time to go.

Stella was being a cow, but Oliver was used to it. He knew she wouldn't take the news well, but he didn't care.

'After all I've done for you,' she screamed, her eyes blazing. Before she knew it, her chin was clutched by his fingers.

'Whatever's been done I've done for myself. You were just a stepping stone. That's all.'

'All that money ; . .' she began.

There was still some fire in her along with the pink gins. She winced when he pinched her more tightly.

His eyes blazed. 'I saw the opportunity. I made you the money. I deserve better reward.'

Her chin hurt, her lips were squeezed out of shape. 'But what about me?'

Oliver Stafford had two sorts of smiles; one sort could make a woman go weak at the knees. The other could strike a chill in the bravest of hearts.

'You've had me, darling. Isn't that enough? Now it's off to pastures new. Fallow pastures you could say.'

He had a new girlfriend, someone fresher and younger than Stella. She'd been his meal ticket to more money, influential people and a better life.

'I made you what you are. I made you wealthy with my connections,' she shouted.

He eyed her sidelong, like he had when first seducing her. 'Yes, you introduced me. But I have their ears now and under my terms, I'm calling the shots. You're just their lackey. I'm not willing to remain so.'

She stared, eyes blazing. 'You'll be sorry. You mark my words.'

'And you will keep your mouth shut,' he said, pointing an accusing finger. He saw the blood drain from her face and knew that for a while she would keep her mouth shut. The trouble was that once the booze was in her, she couldn't control her tongue. It could get her into trouble. What he was up to could do the same. *But I'm cleverer than her*, he told himself. *I know how to handle them.*

He drank a toast to her after she'd gone. Today had been such a good day. He also drank a toast to Mark Smith, head chef at the Green River Hotel.

'And to his butcher,' he added. 'Nice bit of chicken that.'

Draining the glass, he threw it into the sink where it smashed to pieces. That was when he noticed a pan left in soak. A Kitchen Devil, a sharp knife used for all manner of tasks, was left in it.

Oliver scowled. All chefs were trained to put things away – especially knives. And in his kitchen, you did what you were trained to do. His expression darkened. 'You little shit. Wait till I get hold of you, Carmelli.'

He threw the knife on to the steel table where it slid and pirouetted before coming to a halt.

There was also a bag of rubbish left by the door. Carmelli would be mincemeat by the time he'd finished with him. But in the meantime . . .

His hands worked with malicious zeal spreading the rubbish out on to the clean table, rubbing coagulated gravy and fat on its shiny surface. Then he surveyed the cooking ranges to see what other tasks he could set for his errant apprentice.

He looked up when the door opened, saw who it was and said, 'If you've come to try and persuade me to knock it on the head, you're wasting your time.'

So intently was he concentrating on making more of a mess that he almost forgot about his visitor, only remembering as the knife sliced through his throat. After that, oblivion.

Smoke charged with delicious aromas had drifted across Queen Square all evening. Honey breathed in the smells deeply, then sighed. This evening had been heaven compared to the event at the Pump Rooms. Smudger had recovered – if you could count a lack of communication and a glum expression as a sign of recovery. She knew he was disappointed that he didn't win, so she did her best to take his mind off things and gave him a twenty to take himself off to the nearest bar.

She and Clint continued to run the stall, churning out steak and langoustines, pasta and pasties until a few minutes before midnight. Just as the last item of paraphernalia was loaded into the back of the van, Steve Doherty turned up.

'Can I tempt you to accompany me to the nearest wine bar?'

Her tiredness lifted. 'I'm easily tempted.'

His smile was filled with expectation. 'Good.'

They went to a little wine bar called Lautrec's just off Kingsmead Square, one of Honey's favourites. Toulouse Lautrec posters decorated the walls between gas lights almost as old as the building.

'I like these black dolphins,' said Steve, nodding at the paintings whilst the Burgundy glugged from the bottle.

Honey frowned. 'What black dolphins?'

'Those.'

He pointed at the stockinged legs of *La Goulue* and the other can-can dancers from the Moulin Rouge.

'Steve, those are dancers' legs. They're doing the can-can. Can't you see the rest of their dresses and their features?'

He looked embarrassed. 'It's just a load of scribbles – and bubbles.'

She laughed. 'Spots. Spots on a dancer's dress.'

He huffed a bit. 'Can't see it myself.'

'Are you colour-blind?'

'Of course not. Are you?'

'Women aren't usually colour . . .'

She would have gone on to tell him that women didn't generally suffer from colour-blindness, but Steve's phone began chirping like a parrot with laryngitis. Like Wyatt Earp, he was a blur of action as he got it from his pocket. If it were possible to shoot someone with a mobile, whoever was at the receiving end would have been dead by now. As it was, it was just a mobile.

They had only just started the bottle of wine, but she knew by the look in his eyes that they wouldn't be finishing the rest right now. She eyed him speculatively. His expression had changed. A dark thoughtfulness appeared in his eyes. It meant trouble.

'What is it?'

His phone snapped shut. His eyes held hers. 'We've got a murder at the Beau Brummell Hotel.'

Don't be silly, she told herself as a cold shiver ran down her back.

'It wouldn't be a chef by any chance?' she asked.

He frowned. 'How did you know that?'

'I didn't.' In her mind she was wondering where Smudger had gone. 'Just guessing,' she said with a nervous smile. 'It's been that kind of day.'

Three

Beau Brummell was a Regency buck and social climber, a Mr Fix-it to Regency gentry; whatever they wanted, he could get or fix.

The hotel bearing his name was a Victorian architectural hotchpotch of fake Florentine and birthday cake madness. It was situated in Weston Lane on the eastern side of Bath. What it lacked in Georgian elegance it made up for in amenities, chief among them being its own car park. What she wouldn't give to have a hotel car park at the Green River Hotel. But there it was; car parks weren't pencilled in on the eighteenth-century city plans.

Honey counted the cars with undisguised envy. It helped to keep her mind off Smudger, the chicken breasts and the unbridled rivalry between those two, and dare she think it, the question of murder.

'Damn the woman. She's full! Why couldn't the chef have got killed when it was empty?'

Doherty attempted to hide his amusement and kept walking. 'Just so you could gloat that she wasn't full?'

She glowered at him, noticing the smirk that was playing around his mouth.

'She would if it was the other way round. Bling Broadbent is a cow.'

'Now, now, Honey. You're on official business. Serious business. Time to put the claws away.'

'It won't matter to Bling Broadbent. She'll smile and ask how I'm doing and I'll say so-so, and she'll say "Well, actually, dahling, I'm terribly full at the moment." It's dahling when she's sober. An earful of expletives when she isn't.'

She shoved her hands in her pockets, a symbolic act that wasn't lost on Steve.

He grinned. 'This business is more cut-throat than mine.'

He didn't meet her eyes: best to plead ignorance rather than sour a blossoming relationship.

It was two in the morning and although blue lights flashed from police cars, most hotel guests continued to slumber on.

A disgruntled security guard wearing a surprised expression and a wrinkled uniform heaved a wooden barrier to one side.

A glow of amber light fell through the plate-glass doors of the hotel entrance. A policeman stood guarding them. All attention was diverted to a sign saying tradesmen's entrance beneath which a figure bobbed about like a plump hobgoblin.

'Here! This way,' said Stella Broadbent in a loud whisper. She was waving her arms. Gold chains flashed around her neck; diamonds the size of house bricks sparkled on her fingers. Her face was pink. She smelled of French perfume and strong wine.

'Bling Broadbent? I'm Detective Sergeant . . .'

Stella Broadbent's eyes fixed him with the sort of stare that could nail bare feet to the floor. 'Incorrect, sergeant! My name is *Stella* Broadbent.'

Steve apologized. 'This is a night for corrections,' he said with a wry smile. 'I should have said Detective *Inspector* Steve Doherty. My promotion was only recent.'

'Congratulations.' Her eyes narrowed and her pursed lips reminded him of the rear end of a cow.

'Follow me. The rest of your men are already here causing bloody havoc. It's most disconcerting and bloody inconvenient. *Hic.*' She turned and marched away.

Steve raised his hand in a drinking motion to his mouth and looked at Honey.

'You bet,' she murmured. Gossip was rife that 'Bling' Broadbent had relationship problems, drink problems but no money problems.

'This way,' she repeated, ushering them down the side of the building. 'I apologize for using this entrance, but I can't have you disturbing my guests. It's bad for business.' She gave a brief nod in Honey's direction. 'It's good to see that the Hotels' Association is keeping its finger on the pulse.'

Honey gave a weak smile back. 'I think we all know how important it is.'

'More important than whose chicken breasts belong to

whom,' said Stella with a haughty toss of her head. She turned back to Steve. 'My chef was threatened today by her bloody chef. He's a temperamental sod! You should arrest him right now. Stands to reason. That's who did it all right.'

Honey didn't meet Steve's questioning look. To his credit, he handled the situation pretty well.

'All avenues will be explored and anyone that ever threatened him will be questioned.'

'Glad to bloody hear it,' said Stella and hiccupped again. She threw a sour look at Honey before motoring on towards the kitchen.

'I thought you said her name was Bling,' Steve whispered as they followed the hotel owner past an army of green wheelie bins and a large bottle bank.

'Bling is what she wears,' Honey whispered back. 'Didn't you see it flashing?'

'Ah!'

Ungodly hour though it was, she flicked the numbers on her phone. Casper didn't know about this yet. Tourists getting murdered were one thing; that sort of thing really could affect trade. But the murder of chefs – even obnoxious ones – wouldn't cause a devilish fall in profits – would it? There was no reply.

The tape around the crime scene fluttered like bunting at a second-rate carnival. The police were on one side of the tape; the specialists – Scene of Crime and Forensic – were on the other.

The kitchen had a red quarry tiled floor; Honey looked for the bloodstains. There were none. So where was the body?

She craned her neck. The usual gang in jumpsuits were picking around for evidence. Centre of attention was a flat-top Falcon heavyweight commercial oven. There were two of the sturdy beasts standing side by side. The other had five burners. Saucepans could be moved from the cooler edge of the flat top to the red-hot middle, a boon to a busy chef. The last of kitchen heat hung in the air, lying heavy on the chest. So did the smell of the kitchen waste spread over a stainless-steel worktable.

The oven door on the flat top was open. A body was being eased out of the oven and into a body bag.

Had he been cooked?

No! Please!

'Careful now.'

The head of the corpse flopped back as he was lowered into place. A collar of blood seeped from a deep neck wound staining his chef's whites.

'I won't faint,' muttered Honey once she was convinced that Oliver Stafford did not resemble a well-roasted suckling pig.

'What?' asked Steve.

'Oliver Stafford,' she said.

'And Smudger didn't like him?'

She didn't answer.

Zip went the body bag.

Another mutter. 'Thank God for that.'

'For what?'

'That I didn't know him very well. I'd hate to think of anyone I know well having their throat cut.'

'My mother used to cut chickens' throats,' said Fleming, the on-duty pathologist who was already drawing his pension but keeping his hand in. 'She used to knock them on the head with a piece of wood to stun them. Otherwise they run around without their heads.'

'Is that right,' said Doherty with surprising curiosity and not a hint of revulsion. 'Never known humans to do that,' he joked.

Fleming shook his head. 'No. Different nervous system.'

Honey blinked. Did they have to be so offhand about it all? It was as though she were standing in the midst of a freezing cold cloud. Her legs had turned to clouds too; puffy and floating and no longer attached to the earth.

Steve noticed. 'You all right?'

'Is this a nightmare or is it real?'

Someone chose that moment to drop a load of knives that were being taken for testing. The clatter of steel against tiles did something to her nervous system. The cold cloud rolled away.

She found her voice. 'So you're looking for a murder weapon?'

'Looks like it,' said Steve.

Stella Broadbent's impossibly high heels came clattering down the corridor. She looked what she was; pompous, plump and pickled to the eyeballs.

'Excuse me, officer, but I do require you to be finished and off the premises before my guests come down for breakfast. Please do hurry up. There's a good fellow.'

Honey reminded herself that sensitivity wasn't part of Stella's make up. Still, at least the bad language had ceased.

Steve Doherty turned his back on her and addressed Honey. 'I think Forensics will agree that a pretty big knife was used, one with a big blade if that neck wound is anything to go by.'

Stella tugged at his sleeve. 'Don't turn your back on me, you bloody wanker. I want you to sod off. I've got a bloody business to run.'

Steve was as cool as iced cola as he turned to face her. 'Madam, if you continue to use that language I'll have to arrest you for being drunk and disorderly.'

Stella's eyelids flickered like the pop-up numbers on an old-fashioned cash register.

'But . . .'

Steve was adamant. 'Madam, you can have your kitchen back when I'm good and ready. And not before!'

She made an effort to drag herself up to her full five feet four inches. 'I don't know that I will acquiesce to your demands!'

'*Agree*,' said Honey. 'She's not willing to *agree* to your demands.'

'I know that,' Steve muttered, with a frown.

'Sorry. I thought you were having another *bling* moment.'

An angry flush seeped through Stella's rouged cheeks. 'Stop this muttering. Get out of here and arrest that obnoxious sod she employs in her kitchen!'

She made a stab towards Honey with a red-tipped finger-nail.

Steve squared her up. 'All in good time, madam. You will not tell me what to do. I will tell you. First, I want you to round up all members of staff and guests who were on the premises tonight.'

'My guests?'

Her eyes nearly popped out of her head.

'Your guests.'

'But what's it got to do with them? Most of them were asleep in their beds when this happened.'

'Then they can sign a statement saying so. If they're in bed, do it in the morning.'

Stella exhaled a deep breath, so deep she resembled a deflated beach ball. 'Right. I will gather everyone still up together in the lounge . . .'

'And your staff.'

'Yes. My staff.'

'You too. I need to ask you some questions.'

'Myself? But I'm the hotel owner.' Her head spun round as though it were fastened on a clockwork spring. 'Honey! You represent the association. Do something!'

'Stella,' she said, adopting a soothing, sugary tone even though it threatened to choke her. 'Look at it this way. Make a statement in your own hotel or make one down at the police station. Imagine if anyone sees you down there! What are they going to think? Your social standing will be ruined for ever.'

Stella's eyelids fluttered nervously.

Honey continued, her voice becoming as gooey as melted toffee. She was enjoying this. 'Now, tell me truly, which would you prefer?'

'A few questions to kick off,' said Doherty. 'Did the deceased have any enemies?'

Stella held her hand out in front of her. A huge diamond, the one Honey had thought was the size of a house brick, flashed on her finger. 'See that diamond? That's what Oliver was. A diamond among chefs. The best in Bath, perhaps even in the country. That's why other chefs hated him. Isn't that right, Mrs Driver?'

The red lips curled back from the ultra-white porcelain. It wasn't a smile, more of a snarl. Stella Broadbent had seen and heard everything that had gone on at the competition.

'I told you who did it. Speak to her chef,' she spat, one polished claw pointing at some place between Honey's eyes. 'He threatened to kill Oliver earlier today. Ask her! She knows it's true!'

'He didn't mean it like that,' Honey said to Steve. 'He was upset because Oliver had stolen his breasts.'

Steve's eyebrows jerked upwards.

'Chicken breasts. He reckoned Oliver had swapped them. Ours were best quality and theirs were . . .'

Stella sprang from a deflated crouch into a feline attack.

'How dare you! What would we want stealing from a second-rate establishment *and* a second-rate chef?'

Now it was Honey who sprang. Steve got in between them. 'Now, ladies!'

With a bit of help from other officers, the two were prevented from clawing each other's eyes out.

'Take her through there,' said Steve nodding towards the Reception. 'I'll take this one outside.'

'No fornicating with floosies on my premises,' shouted Stella as she was propelled firmly but politely out of the room.

Steve wrapped his arms around Honey, lifted her off her feet and took her outside.

'Put me down.'

He let her go. She landed with a scattering of gravel.

'Cow,' she said. 'She ought to strangle herself with that bloody gold chain. Or put it through her nose like they do with cows.'

'That's bulls,' said Steve. 'They put rings through the noses of bulls not cows.'

'Well, that one's a cow,' said Honey, thrusting her arm in the direction of the hotel entrance. A light came on in a ground-floor room. She could see right into the bar through the elegant oriole window. Stella was perched on a bar stool accompanied by a bottle of something and a large glass. She poured, drank, and poured again.

'And a lush,' she added.

Steve was disinterested. She felt his eyes on her and knew they were full of questions. She knew he'd taken on board everything Stella had said. Too many witnesses had heard Smudger threaten Oliver Stafford. But surely he couldn't be the only one. Chefs were competitive by nature. They made enemies easily. She imagined Steve's questions: How many people had wanted to see Oliver Stafford dead? Is it true that your chef threatened to kill him only a few hours ago?

Drat! She hadn't spoken to Smudger yet. Could she hold Steve off long enough to speak to him first?

'I haven't congratulated you on your promotion,' she said suddenly, smiling and throwing her arms around him. 'How would you like to celebrate?'

He eyed her accusingly. 'Are you trying to change the subject?'

She told herself not to look up into his eyes. *If you do, you're lost.* She did and she was. He had such deep-set eyes, like pools you wanted to dive into – or better still just dive into bed with the attached body.

But she couldn't give in that easily. 'Smudger didn't mean it. He wouldn't kill anyone.'

'I'll need a statement from him.'

She sighed. 'I knew you'd say that.'

Four

S mudger had an alibi – so he said. She caught up with him after having a quick word with Clint, who seemed to know the darkest dives that people might frequent; especially people he knew.

Smudger was exiting a nightclub and looking slightly the worse for wear.

She grabbed his arm. 'A word in your shell-like. Have you been in there all night,' she asked him.

'No,' he replied, shaking his head, his breath covering her in an alcoholic mist. 'I went to Sam Weller's first.'

Sam Weller's was a pub named after the character of the same name from Dickens.

'Are there witnesses that can verify that?'

He stopped in his tracks, looked at her and frowned. 'Why?'

Taking a tight grip on his arm she headed him in the direction of Manvers Street Police Station. 'Oliver Stafford's been murdered.'

He stopped and his face broke into a grin. 'Couldn't have happened to a worse bloke! Give the guilty bloke a medal. Where did it happen?'

'He was found with his neck partially severed and half stuffed in his own gas oven.'

'So someone finally cooked his goose!' He laughed at his own joke.

'It's not funny, Smudger. You were heard threatening to kill him. The police want a statement – now!'

'I've got an alibi.'

'You'd better have.'

He looked totally unfazed. 'After I left you, I bumped into Reggie Banks, an old mate of mine. He can vouch for me. We were playing pool.'

'You'd better be telling the truth.'

'Stay cool! Stay cool!'

Honey seethed, grabbed him forcibly so they were face to face. She almost shoved her finger up his nose.

'Don't tell me to stay cool! I am cool – more or less.'

He shrugged. 'What's the worry? I couldn't stand Oliver Stafford, but I wasn't the only one. I didn't kill him. Why would I?'

Honey eyed him sidelong. 'Professional jealousy? He beat you in the competition.'

Smudger made an indignant snorting noise. 'I didn't need to kill him for that. I've got nothing to prove. I *know* I'm better than him!' He grinned suddenly 'Perhaps it was someone who didn't like his cooking.'

'That's poisonous.'

'So was he.'

She shook her head in desperation. Smudger was a good chef and, like most good chefs, incorrigibly cocky.

A female police officer with glasses and acne took Smudger's statement while another took his fingerprints.

Steve Doherty came in just as they were leaving. He glanced briefly at the fingerprint sample.

'No,' he said, his eyes and experience keen enough to make a swift judgement. 'We'll have to run them through the system.'

'Of course, Inspector Doherty.'

Honey watched as the policewoman's cheeks turned pink.

'One of your groupies?' she asked Steve once the woman was out of earshot.

He grinned. 'They can't resist.'

It was too early in the morning to bring him down with a sharp comment. 'We can go now?'

'You can.' He offered up an apology as to why he couldn't give them a lift back to the hotel. 'Too busy following up leads,' he said, throwing a warning glance at Smudger who was looking far too complacent for someone who'd been prime suspect only minutes before.

She told him it was OK. They'd walk. 'We both need to clear our heads.'

Not too good an idea as it turned out. It was four in the morning and pouring down. The rhythm of the rain accompanied the sloshing of their footsteps. Her shoes were killing her and her hair was plastered to her head. By the time they'd reached the Green River Hotel, they were both wet through.

Smudger had his own flat in Walcot Street, a Bohemian kind of place where antique shops and interesting delis rubbed shoulders with small cafés and owner-occupied craft shops. It was too late for him to go home. The hotel was closer.

Circumstances, such as functions that didn't finish until after midnight, sometimes necessitated him using a room in the hotel. Sometimes he had a few drinks to unwind before going to bed. Sometimes so did Honey.

'We're having a nightcap,' she said.

'It's not night. It's morning.'

It was hardly a protest.

'Who cares?'

She unlocked the door to the bar and pushed it open. The muted smell of rich liqueurs and varied malts came out to meet her.

She handed him the Jack Daniels and took a sip of the vodka and tonic she'd poured for herself.

After sinking into the springy comfort of a leather chester-field, she set her empty glass down on the table in a businesslike manner.

'So! Who did it?'

For the briefest of moments she sensed hesitation.

Smudger's ultra-light lashes brushed his cheeks before he looked up at her.

'Do you want a list?'

'Possibly. Casper will be on the phone first thing in the morning wanting to know details and to hear what I'm doing about it. The Hotels' Association is very touchy about murder. It affects bed occupancy. And bank accounts.'

'Where do I start? I know, I'll start with saying that he was a right arrogant ba—'

'That description covers every chef I've ever known.'

His blue eyes opened wide with surprise. 'Am I arrogant?'

'Are you a chef? A good chef?'

He made a humphing kind of sound before emptying his glass.

She rested her chin on her hand, elbow on the chair arm. Her eyelids were heavy, but she was curious. Bed could wait.

Smudger looked thoughtful, no doubt giving his image a mental makeover.

Honey began to focus more on bed.

'So? Come on. We don't have all night.'

Smudger flicked a finger at his bottom lip as he thought it through. 'He was a bully in the kitchen. Now you can't say the same about me, can you?'

It was a statement not a question. A truthful statement as it turned out. The kitchen staff thought Smudger was fun. Only the suppliers felt bullied by his fastidious inspection of catering supplies – especially the butcher.

'Did he have family?'

'Married with two kids.'

'Poor soul.'

'I told you, he was a right—'

'I meant his wife. Left with two kids. What a shock.'

'Hmm.'

Hardly a word, but there was something about his tone that grabbed her attention.

'What does "hmm" mean?'

He shrugged. 'Just rumours.'

Honey took a guess. 'He was an out-and-out womaniser?'

Smudger looked surprised. 'Who told you?'

'Call it womanly intuition. A woman can tell.' She knew all right. She'd been married to one. Carl Driver had hired a female crew to help sail his fifty-foot yacht. Sailing mid-ocean can get boring. He'd needed something nice to look at; something to do.

'Really?'

'By the tone of your voice. Anyway, gossip travels fast in Bath.'

She'd heard nothing, but someone was sure to know. Smudger was being cagey. She would have quizzed him about it, but her eyelids were getting heavy and her head wanted to assume the horizontal position.

She yawned. Never mind. Her weariness began to get the better of her. She lay back barely aware that her head was sinking lower on to her hand and that her elbow was slowly sliding along the back of the settee.

She didn't hear Smudger shuffle off to bed. She didn't even hear the early shift coming in to prepare breakfast or the guests descending the stairs, lured by the smell of grilled bacon and Cumberland sausages. She heard nothing until the trilling of a ringtone permeated her right ear.

At the same time as blinking herself awake, she tried to work out where she'd left her phone. It took a few more seconds of blinking before she realized that she'd been using her handbag as a pillow and her phone was inside it.

'Hello?'

There was no answer at first – a matter instantly rectified once she'd turned it the right way up.

'Where are you?'

She recognized her daughter's voice.

'I'm in the bar.'

'I thought you'd stayed out last night.'

'No. Here I am.'

'Right.'

The line went dead.

The door to the bar wasn't usually opened until mid-morning. Lindsey, bless her, didn't enquire as to why her mother was lying semi-comatose on a couch in the bar at the same time as bacon and eggs were cooking.

Her worried face appeared around the door.

'Mum, I need to talk to you.'

Honey blinked herself to wakefulness. A couple of match-sticks would have helped, but she didn't smoke so none were close at hand. She imagined they were stapled awake and they obeyed.

It might have been her imagination, but Lindsey looked a little drawn, a little too white even for breakfast time.

Honey pretended to study her reflection in a gilt-edged mirror. She looked as though she'd been dragged through a hedge backwards, her hair lank and lifeless and her mascara smeared across her cheekbones.

'I look as though I've died overnight. Do you think I look forty-something – or fifty-something? Better still thirty-some-thing, though I suppose that's a bit much to hope for.'

Her eyes slid sidelong to the edge of the mirror, the frame and the girl pacing the carpet.

Lindsey was fiddling with her hair, her eyes darting all over the place.

Something was wrong. A mother knows when it is. Over

the years Honey had learned not to rush things. She wouldn't pry. She wouldn't hound her daughter into telling her everything. The aim was to avoid ending up sounding like her own mother. Softly, softly approach was best. Give her time, she'll tell you all about it.

Lindsey began to speak, though haltingly. 'Everyone's . . . talking about Oliver . . . you know, Oliver Stafford. He was murdered last night.'

'So I hear.'

Lindsey looked down at the floor. Honey guessed she was chewing at her bottom lip, just like she'd done when she was ten and had hung a school bully up on a coat peg.

A sense of foreboding trickled down her spine. 'What is it?'

Without lifting her head, those lovely eyes looked up at her from beneath a jagged, tulip-petal fringe. 'I think the police will want to question me.'

The trickling sensation became a mountain torrent. She didn't ask why the police would want to talk to her. Heart thudding in double-quick time, she waited for Lindsey to continue.

'Well,' she said, settling herself back on the chesterfield, nerves on edge, but her expression controlled as she waited for her daughter to continue.

'I knew Oliver Stafford – quite well as a matter of fact.'

Honey nodded as she took it in, knowing instinctively that she was not going to like what was coming next. 'Knew in the biblical sense?' she asked, desperately keeping her voice even.

Lindsey sat down in the chair opposite, legs tightly together, hands resting on her knees.

An unidentified emotion surged in Honey's chest. Anger? Shame? She didn't know.

'You bloody fool!'

At last Lindsey raised her eyes. 'I didn't know he was married. I chucked him when I found out.'

'When?'

'Two months ago.'

'When did it start?'

'Three months ago.'

Honey groaned and hid her face in her hands.

A member of staff tapped at the door. 'Mrs Driver. There's a policeman here.'

'I'll be right out.'

'He wants to talk with Miss Lindsey.'

Five

They gathered in the small conference room at the end of the first landing.

'Any lead on the fingerprints?' Honey asked Steve.

He shook his head. 'That kitchen's like a bus station. Everybody's in and out and their fingerprints are everywhere. None on the knife either, except for those belonging to the deceased.'

Honey asked Lindsey why she'd been attracted to a smoothy like Oliver Stafford. The effort of trying to control her emotions made her voice sound taut even to her own ears.

'He liked history,' Lindsey answered.

This was not quite the answer Honey had envisaged. She couldn't stop her jaw from dropping. 'And that was what attracted you to him?'

Lindsey sighed and gave her that look, the one teenagers seem to have borrowed from their grandmothers; the one that reminded Honey that they shared the same size bra cup.

'Mother, adult relationships are about people having things in common; a bit like you and Steve.'

Honey exchanged a brief glance with Steve. 'OK, yes, we've got crime in common . . .'

'No, you're roughly the same age and I suspect you both have a collection of Abba LPs hidden away in a cupboard.'

'That's beside the point,' said Steve, his expression bereft of familiarity; face taut, jaw firm. 'It's you that's got questions to answer.'

Honey noted the pinkness in his cheeks and touched her own. Hot. Guilty as charged.

'This is about you and this Oliver Stafford.' Honey turned suddenly to Steve Doherty. 'Will she need a lawyer?'

Steve opened his mouth to answer. Too late, his response

was halted by the opening of the door. 'What's going on here? Who wants a lawyer? What for?'

A cloud of French perfume preceded the entrance of Honey's mother, Gloria Cross. She was wearing a linen dress of Italian design cinched with a brown leather belt at her oh-so-slinky waist. Hell of a looker for a septuagenarian.

'Look,' said Steve, a little snappy now because he hadn't yet got round to asking a single question. 'All I want to do is get you to answer some questions about Oliver Stafford; how you met, what he told you, and who his friends were.'

'This sounds interesting. Shift up,' said Gloria, pushing her rear into the spot between her daughter and granddaughter. 'Has my granddaughter turned into a femme fatale?'

'You don't need to be here,' said Steve.

'Of course I should be here,' she retorted. 'I've watched *NYPD Blue*. And *The Sweeney*. I know your sort, Doherty, and I won't have my family being intimidated!'

Steve adopted his good, very, very good cop mode. 'Look, ma'am, all I want to do is ask Lindsey a few questions about the murder victim.'

'Murder? Who got murdered? And don't call me ma'am,' she added, fixing him with a warning frown.

Steve rolled his eyes.

Honey went ahead and explained. 'A chef's been murdered. The one who beat Smudger in the competition yesterday.'

'Is that so? He must have been very good indeed to have beat Smudger.'

Honey interjected without thinking. 'Don't let Smudger hear you say that. You know how temperamental he can be . . .' She groaned. The words had come tumbling out before she could stop them. She leaned close to Steve and whispered in his ear, 'Can you forget I said that if I'm very nice to you later?'

Steve sighed, closed his eyes and rubbed his temples. 'Your attempt at bribery is noted though I'm too dog-tired to write it down. Can you make the being nice after I've had an afternoon nap? In the meantime, a cup of coffee would be good – black with plenty of sugar.'

Honey would have sympathized if Lindsey hadn't been involved. She wanted this over and done with. 'Sod the coffee. You're supposed to be taking a statement.'

He yawned. 'Have pity, Honey. I've been on duty all night.'

'I insist you take my daughter's statement.'

The pad and pen he'd brought with him were in danger of sliding out of his lap. He clutched at them with aching fingers before they escaped.

Grandma picked them up, phoned for coffee then sat herself back down between her daughter and the policeman.

'Right. Let's start at the beginning,' she said, brandishing the pen and pad. 'What made you get involved with this jerk in the first place?'

Lindsey glanced at her grandmother, but spoke directly to her mother. 'As I said, he told me he was something of an amateur historian and you know how I am with history.'

Honey thought of all the times Lindsey had gone to lectures on the Tudors and concerts of medieval chamber music when her peer group were getting legless and laid in nightclubs.

She said, somewhat disparagingly, 'I'm curious to know his chat-up line; what was it? Come and see the size of my codpiece?'

'Costume matters,' said Honey's mother. 'I get turned on by costume drama; did you ever see that Jane Austen adaptation when Colin Firth comes out of the water all dripping wet and his trousers sticking to his loins. My, you could see everything. And then Sean Bean playing Sharpe. What was he like? Especially from the rear; the best butt I've ever seen—'

Honey found her patience failing. 'Mother!'

'Am I digressing?'

'Worse; you're fantasizing.'

After checking Steve Doherty's half grin, she turned back to Lindsey. 'Right, let's start from the beginning. You didn't know he was married?'

'No, I didn't want to get involved with him, but he was such a charmer. And how many men do you know who are interested in history?'

Honey thought. 'John Rees. The guy who owns the bookshop in Rifleman's Way.'

'He's ancient.'

'He's two years older than me,' growled Honey through gritted teeth.

'I know quite a lot of men who are interested in history,'

said Gloria Cross. The most ungrandmotherly looking grandmother had a faraway look in her eyes.

Honey groaned. This was getting them nowhere. 'Mother,
the men you know are *part* of history.'

Her mother drew air up her nose with all the ferocity of a
psychotic vacuum cleaner. 'Hannah, I shall leave if you insult
me.'

Recognizing an altogether vitriolic tone in the way she
pronounced Hannah, her given name, Honey apologized. She
attempted to get her thoughts in some kind of professional
order – professional as in Honey Driver super sleuth, not
Honey Driver hotel owner.

'Sorry. Lindsey, what Steve would have asked if he hadn't
been so rudely interrupted, is where were you last night, say
between the hours of eleven and one?' She held her breath as
she awaited the answer.

The moment Lindsey smiled, Honey feared she was in for
a stark revelation. Why could teenagers sometimes make you
feel as though you were younger than them – or worse – about
to become a permanent resident in an old folks' home?

'Mother, I was here. You were out gallivanting with Smudger
and I was holding the fort. Mary Jane can vouch for me. She
was reading the Tarot cards.'

Mary Jane, ex-resident of La Jolla, Southern California,
was a doctor of the paranormal who had touched down in the
UK on a regular basis for years but had since decided to stay.
Her reason for making the Green River Hotel her place of
residence was the fact she claimed that one of her ancestors,
Sir Cedric Dixon, frequented the place. He'd been dead for
nigh on four centuries but didn't seem to know it yet. Perhaps
he might have done if Mary Jane would stop conjuring him
up at the slightest opportunity.

'Well, that's good enough for me,' said Grandma getting to
her feet. 'Mary Jane may be a little eccentric, but she always
tells the truth.'

To Honey's ears it sounded a bit of a contradiction, but she
gave it no mention. Lindsey's revelation had left her feeling
let down. She couldn't stop the anger. She couldn't face the
disappointment of not knowing, not being told. This sort of
thing happened to other people's daughters. Not hers. Not her
beloved Lindsey.

Steve chose that moment for his head to fall against her shoulder. He was sound asleep.

The women looked at him. Lindsey carried on. 'By the way, Casper phoned.'

'Oh! The word's got round.'

'He asked you to call in when you're passing.'

Honey bit her lip. Casper would want to know the details of the murder.

She cupped Steve's face in her hands and laid his head back as she got to her feet. 'I'd better get round there.'

'What about him?' Lindsey jerked her chin at the sound-asleep policeman.

Her mother thought about it. 'He's quiet enough.' She took the notebook and pen from her mother and placed it back in his lap. 'Wake him up when he starts snoring.'

'Are you going to see Casper?'

'Yes. And then I'm off to ask Bling Broadbent a few questions. That cow! Do you know her car park was full last night?'

Lindsey smiled ruefully. 'Now, now, Mother. Remember to play nicely.'

'I'll play rough if I have to, and talking of rough . . .'

Doherty's jaw dropped open and a resounding snore erupted from his open mouth.

'Shall I . . . ?' asked Lindsey.

Honey shook her head. 'Not yet. Give me a head start. Then wake him.'

Six

On her way to the underground garage where she parked her car, Honey conjured up how best to put 'Bling' Broadbent in her place. Arresting her on suspicion of murdering her own chef would be good. The delicious vision of wiping that supercilious smile from Stella's bright red lips would not go away. A citizen's arrest! Unfortunately she had no evidence to support that particular theory except that she'd heard the rumour that Stella was a middle-aged nymphomaniac. Jealousy was always a good reason for murder.

As she folded her legs into her car, she daydreamed that Smudger had won the BITE competition. Now that would have sent the woman heading for cover! Stella was one of those people who *had* to be like the Christmas fairy, always on top of the tree looking down her nose at everyone else.

Her reverie was interrupted by yet another call from Casper.

'I need you here . . .' He spoke low, deep and slow, the last word as drawn out as the string on a bow.

'I'll be right there as soon as I've spoken to Bling, I'm sorry, Stella Broadbent.'

'Here. Nowww!'

There was something pleading in his voice. There was class, there was confidence, but today there was also something else. Puzzlement? Confusion?

Eyes left to a notice board and her intention of calling on Stella Broadbent flew out of the open car window. Bonhams were holding an auction of collectables at their premises on Old King Street. Clothes were included. Collecting antique clobber, especially antique underwear, was her great passion. Her eyes stayed fixed on the notice board.

She spoke into her hands-free phone. 'I won't be long.'

'Honey? Honey?'

A car pulled off the single yellow lines in Queen Square and she pulled into it, turned off the engine and locked up. Like a bear following a honey trail, she dodged the traffic to the other side of the road and into Bonhams.

'More voluptuous underwear, hen?' asked the Scottish clerk behind the counter. His smirk of approval was lost within the confines of a bright ginger beard.

The last time she'd been in Bonhams, she'd purchased a particularly large pair of undergarments, said to have been worn by Queen Victoria. Alistair remembered the purchase. He knew what items interested her. He knew what everyone collected.

She paid for a catalogue.

'Anything interesting?' she asked as she thumbed through the shiny pages. If there was anything, the employees of the company would have spotted it. Experience equals grandstand knowledge.

'I did see a very nice pair of garters fashioned from French lace and festooned with ribbons in a particularly fetching strawberry shade.' He spoke slowly and eloquently, the richness of his accent turning the verbal equivalent of flat pancakes into fruit-filled Genoa.

'You sound as though they quite took your fancy.'

Standing at six feet plus in his lace-up shoes, Alistair smiled through his thick red beard. 'Not for me, hen. I would have preferred blue myself – to match my eyes you understand.'

'Anything else?'

He clapped his hands over his breasts. 'A pair of salmon pink Berlei's from the fifties.' He used his finger to describe them. 'Sewn round and round, and round into a conical shape, just like the ones Madonna used to wear at the height of her career. Only bigger. Much bigger.'

Her phone rang again as she headed into the auction room. Bidding had already started. She didn't have time for a proper look round so would have to trust Alistair's judgement. The garters came first. Bidding started at twenty pounds, a ludicrous amount for apparel never likely to be seen.

Bidding climbed steadily. There was a middling crowd. If she craned her neck she'd see who she was bidding against. But she wouldn't. Bidding called for deep concentration. All that mattered was getting what you came for.

She waited until the bidding reached thirty-five before going in at forty.

'Forty. Do I see forty-five? Forty-five anywhere? Now, come on. These were said to have been worn by a dancer at the Windmill Theatre in London. During the war it boasted that it never closed. Got to be worth more surely?'

The auctioneer's eyes scoured the room for a potential punter. No one stepped in. She smiled. The garters were hers.

'Going once, going twice . . . Fifty, madam? Fifty pounds. A fresh bidder at fifty pounds.'

Honey bid fifty-five. The other party bid sixty. Honey bid sixty-five. Her rival bid seventy.

Seventy? For a pair of faded garters?

Despite the condition of the intriguing items, she might have pushed the bidding further if her phone hadn't rung again.

'I need you here right now!'

Casper!

'Casper, there's just one more lot—'

'Honey. I have a man here who I think you should speak to. Remember, my dear, you're the one liaising with the police on behalf of the Hotels' Association. Do I have to remind you of the benefits . . . ?'

Perks came with the job. She got priority bookings via the committee, recompense for involving herself in tourist-related crime. 'I'll be right there.'

She sighed. So much for the garters. There was still hope for the salmon pink brassiere with conical stitching.

Alistair had come out from behind his counter and was standing at the back of the room. She knew he would be bidding on behalf of people who for whatever reason couldn't be there. It was a fair bet none of them were involved in a murder investigation.

She handed him her bidding card. 'Last bid for lot one hundred and thirty-two. Go up to fifty for the Victorian christening dress and ten pounds for the satin corset.'

'Och! You couldn't resist the brazier could you, hen.' His lips grinned. His eyes remained fixed on the auctioneer.

'No, I couldn't. Aren't you going to ask me if I'll be wearing them?'

'Oh, no. You won't be doing that, hen. Not unless your breasts are considerably more than an honest man's handful. Though you could use them as a bowling ball carrier . . .'

Her eyes widened. 'That big?'

He nodded. 'What the Germans would call a *Büstenhalter*.'

Enough was enough. 'Don't bother.' She grabbed the ticket from the bunch he was clutching and tore it into shreds.

'See you, hen,' said Alistair, his eyes still fixed on the auctioneer and his head nodding in time with the bids.

Casper's hotel, La Reine Rouge, was a stone's throw from Pulteney Weir and a pleasant walk from the auction rooms.

A party of Dutch kids on a school exchange trotted past chattering happily as though they were the only people in the world. Whether they noticed the grandeur of their surroundings was questionable. They were away on a jolly and that was all that mattered.

She darted between people aiming digital cameras and barely missed being run down by a hire car driving on the wrong side of the road. The driver wound his window down.

'Excuse me, can you tell me where the Pump Rooms are?'

She pointed round into Quiet Street. 'That way, but you'll have . . .' Too late. The window was wound up. The last she saw was the car mounting the pavement barring its access to Quiet Street. Horns were blowing. People were shouting. Quiet Street was far from quiet.

Never mind. The air was balmy, summer was here and everyone was out enjoying themselves.

Neville, Casper's head receptionist, was on duty behind the highly polished mahogany desk. Honey glanced at her watch as a brass-faced grandfather clock struck eleven. So did the wall clocks lining the stairs to the upper floors. Casper collected clocks.

Neville was resplendent in a red silk waistcoat embroidered with birds of Paradise. Regency style was *de rigueur* at La Reine Rouge, suiting the ambience of the elegant building. The tourists loved it.

He never gave her the chance to say good morning. 'If you think this is a flamboyant outfit,' he said, pointing to his waist-coat and tight breeches, 'wait till you get downstairs.'

The phone rang and he picked it up. He plastered his hand over his mouth before attempting to answer the phone and pointed to the stairs leading down to Casper's office.

Intrigued, Honey made her way down, knocking before entering the subterranean suite that served as offices.

The first thing she saw on entering was Casper's worried expression.

'My goodness. You look as though you'd seen . . .'

Casper's visitor rose from his chair.

Honey's jaw dropped. Her head tilted back to accommodate the man's height. A six feet seven man dressed as a warrior? He was also carrying what looked like a spear. An assegai? She was looking at an honest to goodness Masai warrior. In Bath. A tourist?

She heard Casper clearing his throat. He probably couldn't believe it himself.

'This gentleman tells me he has important information regarding the murder of Oliver Stafford.'

Honey nodded slowly whilst she tried to find her voice. Now it was her turn to clear her throat.

'Is that so . . .'

'Call me Obediah Jones,' said the man. He offered her his hand.

'Right!'

She found her voice in time to say hello and pleased to meet you without sounding too stupid.

'Do you think we can sit down?' she said, her neck already aching from having to adopt such an acute angle.

'Certainly.'

His accent was negligible which was not what she'd expected.

'And this evidence, Obediah, can you tell me exactly what it is?'

The multi-coloured beads festooned around his neck jangled when he nodded. 'Most certainly. I heard my wife arguing with Mr Stafford. She was calling him many rude names and threatening to destroy him if he didn't continue to "play ball".'

Honey stared. She looked at Casper for help. He looked just as shocked as she felt. Bath welcomed tourists from all over the world, but Masai warriors were definitely a bit thin on the ground.

'And your wife is . . . ?'

'Stella. The story is that she was on safari and I was the guide for the group around the Masai Mara. We married in Africa, but she pretends that it never occurred. I followed her back here to claim my rights.'

'That's wonderful!' said Honey with delight.

'Not so wonderful. I was paid to do it.'

'That figures.'

'But I overheard this argument.'

'He's given me the details,' said Casper, a perplexed look sullying his usually calm expression. He related a few details.

'I can't go to the police about it. You see, I shouldn't be here. My work permit has run out.'

The truth was obvious. He wasn't a real Masai warrior, just a very tall man dressed up to look like one.

Honey asked the obvious question. 'Who paid you?'

He shook his head. 'I cannot divulge my client's particulars. It's private.'

Honey took a deep breath and reminded herself that this was a serious business. Murder was involved, plus the reward of substantial bed occupancy at the Green River Hotel for taking on the job in the first place. 'And you definitely heard her threaten Mr Stafford?'

'I managed to sneak through. I heard her screaming at him to do as she said. There was no security guard on duty when I arrived. I think he was asleep – at least at first. And then he was not.' He frowned. 'The guard appeared quickly. But I hid.' He explained about his escape into the car.

Honey made a mental note to have a word with the security guard – that was after she'd had a word with 'Bling' Broadbent.

'You have to tell the police,' said Honey.

A sense of panic moved him. 'You tell them,' he said, backing towards the door. 'I don't want to get involved. That's why I came to see you and not them. '

'Do we have your address?'

'I'll be around.' He was gone, the door swinging behind him.

'Oi!' Honey raced after him whilst Casper reached for the phone.

Once outside, she looked up and down the crowded street. There was no sign of Obediah Jones. Traffic was flowing well. He could have jumped into a taxi or even on to a bus. Steve Doherty would have to deal with it. They had to find him again. They also had to find out whoever had paid him to dress up.

Seven

The atmosphere between mother and daughter was subdued. They were each carrying out their duties around the hotel efficiently, only speaking when the need arose and never, ever, alighting on the subject of Oliver Stafford. The relationship rattled between them. It had happened but both were having difficulty dealing with it.

Getting out cleared Honey's head but because this case was so personal, the details never ceased to whirl in her mind.

She and Doherty were having a lunchtime drink in the public bar of the Garrick's Head next door to the Theatre Royal. Just for once it was Honey who had called him to arrange the meeting.

'His wife could have hired a hit man,' Honey said.

'It's possible. Or Mr Mark Smith could have done it.'

'Nooo!' She said it emphatically and low. 'Not Smudger. Anyway, his alibi checks out.'

'For the most part. Did you know he visited Stafford's wife on a regular basis?'

Honey looked away. She hadn't known about her daughter's relationship with that rat Stafford, and she hadn't known about Smudger's relationship either. It rankled that neither her daughter nor her chef trusted her with their secrets.

'I'll take that as a "no",' said Steve. 'How are your hotel bookings?'

'Great.' She continued to admire the Regency decor, the old posters and pictures of stars who'd trod the boards of the old theatre. The famous Sarah Siddons and David Garrick himself had played to packed houses in Regency times, and Sarah Bernhardt and Lily Langtry at a later date. The big names still came, taking a break from the stage with a gin or two.

Honey knew she was dwelling on this case, but she couldn't

help it. Even if Casper wasn't putting bookings her way as reimbursement for police liaison, she would still be doing the job. But should she be? Was she neglecting her family – notably Lindsey? She wanted to find Stafford's murderer for no other reason than to serve her own misgivings. The high-flying chef was a sexual predator; that alone could have resulted in his murder. No stone must be left unturned. After that? Well . . . she'd wait and see how she felt.

'You need more fun in your life,' Steve said suddenly.

Still with her eyes on her drink, she nodded. A thought occurred to her and suddenly she began to smile.

'Any luck tracing our Masai warrior?'

He shook his head. 'I don't think Obediah Jones is his real name. Your friend Stella and her premises have been the target of a hate campaign for some months. Someone's responsible for it all.'

'They most certainly are.'

'Never mind. We'll find him.'

'First stop, a few questions at the Beau Brummell?' she asked brightly.

'Did I invite you?'

'No. I invited myself.'

Eight

The Beau Brummell Hotel always struck Honey as a three-star building striving for five-star excellence. She admitted she was biased. She loathed Stella Broadbent. Couldn't stand her. Not at any price.

And the bitch had a car park.

The car park was covered with honey-coloured gravel. Today it dazzled under bright sunlight. Honey put on her sunglasses.

'The sun's not that bright,' said Steve.

'I'm doing it to protect my eyes from Stella's jewellery,' she growled.

A few hire cars were parked out front. So was Stella's sporty Mercedes alongside a white Rolls Royce.

The same security guard was still in situ looking less surprised and more wakeful.

'You back again?' He was making an effort to sound welcoming, but it came across only grudgingly.

'Yes. To see you,' said Steve, flashing his warrant card. 'You haven't made a statement yet.'

The man shrugged his bulky shoulders. They were rounded and heavy like the rest of him; not so much a good physical specimen as a very large one.

'I didn't see anything.'

'You were here all night?'

'Yes.'

The man's eyes flickered. Honey noticed and pounced. 'But you must have taken a leak. Or supper? Or fallen asleep?'

He turned on her. 'I didn't fall asleep.'

He sounded defensive. She knew he was lying. His complexion turned apple red.

'I want a statement from you,' said Steve, pointing at him with a stabbing action.

The big man seemed to shrink in size.

'I can't wait to see her face when we mention Obediah,' said Honey as they approached the entrance. 'It's the stuff of tabloid journalism – middle-aged woman acquires warrior husband . . . I know it's not true, but . . .'

'Honey, behave yourself or I won't let you stay.'

'Did you say stay or play?' She nudged his arm.

'Behave.'

Stella was in Reception. Honey had the impression she'd been waiting for them, watching as they'd questioned the security guard.

'I have a few more questions,' said Steve, once the formalities were out of the way.

She studied her watch. 'Well, I can only spare you twenty minutes. I'm interviewing for the post of head chef you see. I know it may sound a bit mercenary so soon after Oliver's death, but I am off on holiday in two months and need to have everything running smoothly by then.'

Honey sucked in her lips to stop herself from bursting out laughing. 'Where are you going?' she managed to ask.

'Borneo to see the orang-utans. I'm very keen on conservation. One can adopt or sponsor an orang-utan, you know.'

'How romantic.'

Stella's wonderfully made-up face never gave into expressions – especially nervous ones. It cracked into a smile on occasion, mostly when she was taking the money of overcharged guests. She tried to smile now. It still came across as nervous.

'Perhaps we'd better go into my private lounge.' She said lounge as though she were swallowing a lozenge. 'Perhaps you'd like to wait here,' she said to Honey.

Honey's smile was for real. She was enjoying this. 'Oh, no. I'll come in too. I need to hear the evidence and I particularly wanted to ask you about . . .'

'Best you stay here,' said Steve with a warning look.

Honey was left gaping. *How could he do this to her?*

'I've got no time to make you coffee, so don't ask,' said the receptionist. Her tone was as plumy as her uniform. The name emblazoned on her breast, Perdita Fordingby, only added to Honey's perception of the type of person she was.

Honey plastered on a smile. 'Your congenial hospitality is quite overwhelming.'

The receptionist sniffed and flapped some papers. 'Well, there you are then.'

It was obvious the meaning was lost on her.

'Perhaps you threw it in the waste bin,' Honey remarked over her shoulder.

The girl frowned at the papers she was holding and looked around her. 'What?'

'Your brain,' said Honey, and went outside.

Now what?

The nose of a butcher's van poked out from around the side – just below the sign saying 'Tradesmen's Entrance'.

The driver came out and got in. One careful owner description wouldn't apply to this particular vehicle. Chippings flew up from beneath the squealing tyres as he accelerated from 0 to 40 in half a second.

'Oi!' she shouted as a sharp stone hit her on the cheek. 'Ow!' She gingerly touched the sore spot and felt blood. The flow trickled down her cheek. 'Damn.'

She was wearing a taupe top with a contrasting white collar. Two minutes and it was likely to turn polka dot. Loath to reacquaint herself with the smug-faced receptionist, she headed for the entrance to the storerooms and kitchen. From her last visit she remembered there being a staff toilet in the vestibule outside the kitchen. She could wash the blood from her face there.

Muffled conversation came from the other side of the kitchen door. She pushed open the one to the toilet, turned on the water and dabbed at her face. The water turned pink. She looked for a paper towel to staunch the blood. There was none. Toilet paper? None of that either. She spotted a pillow and a sleeping bag rolled up in the corner. A slow smile spread over her face. She'd been right. The security guard had been lying.

She still needed something to staunch the blood, so headed for the kitchen, knocking on the door before going in.

A chef and a man of around sixty wearing a denim shirt and matching jeans stopped talking and looked at her. Honey gave them both the once over. The chef was wearing a red bandana around his head instead of the traditional toque. The other man was trying to be something he wasn't. His shirt was too small for his robust flesh. So were his trousers and the toupee that sat like a pancake on top of his head. In short, this was a man who overate on a regular basis and saw himself as Stan Laurel rather than Oliver Hardy.

Piles of vac-packed meat sat on the table in front of them. At the other end of the table were round white tubs. She glanced at them and saw the handwritten labels.

Coronation Chicken. The chef had been batch cooking. Four days' supply of the tubs would go into the cooked meats' fridge for immediate use. The rest would be frozen down and brought out when needed.

Her attention returned to the two men. The older man looked determined; the younger looked intimidated, as though the other guy had said something he didn't want to hear.

'Sorry,' she said. 'But there are no paper towels in the loo – or any paper at all for that matter. I've cut my face.' She lifted her fingers momentarily to indicate the bleeding.

The chef handed her a piece of kitchen towel. 'What happened?' He sounded genuinely concerned.

Honey explained. 'The driver of the butcher's van is out to get a place on the Ferrari racing team.'

The big man in the toupee faced her. 'Do you mean my van?' His whole demeanour was bluff and blunt.

'Are you Roland Mead, meat trader?'

'Aye.'

'Then I do. That driver's a maniac.'

She felt the big man eyeing her with sceptical disdain, one eye narrowed. The other eyeballed some point between her chin and eyebrows, as though seeking a secret doorway into her brain. He seemed to weigh things up before speaking. Sympathy wasn't on the menu.

'If you're looking for compensation, you'll get nowt from me.'

He spoke in a broad Yorkshire accent – or it could have been Lancashire. Honey had never been too hot on northern accents. He turned to the chef. 'Give me a call if you want to reconsider my suggestion and I'll sort things out.'

He threw her a warning glare before exiting the kitchen through the opposite door.

'What a charming man.'

'*Not!*' said the chef, a dark-eyed, dark-haired youngish man. The name embroidered across his chest in flowing script said Richard Carmelli.

Italian in looks, Italian in name.

'I take it that's his Rolls Royce out front?'

The chef grimaced. 'Well, it certainly isn't mine. Not on the wages I get here. Do this, Richard. Do that, Richard. How about a rise, Mrs Broadbent? Certainly not, Richard.'

'Yep. That sounds like Stella. Generosity has never been her middle name.'

She wondered if Oliver Stafford had asked for a rise after winning the competition. Could Stella have slit his throat in one sober, angry moment?

The young chef interrupted her thoughts.

'Is your face all right now?'

She dabbed with the kitchen towel at the sore spot and looked at the results. 'It seems fine.'

'Good. We've had enough blood spilt on this floor.'

It was impossible to tell by his tone whether he was glad or sorry that Stafford was dead. She chose to take the negative line.

'I take it you didn't like Oliver Stafford.'

He nodded. 'That's about right. And I've got the scars to prove it.'

'Are you serious?'

'The man was a jerk. Ask his wife.'

Asking his wife anything was something she would try to avoid and not just because the poor woman must be upset. Her own daughter had been one of the 'other women'. Even though Lindsey had been innocent of knowledge of his marital status, it made her angry; angry at Lindsey, but also angry with Oliver. And then there was Smudger. She still hadn't got up the courage to ask him about his relationship with Oliver's wife. There seemed to be enough on her plate at present.

'He had this thing about being superior to any other chef in the city,' Richard went on, pacing backwards and forwards to the open fridge with bundles of the vac-packed meat. 'That meant taking anything they valued – and I'm not just referring to recipes.'

Honey frowned. 'I'm not with you.'

Richard picked up another pile. 'Wives. Girlfriends.'

'You're joking.'

Richard shook his head. 'Oliver had a big appetite – not for food mark you. He took care of his health and went to the gym and all that stuff – when he could fit it in. He wanted *things*. The trappings of success. Money, flash cars and women. Material Man; that was our Oliver. He wanted to prove to the world – or rather other chefs – that he was better than them in every possible way. Oh . . . and he was a bully.'

Honey jumped when he slammed the fridge door. There was no need to ask Richard whether he'd been the victim of Oliver Stafford's tantrums. Actions spoke louder than words.

'Where were you on the night he died?'

Richard stopped transferring the meat to the fridge and laid his palms flat on the stainless-steel table top.

'That bastard came back here, crowing about beating the pants off the other chefs. He'd been drinking champagne with Mrs Broadbent and was full of himself and left me to tidy up before going off to drink some more. He reckoned he was going places and the likes of me wouldn't be allowed in his kitchen. He started pushing me around. Once he'd gone off to do more partying, I shoved off home. I'd had enough.'

Honey remembered the mess in the kitchen. 'Is there a witness who can verify that you went home?'

He nodded. 'Two witnesses. The security guard and my girlfriend, Sasha. We've got a bedsit in the Old Dispensary.'

'Why do you think he was boasting like that?' she asked him.

Carmelli grimaced. 'He reckoned he'd played his cards right and was becoming a partner in the hotel. I couldn't see it myself. Why should he be?'

Why should he indeed? Honey looked at the table. Some packs of meat remained.

'You've forgotten some.'

'That's pork. They're stored separately to steak.'

'The Coronation Chicken smells nice.'

'It's not as good as you think. Oliver made it. I'm ditching it and making my own. Have some. Compliments of the house.'

She thanked him. Because 'the house' was Stella Broadbent, she wouldn't normally have accepted it. But Richard had such a captivating smile.

She tucked the tub into her bag. The bag was a wonder; she could hide a puppy in there. The bag came with her everywhere. 'You were saying?'

'Oliver. Yes.'

She sensed he wanted to get Oliver Stafford and all that he'd stood for off his chest.

'The chefs whose girls he was knocking off, were any of them competitors in the cooking competition that he won before he died?'

'Brian Brodie's wife. It didn't stop Brian from hanging around Oliver's coat-tails though. Oliver was Brian's role model. Poor sod!'

She left a beat before asking the young chef the pertinent question, the one that might cause him to grind his teeth or use the 'f' word. 'How do you feel about not getting Oliver's job?'

Turning to face her, Richard Carmelli cocked his head – a sure signal for sudden or deepening suspicion.

'How come you're so curious?'

She thought about blustering, but decided to speak the truth. 'I liaise with the police on behalf of Bath Hotels' Association.'

Abject realization came to his face. 'Oh! You work for Smudger Smith – sorry – I mean Smudger Smith works for you.'

Far from needling her, the comment had hit on a well-known truth; a hotel and restaurant's reputation depended largely on its chef.

She smiled and decided she couldn't help liking this young man. 'No need to apologize. It does seem the other way round on occasion.'

'Right.'

She sensed her source of information was closing down. It occurred to her to offer him a job at the Green River if anything came up, but decided now was not the appropriate time. In any case, she'd have to ask Smudger.

'Thanks for your help.'

'No problem.'

'Thanks for the kitchen towel.'

She asked if Oliver had been confident about winning the competition.

Richard nodded. 'He was before he heard that Casper had replaced Sylvester Pardoe. Pardoe's good, but Casper is fastidious. Nothing gets past him.'

He was absolutely right. On his death Casper could donate his taste buds to science, they were that sensitive.

'So why did Pardoe opt out?'

'Couldn't say. Sorry. Have to go. Work to do.'

She couldn't help feeling she'd been dismissed. She also couldn't help noticing that Richard's attitude towards her had changed suddenly. She made a mental note to check out Sylvester Pardoe.

After she'd gone, Richard Carmelli glared at the last packs of meat sitting on the table. His fingers tightened around the knife handle. He hadn't meant to say that much. He certainly hadn't meant to mention Sylvester. Now he regretted it. *Damn! Damn! Damn!*

He thudded the knife into the meat again and again. Blood oozed out through the jagged openings, ran across the table and dripped on to the floor. It spattered his fresh whites; it flicked up into his face. Once the packs were no more than a sodden mess, he threw down the knife, rested his elbows on the table and dug his knuckles into his eyes.

Nine

It was mid-afternoon and Honey Driver was in the centre of Bath beating on Casper's door. Not literally of course; she was merely entering the elegant foyer of La Reine Rouge intending to ask Casper for Brian Brodie's address and also that of Sylvester Pardoe, the two names Richard Carmelli had mentioned.

Her mother had arrived at the Green River Hotel just after lunch, full of information about her latest beau and his white Rolls Royce. It wasn't the first time her mother had found herself a guy. Her demands were minimal when it came to character or age; as long as they were rich and still breathing she didn't give a hoot.

In her haste to escape the gory details, Honey had grabbed the first pair of shoes she laid her hands on and raced out. They were the wrong pair, too high and too pointy. Now her feet were killing her.

Her phone caused her to hesitate between the outer and inner doors of La Reine Rouge to answer it.

'You've got the brazier,' said Alistair, the clerk from the auction rooms.

Her immediate vision was of a cast-iron tripod contraption with a receptacle at the top to take the burning coals.

'Not me, Alistair. I didn't bid for any brazier. I've got central heating.'

'The upper-decker wobble checkers. The *Büstenhalter.*'

The cone-shaped monstrosity, fifties brassiere, the cup sizes big enough to take a pair of prize-winning turnips or tenpin bowling bowls.

'Alistair, you've made a mistake. You saw me tear that slip up.'

'Sorry, hen. You must have torn the wrong one up and I

was a bit too busy to notice. You've got yourself a brazier big enough to fit the Fifty-Foot Woman!'

This was not good news. Yes, she collected old-time under-wear and conical-type bras had come around in recent years. Take Madonna. She'd worn one, though not a pair like these. From what Alistair had told her, no one could look sexy in *this* particular pair, with the possible exception of a Jersey cow.

No point in arguing. 'I'll be round for them.'

First, the information. The fact that Oliver Stafford had been a ladies' man didn't surprise her. She remembered the look of him; average height; solid, trim build; classic features; come-to-bed eyes; mightily self-assured and oozing sexuality. A Mr Super Stud, especially in his own eyes.

Thinking of him set her teeth on edge. How many women had he seduced? She shuddered at the thought of it, not because of the number; but one of those females concerned her. Lindsey. She didn't stop to ask herself whether she should tell Steve of her conversation with Richard Carmelli. Sod him! He'd blanked her out at the Beau Brummell Hotel just because she had wanted to make 'Bling' Broadbent squirm. Now it was her turn. She wanted to find Oliver's killer before Steve did, though she'd still need his help. If she trod carefully she could do it.

She'd asked Steve what Stella Broadbent had said about the Masai warrior.

'She confirmed what we'd already guessed, that someone hired him from a strippergram agency and that it was all a huge joke.'

'And where is our intrepid warrior?'

A lock of hair fell over his eyes when he shook his head and made Honey tingle.

'Don't know,' he said. 'Someone was out to make her look stupid. Apparently she'd been experiencing a lot of that kind of thing, you know – wrong deliveries, guests not turning up, parties of school kids arriving for cream teas.'

Honey couldn't help smirking. Stella's upmarket hotel and school kids were worlds apart.

Casper was perusing a copy of the *Western Daily Press* when she was ushered into his presence by Neville.

'Have you seen this?' he demanded without looking up, his tone strident and none too pleased.

She didn't wait for a chair to be offered but sat herself down. She sighed. 'Well, it's only to be expected that it would make the front page.'

The paper rustled indignantly as Casper reappeared. 'But that's just it. We have most certainly *not* made the front page.'

Honey frowned and screwed her head to one side so she could get a look at the front page. The headlines were there: Prize-winning Chef Found Murdered.

'Yes, it is.' She dabbed her fingertip at the headline.

Casper sniffed disdainfully and fixed her with an accusing glare. 'I meant the competition results. No mention of Bath International Taste Extravaganza until page three, and then only a few oddly chosen words. Grande Epicure chef wins local award. *Local* award! How dare they? And on page three!'

Honey raised her eyebrows at the series of exclamations. It was on the tip of her tongue to quip that topless models usually graced page three in the tabloids and that it could be an advantage. Some people had got into the habit of automatically turning to page three, though such models were confined to the nationals. Provincial papers didn't go in for things like that. They had a reputation to maintain, besides the likelihood of giving their more senior readers a heart attack.

She sighed and decided to get straight to the point. 'That's what I wanted to talk to you about; the competition. I need the address of one of the chefs who took part in the final cook-off.' She got her notebook out from her bag. 'His name's Brian Brodie. I'm also interested in Sylvester Pardoe, who I understand you took over from.'

'Correct.' Using just the tips of his fingers, Casper folded the newspaper and placed it to one side. Layering his hands beneath his chin, his piercing eyes fixed her with a challenging stare.

'I don't think I need to tell you that we could do without this very adverse publicity. The committee and I had envisioned an approach from a television channel – you know the sort of thing – cook something up in twenty minutes from basic ingredients. They tell me such programmes do very well. As I am not in the habit of watching television, I have to accept this information second-hand, but I presume the food tastes good enough. Not that it matters that much. It's the publicity that counts.'

'Add butter, salt, sugar and oil and anything tastes good,' Honey murmured. It was true. Every television chef she'd ever seen enriched their dishes with some or all of those ingredients.

Casper shrugged. 'Whatever. We could still be in with a chance.' Casper leaned forward, his eyes more piercing than before. 'I want you to deal with this, Honey. I want it wound up and finished with before we get a call from the BBC or any of those other wretched people.'

As usual Casper was at pains to ensure that the City of Bath's prosperity was not blighted by bad publicity. He handed over a list of names. 'Finalists and semi-finalists.'

She saw Oliver Stafford's name and address. She also saw Smudger's.

'And Pardoe?'

He almost purred the information. 'He was a judge. I replaced him.'

'But why did he opt out?'

Casper waved an elegant hand. 'Wasn't up for the job? Got last minute jitters I suppose.'

'Do you have his address?' she asked.

He sighed.

She sensed he'd scheduled their meeting to last no more than five minutes. Casper was as fastidious about time as he was about appearance. Everything had to be perfect.

He pressed a button and Neville appeared.

'Get me the folder regarding the BITE competition,' he ordered.

Neville scurried off but was back in no time. Casper passed her a piece of paper.

'Here.'

Closing his eyes, he laid his head back and spun his swivel chair. The interview was at an end.

Honey thanked Neville on her way out.

Sylvester Pardoe ran a restaurant in the Cotswolds. Instinct told her to speak to him first. The coincidence of him opting out of the judging intrigued her. She'd bear it in mind, but for now, back to her hotel.

Her feet were killing her, her toes squashed to distraction

within the wickedly witchlike toes of the spikily heeled shoes. It was a case of barefoot or a taxi and there were no taxis around.

A third alternative came jogging into view. Some clever soul had started up a sedan-chair service from the Royal Crescent and all places en route down into the city. Luckily for her a guest of La Reine Rouge had taken advantage and was being dropped outside.

Slipping her sore feet out of the instruments of torture, she waved them over.

The two men carrying the sedan chair were dressed in period costume, tricornered hats, thigh-length waistcoats, knee-length britches and white stockings. They seemed only slightly breathless. Luckily for them the trip had been downhill all the way. Just as luckily, their passenger was on the plus side of eighty and the minus side of one hundred and ten pounds.

Honey eyed the chair with curious intent. Should she? In the hope of losing weight, she made herself a promise to walk as much as possible. Bath was a compact city, surrounded by green hills and nestling at the side of the river. But it was getting close to rush hour. Traffic was building up and she'd give anything to rest her aching feet. Besides that, she needed time to think and a gentle jog home might be just the thing.

'Hey,' she said. 'Can you take me to the Green River Hotel?'

They eyed her up and down as though she were the sexiest bird they'd seen all day. For a brief moment she felt flattered until the truth hit her. They were working out whether they could lift her. She felt like a side of pork in a Guess the Weight Competition.

'It's flat all the way,' she added by way of incentive. 'Well, most of the way.'

They exchanged looks and took a few deep breaths.

'Right you are, madam,' said one of them, a ruddy-faced chap with thick dark eyebrows and shoulders the width of a decent-sized doorway. 'That'll be fifteen pounds.'

She balked at the charge calculating that a taxi would be less. A taxi would also be quicker, but not nearly so much fun. And her feet were hot – almost steaming. And there was that thinking time. Watch the crowds enjoying themselves and plan what to do next.

'OK. Fifteen pounds. And don't spare the horses.'

The man's face visibly paled. 'You don't mean that, do you?'

She shook her head and smiled. 'No. Just kidding. Take it as slow as you like.'

She paid her money, they took their places fore and aft between the shafts, and she clambered in.

The sedan chair swayed and rocked in time with the trotting bearers. The inside was lined with blue brocade. If it wasn't for the traffic wardens and fat women in tight shorts, she could almost believe she'd travelled back two hundred years.

At sight of the passing sedan, heads turned and hands scrabbled for digital cameras.

The swaying of the chair was making her seasick. Fix your eyes on a steady point; that's what Carl used to say. Carl had been a keen yachtsman. But it wasn't only the sails that had got pulled down on a regular basis. Underwear rated pretty high on his list too.

She tried taking her own advice. Nothing seemed fixed. It hadn't worked when she'd gone sailing with her deceased husband, and it didn't work now.

So concentrate on something important.

Gulping down the bile, Honey sank back against the upholstery and thought about the dead chef. What had been her immediate impression of him? Good-looking. Yes, she had to admit it. She could understand why women fell for him. She recalled the wicked wink and the way his eyes had swept over her. She'd blushed. Oh, yes, Oliver Stafford had been a charmer whose glance and sweet words could make a woman feel on top of the world. Not a woman of her age of course. Older women didn't fall for flattery quite so easily.

A shout from the street caught her attention.

'Hey, is that someone important in that there chair?'

Important? Yes! This could be fun. She'd play at being important.

Sitting bolt upright, she adopted the regal pose; nose high and hand waving at the crowd like a slowed-down metronome.

Of course I'm important, she told herself and felt her spirits soar. It was the best she'd felt in weeks.

They passed from the busier hub of the city and into Great Pulteney Street. Minutes from home. Seconds in a taxi.

Guests coming out of the Green River Hotel stopped in their tracks, staring at the liveried bearers and the swaying chair. Some ran back inside and returned with more gawping tourists.

The crowd loomed closer, cameras at the ready, batteries whirring in unison.

The bearers set down the chair. Coming to a sudden halt brought Honey down to earth.

'I feel sick,' she said as she squeezed herself out of the narrow door.

'It's the motion,' said one of the bearers. 'A lot of elderly people have trouble with it.'

She threw him a killer glare. 'Thanks a bunch.'

Suddenly Lindsey pushed her way to the front of the crowd that had gathered around the chair.

'Mother!'

'I'm all right, dear. I just need a bit of fresh air.' She patted her face and waved her hand. Her cheeks felt hot. It seemed the whole world was a carousel, spinning slowing, and she wished her eyeballs would stop pretending they were hitting tilt on a pinball machine.

Lindsey's expression was unchanged – something between exasperation and irritation.

'You might be OK,' she murmured, 'but Smudger isn't.'

Bump! Her eyeballs and everything else was back to reality. 'What now?'

'I think he's going to murder the butcher.'

'Really?'

Unbelievable.

The Davis brothers had been her meat suppliers since the very beginning. They were old-style butchers and gentlemen, and although Smudger sometimes had a go at their delivery drivers, he'd never had a serious set to with the butchers themselves. True the steaks were sometimes returned if he wasn't impressed with the ratio of marbling to meat, but on the whole things were congenial. And why shouldn't they be?

'Poor Mr Davis,' said Honey as they headed for the kitchen.

Lindsey put her right. 'Not Mr Davis. Mr Mead.'

The kitchen door swung on its hinges. Smudger appeared looking as though his head was about to blow off.

Honey prepared herself.

Smudger was red in the face and glared when she came in. 'Tell whoever the duff nut is on Reception that the next time they send a supplier into my kitchen without telling me first, I'll pickle their nuts in vinegar!'

Lindsey mumbled an apology.

Honey felt rather than saw her daughter's awkwardness.

'No nuts,' said Honey. 'Lindsey didn't know he didn't have an appointment.'

Eyes like billiard balls, Smudger glowered. 'Just don't!'

Muttering to himself, he stormed back to the kitchen.

Honey raised her eyes to heaven. *Why do I put up with it?* The answer came in parts. Number one, he was a good chef. Number two, firing him and employing another meant getting used to someone. Compatibility was important. And Smudger and she were compatible – most of the time.

She considered all this as she and Lindsey returned like smacked pooches to Reception.

Sighing, Lindsey picked up a pen, fiddled with it and poked it through her hair to an itchy spot on her scalp. She avoided meeting her mother's eyes, bit her bottom lip and looked apologetic. 'The phone rang before I could tell Smudger that Mr Mead wanted to see him. As I answered it, he sneaked through into the kitchen.'

Honey rolled her eyes. Placating difficult customers was as nothing to placating difficult chefs. Like wild animals they were extremely territorial. No one was allowed into their space without permission.

'OK, OK. I'll sneak out there and go on bended knee.'

Usually, Lindsey would have responded, saying something like, 'He's only a chef not the queen,' or 'He only bites when there's a full moon.' Today she said nothing and didn't meet her mother's eyes. Honey knew how she was feeling; neither of them showing a willingness to cross the awkward zone appearing at the time of Oliver Stafford's death and Lindsey's confession.

It was gone two in the morning and Brian Brodie sat alone at a table in his own restaurant staring at a dark spot on the wall where the damp was coming through.

He'd sat staring a lot since Oliver Stafford's murder, wondering what he should do. Was there any real point in talking to the police?

The sound of something moving in the kitchen made him shiver. He knew instinctively who it was. Flight and fight fought unequally inside him. He couldn't do either. He just had to stand and face the music, simply because there was nowhere and no one to run to.

Shaking like jelly, he got up slowly, droplets of sweat hot on his forehead but freezing instantly. His hands were moist. He rubbed them down his thighs as he stared in the direction of the kitchen. He had to go out there. He had to see. He had to explain that he wouldn't relate anything Oliver had told him.

The kitchen was warm and almost dark. By the blue hue of the fly zapper hanging in a dark corner, he looked around him. The stainless-steel equipment shone icily cold in the bluish glow. Shadows fell blackly on to the tiled floor. The kitchen was empty, and yet he wasn't sure . . .

'I've not spoken to the police,' he said, his voice tremulous and a looseness in his bowels. 'I won't say anything.'

No response. He sighed with relief, his heart hammering against his rib cage. No one. No one at all.

He went across to the oven. Tins of dough were rising prior to being baked into bread. He peered in; saw two tins were pushed too far to the back. They'd burn once the oven came on. He reached in, his head resting on his arm, half in and half out of the oven. That's when the heavy object came down on the nape of his neck, severing his spinal cord.

He lay like that amongst the proving loaves until five o'clock when the timer clicked and the oven came on.

At breakfast time, Honey was humming her way around Reception. On spotting Lindsey she felt a surge of motherly love, that old protectiveness that makes a tiger out of a pussy cat.

'Lindsey, I'm sorry . . .'

The phone rang. Lindsey pounced on it and her mother knew why. The phone ringing was like a chance to draw breath, prepare herself for home truths and all the old tears and apologies between parent and child.

Lindsey's expression altered as she took the call. Raising her eyes she looked directly at her mother.

Honey's nerves went on full-scale alert as she read Lindsey's expression. Something bad had happened.

'It's Steve Doherty. Another chef's been found murdered.'

'Jesus!' Honey closed her eyes and tried not to imagine another cut throat, another life lost.

Lindsey seemed to read what she was thinking. 'It's not the same as the other one.'

Honey opened her eyes. Lindsey looked right back at her but didn't say a word. Honey read her expression. Not the same method, she read there. But something worse. Much worse.

Ten

A t first they wouldn't let her in. 'Extenuating circumstances,' said the uniformed constable standing outside. He wouldn't let on what extenuating circumstances, but a nervous tic developed beneath his right eye when she pressed him. Never mind. She'd find that out in due course.

To while away the time she went around the corner to Bonhams in order to collect the 'brazier' as Alistair insisted on calling it. She loitered on the way welcoming the smell of greenery in Queen Square where office workers and young women with babies were sitting on the grass in the sun. The trees were rustling in the breeze and the traffic was lazy but not too congested.

An empty bench lured her into sitting down for a while. She rummaged in her bag and brought out Sylvester Pardoe's address in the Cotswold town of Broadway, a place of *haute cuisine* and high prices. OK, this was a police investigation, but there was nothing to stop her phoning him and enquiring as to the reason why he'd dropped out of the judging panel. She could say she was a journalist and not give her real name.

Strike whilst the iron's hot.

'Hello?'

The voice on the other end of her phone put her through to Sylvester Pardoe. She rattled off the lie, but wished she'd thought it through a bit more when he asked her for her name.

'Mary Jane Jefferies,' she said, and automatically gave the name of the hotel. 'I suppose you know that the winner of the competition was murdered,' she added. 'Would you like to comment as to why you withdrew? I mean, did you have a premonition that something bad would happen?'

She winced at her own lies. They sounded so lame.

There was a pause.

'Are you for real?'

Honey panicked. 'Of course I am. Why shouldn't I be?'

A pause again. She could almost feel his distrust coming over the airwaves.

'Personal reasons.'

'May I ask what they were?' Honey asked.

'No. You may not.'

The line went dead.

'Friendly,' she muttered, pushing her phone down inside her bag. What next?

It was a hop and a skip from there to Bonhams and the ugly bra that awaited her, but a few more minutes to unwind wouldn't go amiss.

A man she thought was vaguely familiar joined her sitting at the far end of the bench. Unfolding a brown paper bag from his pocket, he began to eat a crusty roll. Recognizing a free lunch when they saw one, a host of pigeons converged around his feet. One of them was more resolute than the others, attacking its comrades each time they dared dive at the same crumb it fancied.

The man laughed at their antics. She looked at him. He looked back.

'I knows you,' he said in a broad West Country accent.

Honey frowned. Did she know him? Did she want to admit knowing him? He had rustic cheeks and thatched eyebrows.

'You knows who I am,' he said expansively, spreading his hands palms outwards.

She stared blankly. *Did she?*

'Of course, of course, of course,' he said, on seeing her expression. 'You don't recognize me without me clothes.'

There was something about that statement that wasn't quite right. He was wearing corduroy trousers and a denim shirt. He wasn't *without* clothes. He was *wearing* clothes. And she didn't recall seeing a red-faced man naked – not lately anyway.

'I'm sorry?'

He reached down and retrieved something from the paper carrier bag he'd placed on the ground. He placed it on his head.

Honey recognized the tricornered hat of the sedan-chair bearer.

'Now you knows me,' he said, with a cheery grin.

'Ah, yes. Of course I do,' she said brightly. 'How long have you been in the sedan-chair business?'

'Not long. Good business though. Good lifestyle. I used to run a pub. Got fed up of that though. Good class of customers, but that don't mean they ain't no bother. We had bother all right, though not too often. You got a hotel?' he asked, seemingly as an afterthought.

She told him she did.

'Got chefs to deal with then. They can be right aggro, they can. I remember one real bad set-to. Two chefs going hammer and tongs at each other in my bar. Award-winning chefs too, they was. They'd 'ave killed each other if I 'adn't stepped in and sorted them out.'

'I can see that.' She certainly could. His broad shoulders matched his broad Somerset accent.

Her appraisal was too evident. Looking pleased as Punch, he rolled his shoulders. 'I need broad shoulders for what I do now. And they suits the costume don't you think?'

It was on her mind to say that the tricornered hat and the Marks and Spencer polyester-mix trousers didn't go that well together. He seemed to read her thoughts.

'I'm on half-day today.'

She had visions of one bearer struggling with the sedan chair all by himself.

'There's three of us. We take it in shifts. You know one of our bearers.'

He handed her a business card, the sort created by any half-decent software package.

'I do?' She looked for enlightenment on the grubby card. All it said was Sedate Sedans and gave a telephone number.

'Clint. You know. Rodney Eastwood.'

Her jaw dropped. Clint did the washing-up on a casual basis, was a bouncer at the Zodiac in the wee hours, and helped out at Oxfam when needed. She shook her head in amazement. 'How many jobs does that boy have?'

The man grinned. 'At least he works for his bread. Can't say fairer than that, eh? There ain't no shame in having more than one job. I got more than one meself. Sometimes I do a bit of furniture bumping for antique auctions, you know, lifting stuff from lorries and getting it into their auction rooms.'

A vision of voluptuous underwear sprang to mind. Lot 69 or whatever it was. Honey made her excuses to leave.

'I'll see you around some time.' Bits of his conversation – a certain bit in particular – caused her to pause.

'You don't happen to know the name of the chefs who were fighting, do you?'

'Once met, never forgotten,' he said with a jerk of his head and a shake of a finger. 'Oliver Stafford and Sylvester Pardoe. Hated each other they did. Pardoe was a regular customer. Stafford was chasing one of my barmaids.'

'Par for the course from what I hear,' she said, walking backwards before turning to head more quickly in the direction of Bonhams.

'Any time you want two burly men to pick you up, just give us a ring,' he shouted after her.

Misinterpreting what was actually being said, curiosity popped on to lunchtime faces.

Blushing like a virgin bride, she ran past the mothers with babies and the office workers with Brie-filled baguettes and Diet Pepsi. She arrived at Bonhams still red in the face but more so from breathlessness than embarrassment.

Alistair was sitting at his desk some way behind the counter.

'I came for my purchase.'

He got up slowly from his chair, stretching each limb in turn and not moving towards her and the counter until he was sure he'd reached full extension.

'I thought you might have put them into the next auction seeing as you don't want them,' he said, eyeing her in his slow, perfunctory manner.

'The thought did occur to me, but then I considered making them part of a fancy-dress outfit – you know – Madonna on Tour.'

Alistair pursed his lips and gave her what her mother called an old-fashioned look.

'You won't want to wear these, hen. Not unless Madonna has put on a wee bit of weight since her adoring fans last saw her.'

With slow deliberation, Alistair pulled the unwanted article from beneath the counter.

Honey stared. They were salmon pink and conical, ever decreasing circlets of stitching finally ending in sharp points, as unlike breast shapes as it was possible to be. And they were large. Not handsome, lustful large, but horrendous, Hammer Horror large.

She shook her head as she held them up before her face, her arms at full stretch. 'I don't know anyone that size.'

Alistair had that deadpan expression even when he was happy, or sad or just nothing. But his eyes twinkled, though his voice was flat as a pancake.

'Do you go tenpin bowling?'

'I have done.'

'Do you have your own bowls and are in need of storage bags?'

She shook her head.

Alistair shook his too.

Honey held them up at eye level and eyed them thoughtfully. 'A pair of hanging baskets?'

Alistair nodded. 'They'd take a good few geraniums.'

Eleven

Ambience, thought Honey as she entered the latest catering establishment to boast a dead chef in its kitchen. Steve had been loath to give her the details, except the name; Brian Brodie. His restaurant was the Samuel Pepys, named after the great seventeenth-century diarist.

'That's two chefs who took part in the Grande Epicure dead in suspicious circumstances,' she said excitedly, her mind working overtime. 'Two dead and one to go.'

He looked puzzled. 'What's this "Grandie" thing got to do with it?'

'Grande Epicure. It's a competition run in France for top-flight chefs. The competition's very hot. A chef would kill to win it.'

There followed a pause.

'Would they now. Was your chef one of the participants by any chance?'

She made a face. Why couldn't she engage her brain before opening her mouth? The genes, of course. Her mother was just the same.

'He had an alibi.'

'For both murders?'

She stuck her neck out. 'I'm almost certain.'

'Almost?'

Suddenly she didn't like the tone of his voice. 'I trust Smudger.' She knew she sounded defensive, but she believed in supporting her staff. This usually amounted to inter-staff disputes or customer grievances. Murder wasn't usually on the list.

Now she had something extra to tell him. Sylvester Pardoe and Oliver Stafford had had a fight.

Before leaving the Green River Hotel, she'd told Lindsey to inform Casper of the latest murder. She was expecting him to ring and had prepared herself accordingly. No sign of being uptight would filter into his voice, but he wouldn't be pleased. She'd bet a pound to a penny on that.

Her phone played a snatch of the 1812 overture, a thunderous and apt introduction for a man like him.

'Casper.'

'Are the press there?'

She glanced out at the small crowd gathering on the pavement; recognized a few freelance reporters and photographers.

'I'm afraid so.'

Casper grunted an acknowledgement. Casper St John Gervais never allowed sympathy to get in the way of practical considerations. Still, what he said next was a bit surprising.

'On the plus side the Samuel Pepys will have its fifteen seconds of fame.'

Well, that was to the point. Honey couldn't help a hint of sarcasm creeping into her voice. 'Quite so, Casper. I can just see a full-page advertisement on the Dining Out page in the *Bath Chronicle*.'

'Quite. Let me know the details tout suite.'

He rang off.

She pulled a face. She really couldn't believe that Casper *would* consider an ad for the Dining Out page. But the man was mercenary. For her part she was feeling regretful on two counts. Number one, she had just been about to make a breakthrough with Lindsey in their strained relationship. Number two, she wished she'd visited Brian Brodie before this happened.

The Samuel Pepys was a place of terracotta floors and exposed stone walls. An interior designer from a Chelsea background and the right connections had been engaged to upgrade the decor when Brodie, the chef/owner, had bought the place. Oak Windsor chairs had been replaced by designer wickerwork, stained dark tables by light oak and dripping candles by twelve-volt LED lighting.

'Must have cost a fortune,' Honey said as she took everything in.

Someone went to fetch Steve who was still exchanging details with the initial forensic team. She spent the waiting time peering at a wall-mounted menu.

British based cooking . . . emphasis placed on home-grown produce . . . free-range Suffolk chickens, Dublin Bay prawns and Wye Valley salmon and asparagus . . . happy lives . . . optimum taste.

'I doubt the chickens, prawns and salmon would quite see it that way,' she muttered, then realized what she was doing. 'I must stop talking to myself, I must stop talking to myself . . .'

'Honey. Are you talking to yourself?' Steve had been fetched quicker than she'd expected. Day-old stubble contrasted with deep-blue eyes and too-long dark hair curling over his collar. A little longer and he'd need to tie it back 'Tom Jones' style – Tom Jones the eighteenth-century rake rather than Tom Jones the singer.

Her smile was as ready-made as baked beans and not quite natural. 'Whatever makes you think that?'

His eyes ran over her like maple syrup over ice cream. 'You're looking good.'

She was wearing jeans and a sailor-type top with an interesting neckline; just a hint of cleavage rather than the Rhône Valley.

'It's the latest thing for murder scenes, straight from the Paris catwalk.'

'Nice.'

Nice was the height of flattery coming from Doherty and made her glow. It also made her fancy him more, though she wouldn't tell him that. He got too cocky if he thought he had the upper hand. Letting him know how much she fancied him would definitely be giving him the upper hand. She turned flippant. 'So what's on the menu?'

'A dead chef. Cooked to perfection.'

She pulled a face. 'Are you serious?' All her enthusiasm for telling him about Pardoe turned to smoke.

'Yep. As crisp as a turkey, though without the trimmings.'

It wasn't funny and he hadn't meant it to be. His expression was deadly serious. He had to cope with this. Being flippant helped him do that.

Honey gulped down her revulsion and followed him. They went through a door that led into a corridor with a red quarry tile floor. Halfway along another door opened into the kitchen.

The aroma of roast pork drifted out each time it swung open. She sniffed and immediately felt sick. There was something odd about it, a hint of toasted aftershave. She didn't need anyone to tell her the nature of the meat.

Steve held his arm across, roughly at the same height as the police incident tape. 'You can't go in. None of us can until this lot have done their thing.'

On the other side the Scene of Crimes people and Forensics were doing exactly that. The Medical Examiner was first to emerge. It was his job to formally state that the victim was dead, though how anyone could not be dead after roasting on gas mark 7 would be a miracle.

He spoke directly to Steve.

'Most definitely dead. Blow to the back of the head. Can't say when, but can say when his head began to cook. He was already dead when the oven came on.'

Honey felt her stomach heaving. How could anyone say that without throwing up?

Steve looked perplexed.

The Medical Examiner went into detail. 'The oven's got a timer on it. The commis chef says that it's always set to turn on automatically at five o'clock in the morning. They make their own bread you see.'

The thought of bread and the smell of roasting meat on an empty stomach was too much. Honey was vaguely aware of the floor coming up to meet her nose.

She was also vaguely aware of being hurried along the corridor.

'He got hit on the back of the head and fell forward on to a shelf,' Steve explained once she'd come round and had vowed never to eat pork ever again. She was sitting in a fashionably minimalist club chair, Steve's arm hovering protectively around her.

As her eyes began to focus, they alighted on a slim blonde with an orange suntan and a skirt that showed more than it covered. She was sobbing into a man-sized handkerchief – or it could have been a napkin. She caught herself hoping that the restaurant had a good laundry service.

Steve saw where she was looking. 'That's Sandy Brown, Brian Brodie's girlfriend.'

She recalled her conversation with Richard Carmelli, the

commis chef at the Beau Brummell Hotel, but couldn't remember the details too clearly.

'Not his wife?' Her voice sounded hollow as though she were speaking from the bottom of a rabbit hole.

His smile kind of floated in and out of her vision as he shook his head. Her eyelids felt heavy.

She sighed. 'I feel like going to bed.'

His smile smothered his face. He whispered in her ear. 'Just name the time and the place.'

She threw him a you-should-be-so-lucky kind of smile designed to put on the brakes. Her hormones were going full gallop and won the day. 'I don't suppose I'd kick you out,' she said as an afterthought. He liked that. She could tell by the way his fingers brushed against the side of her breast. And the smile. Christ, how could he smile with all this going on? That poor chef. Even at his most irritating she had never considered roasting Smudger in his own oven.

'Come on.' Steve sounded concerned.

She made a firm effort not to fall against him as he helped her to her feet.

'I'll be OK.' He looked a bit put out when she waved him away, but her attention was firmly fixed on the sobbing girl.

The male members of the team investigating the murder scene were also paying attention to the delectable Sandy. The girl's skirt stretched like a black bandage across her willowy thighs. A white cotton gusset winked with each strangled sob and the crossing and recrossing of her mile-long legs. She was wearing an off-the-shoulder white top which was too tight to be decent. No bra. Her nipples were like dark eyes peering through a fog. She was about twenty.

Sandy Brown was sitting at one end of a wickerwork sofa. The wickerwork was bronze, the cushions beige and sprinkled with gold thread. Very tasteful. And very expensive, Honey guessed.

She fingered the chair arm and the cushion before sitting down.

'It's Fiona Davenport,' said the girl, referring to the trendy sofa almost as though it were a star of stage, screen and television.

Honey made a face. 'Wow.'

'Brian liked nice things.'

It occurred to Honey to ask in more detail how Brian Brodie could have afforded the services of an interior designer whose efforts got featured in *Country Living* and *House Beautiful* magazine.

'The restaurant must have been doing extremely well.'

The sobs had turned to a well-rehearsed simper. 'The best in Bath. He did ever so well.'

But not well enough, thought Honey. Her eyes flitted over the restaurant, mentally counting the number of *couverts* and coming out at around forty. Forty at around forty pounds per head? One hundred pounds per head? And how often was the restaurant full? Generally it was safe to base the turnover rate at around twenty-five per cent capacity. But the hospitality industry was notoriously optimistic.

The girl blew her nose loudly. Honey winced. Just as she'd guessed, close up the large handkerchief turned out to be a table napkin. Not hygienic but forgivable in the circumstances.

'Was Brian ever married?'

'He was.'

'So how long had you two been together?'

'Two weeks.'

Honey inwardly groaned. 'I see.'

'His wife left him two years ago,' sniffed the girl, pre-empting Honey's next question.

'And you moved in with him as soon as you met?'

The girl pulled a face. 'Not until his other girlfriend moved out.'

Honey sized her up. She instinctively knew that this was not the girlfriend Oliver Stafford had been having an affair with. This was eye candy. Not even that. More like a cuddly toy, something dumb and cute to cuddle up to.

'Would you know who'd want to kill him?'

The girl shook her head. 'He was a lovely man.'

Steve threw her a quick nod of understanding. There was nothing this girl could say to assist them in their inquiries. Honey nodded back. Steve turned to the gathered professionals.

'Anyone available to take this girl home?'

A host of hot-blooded male Scene of Crime Officers, plus two paramedics who'd been called out and had stopped for coffee, rushed forward like a human tsunami. The paramedics won.

'You need a lie-down, love.'

They steered her towards the waiting ambulance.

Honey and everyone there looked on. 'I suppose that's what they call care in the community,' Honey remarked to Steve.

He grinned and passed her a glass of cold water poured from a blue glass bottle. He also ordered her to stay put whilst he oversaw the removal of the corpse and the reintroduction of his wayward officers to their duties.

Honey laid her head back, closed her eyes and gathered her thoughts. Two chefs dead. Both had taken part in the same competition. Only one of them had won so there was no case of jealousy to answer here. So why these two chefs? Perhaps there was going to be another competition and one chef was singling down the opposition beforehand. *Please don't let it be Smudger.*

Her thinking was disrupted.

The uniformed police guarding the door were arguing with two big pieces of brown furniture that had sprouted heads, arms and possibly even legs. She couldn't quite see from the laid-back angle, so jerked herself upright so she could see more clearly.

The police were telling the walking wardrobes that they couldn't come in. The wardrobes were talking back and saying they had every right to come in and collect their property.

Closing her eyes, she resumed the reclining position. It was none of her business. She had no rights getting involved; and then one of them mentioned the magic words.

'It's our salamander and the payments are in arrears.'

He did ever so well.

Honey shot up from sit to stand in two seconds flat and charged over to the new arrivals. Sandy Brown knew nothing.

'I'd like a word with you guys.'

The big guys turned their ugly mugs in her direction. So did the boys in blue.

'Steve Doherty will OK it,' she said to the latter.

The two wardrobes, arms bursting from the sleeves of coal

black T shirts, ambled into the restaurant. They looked her up and down.

'I'm working with the police,' she said. 'There's been a murder.'

Their chins seemed to retract into their jaws. 'That's nothing to do with us,' one of them said.

'So you won't mind answering a few questions.'

She studied them as they thought it through. They'd looked almost identical when viewed at a distance. Up front there were subtle differences. One had a cauliflower ear and the other had a broken nose.

Ripped ear exchanged a look with broken nose before proclaiming their decision. 'S'pose not.'

'How much did Brodie owe you?'

Broken nose adopted an indignant look. 'Not enough to kill for. We don't do things like that. We just repossess.'

'Yeah, repossess,' echoed his partner.

'We want the salamander.'

'Yeah. The salamander.'

They both spoke as though their tongues were too big for their mouths. And they were very round. Tweedledee and his brother Tweedledum.

'Do you know what a salamander is?' she asked them.

They looked at each other before one of them answered. 'It's something in the kitchen.'

'A grill,' she said. 'Wait here. I'll check that the police are finished.'

Luckily for the repossession guys, the salamander – chef terminology for a large wall mounted grill – was in a separate part of the kitchen that could be entered through another door so they wouldn't be contaminating the crime scene. After disconnecting the gas, the two guys unbolted it and heaved it on to their shoulders like a small coffin.

'I should be humming the funeral march,' she said to herself as she watched them progress sedately out of the door.

One of Steve Doherty's team heard her. 'Sorry. Did you say something?'

'Tell Steve I have to go, but I'll be seeing him.'

He promised he'd do that.

Despite him being busy, Honey hoped that he'd call and ask her out tonight. Depending on staffing levels, the dishwasher and whether she could find something to wear, she'd be up for that. He was in need of a night out after a day like this. So was she.

She stepped out of the restaurant, and walked along Quiet Street, a stone's throw from Queen Square.

The city air drove the smell of death from her sinuses. She thought about sitting a while in Queen Square again. That was until she saw her mother coming the other way, arm in arm with a man whose identity was vaguely familiar.

No thanks, she thought, heading off in the opposite direction and considering the possibility of turning vegetarian.

Twelve

Having avoided her mother and 'lover boy', she made for a seat in Abbey Churchyard reckoning she needed the break after what she'd been through. The smell of singed flesh still lingered in her nostrils.

Purchasing a coffee from Starbucks en route, she sat down preparing to enjoy the passing scene. It was like taking a seat at the United Nations, but without the speeches. Everyone was enjoying themselves.

A crowd of French students huddled together whilst a colleague took a photo. Their smiles were cheesy. Were they saying 'cheese' or 'fromage'? Whatever, they were interesting to watch, chic even in their youth.

Steve rang. 'Are you OK?' He sounded worried. She pictured him trying to disguise the fact. It made her feel better though slightly naughty. For a second she toyed with the idea of encouraging even more sympathy. No, not fair. She made an effort.

'Fine. No breakfast this morning. You know . . . an empty stomach and all that.'

'Get some fresh air.'

'I am. I'm sitting in Abbey Churchyard.'

'Alone?'

'In Abbey Churchyard? Are you kidding?'

'I meant close companions.'

Was he jealous? The idea was quite thrilling.

'None.'

'By the way, you dropped something when you keeled over.'

Did she? She couldn't remember and hadn't noticed. Her keys? Her purse?

'I hadn't noticed.' She did a brief rummage of her copious tan shoulder bag. Everything seemed in order.

'Hmm.'

For a brief moment she was sure she heard a trace of amusement. What the devil could be so funny after finding Brian Brodie like that?

'Never mind,' he went on. 'I'll bring it along to the Zodiac tonight – if you're up for it. I'll be there.' He sounded tired.

The Zodiac was one of their favourite haunts; subterranean and dingily impersonal. It was open until the wee hours and was a place where hard pressed hoteliers, restaurateurs and pub landlords gathered to unwind once their own businesses were closed.

'I'm afraid it's got to be later in the evening.'

'Yeah, I guessed that.'

He hung up.

There was nothing she could do about the time. During their brief relationship, he'd insinuated she was too controlling wanting to oversee everything at the hotel until most guests had gone to bed. She hadn't argued with that. Delegating responsibility wasn't her thing. If that was controlling, then that was her.

Tonight he'd brief her on what he knew so far. She wondered about Brian Brodie's previous girlfriend. Funny him being shacked up with girlfriend number two so soon after girlfriend number one had left. Seemed like him and Oliver Stafford were tarred with the same brush. Both liked to play around. What about Sylvester Pardoe? She made a mental note to check up on him as soon as the hotel and other pressures allowed.

Now what was it Steve had picked up that she'd dropped? She delved into her bag again. Nothing important was missing. Never mind. He might be mistaken.

The facade of the Green River Hotel gleamed like gold in the late afternoon. It was her favourite time of day. She looked along Pulteney Street, admiring the hard black shadows falling from one side of the street, and the honeycomb colour of buildings on the other. Mary Jane, their resident doctor of parapsychology was right. If you squinted it was easy to imagine women in bonnets and empire-line dresses, and Regency bucks in tight-fitting trousers and riding boots. The smell would be different though; waste from a horse's rear end rather than the exhaust pipe of a BMW.

Lindsey looked up from behind the desk. She managed a weak smile.

'I didn't expect you back so early.'

Her expression made Honey think she'd taken her off guard. She looked slightly panic stricken.

'Now what? What's gone wrong?'

Lindsey looked hurt. 'Nothing's gone wrong.' She sounded defensive.

Honey counted to ten and drove the suspicious thoughts away. Lindsey had made one big lack of judgement. Honey was still trying to deal with her disappointment, but it wasn't easy. She didn't mean to march so swiftly to the counter. She also didn't mean to be so obvious about trying to see what Lindsey was hiding.

'These are for you,' her daughter said, bringing out a bunch of roses from beneath the desk.

Normally Honey would have had to scrutinize a tiny booklet type of card to see who had sent her the flowers. In this instance she didn't need to. The card was flat and white and said simply: *'To my mother. With love.'*

Honey bit her lip. Dark red roses with velvety petals always brought a lump to her throat. Carl had bought her such roses back in the good old days before they'd got married. He'd bought her the same for each and every anniversary and when Lindsey was born. Then they'd stopped and bunches of indiscriminate flowers had arrived via Interflora, yellows and pinks and purples. She'd known he hadn't chosen them; knew that what had been something special had become no more than a duty.

Silently, Honey wrapped her arms around her daughter. 'I'm sorry.'

'So am I,' said Lindsey, hugging her back.

They both sniffed as they parted.

'Any messages?' Honey at last asked.

'Nothing important.' Lindsey suddenly turned all furtive, looking around her and dropping her voice to just above a whisper. 'Mary Jane wants to see you.'

'What's wrong?'

'Shh! Grandma will hear you.' She took the flowers. 'Here, let me take them. I'll put them in water.'

Honey found herself shoved into the storeroom behind

Reception. Mary Jane was sitting cross-legged on the floor. How a woman of her age ever got in such a position was a mystery. It was a wonder she didn't break something. She was in one of her trances, head back, elbows bent, hands palms upwards.

'What's going on?'

'As you are no doubt aware, Grandma's got a new boyfriend,' said Lindsey.

'Yes, and he's got a Rolls Royce. You know how she is about that particular make of car. I'm not opposed, it'll keep her off my back.'

As she made to leave, Lindsey pulled her back 'Grandma's not a very good judge of character.'

Honey eyed her daughter and paused that bit too long. Her mother stepping out with Mead the butcher was surprising. But this was no corner-shop outfit he owned. He had 'brass' as northern folk might say; warehouse interests, property and foreign supply depots.

'Anyway,' Honey added without thinking. 'We all make mistakes with men at some point in our lives. Some of us worse mistakes than others. It's probably hereditary.'

'OK. So perhaps I inherited my recent lapse from her,' said Lindsey in the glum manner she'd adopted of late.

'I'm sorry, I didn't mean . . .'

An indignant Mary Jane threw her hands up in the air, her batwing sleeves causing one hell of a draught.

'Nice flowers,' she said, opening one eye. 'However, I'd appreciate it if you guys could shut your traps. Give me silence and I'll tell you what the future holds.'

Honey shrugged at Lindsey. In response her daughter dragged her over to the door and whispered, 'Mary Jane's already done the tarot and given a verdict. She reckons Grandma's new boyfriend is up to no good. And he's younger than her.'

'Younger as in?'

'At least sixty.'

Honey heaved a sigh of relief and waved her hand in front of her face. 'Thank goodness for that. For a moment I thought you were going to say that he was forty-six.'

'I'm worried about Grandma,' said Lindsey.

'She's old enough to look after herself.'

The old saying 'There's no fool like an old fool' ran through her mind like Wall Street ticker tape.

'I don't know what she sees in him,' whispered Lindsey.

'He drives a white Rolls Royce.'

Lindsey nodded sagely. Everyone knew that Gloria Cross went weak-kneed at the thought of a man with a Rolls Royce. It proved he had the bank account to afford the fuel and parking fines.

Honey gave what she thought was a philosophical appraisal. 'Perhaps the guy's upfront and just wants a bit of company. He's not likely to be after her body at her age – unless he's an undertaker. And he's not.'

Lindsey was blunter. 'No. We know he's not. He's a butcher.'

'Butcher by trade, butcher by nature,' Mary Jane said suddenly.

Cripes! Honey rolled her eyes. Suddenly she wanted to be up on the ceiling, away from all this madness.

'I think he's got an ulterior motive,' said Lindsey.

Honey folded her arms, resigned to listening no matter what. 'OK. Shoot.'

'I think he's after our meat order.'

Thirteen

That night her mother and Roland Mead came to dine in the restaurant and, of course, she couldn't avoid being introduced.

His handshake felt warm and moist and lingered too long. His smile stripped the clothes from her body.

'I'm going to chance the steak,' he said in a way that left Honey in no doubt that he intended finding fault. 'It won't be up to my standards no doubt, but I'll be lenient in my judgement.'

His smile was wide, his toupee neatly straight, and his eyes dove down the front of her dress. Her mother seemed too enthralled with him to notice.

'My daughter's a widow too,' said Gloria Cross with surprising frankness. 'And the silly girl's had such wonderful opportunities. You would never believe how many eligible men I've introduced her to. Rich, of course. All professionals. But will she listen? No! She's like all these youngsters nowadays. They all know better than their elders.'

'Happen you're right, petal. There's no substitute for the University of Life.'

Honey cringed when he kissed her mother's hand. Bowing slightly from the waist sent his toupee tipping forward.

Her mother went off to powder her nose. 'Won't be long, my big Aberdeen Angus.'

Roland turned his attention back to her. 'Your mother likes bulls. I keep bulls – Aberdeen Angus. They're chunky, slow-growing and well-muscled.' His grin suited his trade – thick and meaty. 'A bit like me.'

'Is that so?' It was quite true that Mead was as big as a bull. The look in his eyes was pure big bad wolf.

Roland Mead had the kind of smile that's not really meant

for anyone but himself. There was a definite flicker of interest as once again his gaze dipped into her cleavage.

'Must say I agree with your darling mother,' he said, his wet tongue lashing along his slippery lips. 'You need a man. A big man I should think. One built like a bull.'

'I'm engaged,' Honey blurted out, making a mental note to have a word with her mother. *What did she see in this man? Ah yes! A white Rolls Royce.*

She wondered what her mother would say if she knew he was paying court to her. The guy didn't know who he was dealing with.

Later on she wriggled herself into a little black dress that always made her feel slimmer. Whether it *actually* did that was another matter. But never mind. Every little bit helped.

Two bubbles of fat spoiled its smooth lines just a bit higher than her hip bones. Love handles people called them. Love? Were they kidding?

She retrieved a certain item of underwear from their hide-away at the bottom of a drawer.

It's only temporary, Honey told herself. I'll lose four pounds by the end of next week. Definitely.

As she pulled on the slinky spandex, she averted her gaze from the full length mirror and flipped her mind back to basics. Was it really just a coincidence to believe that Roland Mead had wangled his way into Smudger's domain and now he was paying court to her mother?

She wasn't meeting Steve until late, so hung around welcoming guests and diners into the restaurant, one eye always on her mother's bewigged man friend.

She warned Smudger beforehand.

'He's going to order steak. You know the score.'

Smudger grimaced. 'Judge a good restaurant by its steak.'

'He's just trying to get our business.'

Smudger's jaw dropped big time and he spluttered as though about to explode. 'That bloke supplies meat to this place over my dead body!' With a loud bang, he brought a steak mallet down on to a piece of pale pink veal.

Honey retreated.

The smell of night and the lights of the city beckoned. Restaurants close to the Theatre Royal were still busy. So were the pubs, their doors wide open, their patrons spilling out on to the pavements.

As usual the eyes of the doorman at the Zodiac peered out through a slit at eye level before letting her in.

'Are you in fancy dress?'

She recognized Clint's voice.

'No. Should I be?'

'It's optional.'

'Then I choose not to participate. Let me in.'

It was quite a shock when he opened the door to see a slit of a mouth and his eyes – similar to the view she'd had through the door. Head to toe he was dressed in bandages.

Honey looked him up and down. 'Have you had an accident?'

'Course not! I'm an Egyptian mummy.'

'So I see. Have you been raiding my first-aid box?'

He grinned. 'I'd need a lot more than one box of bandages to cover me. The boss hired this for me from a proper fancy-dress place. He reckoned it suited my image.'

Honey nodded a questionable agreement. Clint had a shaved head and scary tattoos. He also wore earrings and a ring through his nose.

She made her way to the bar where she perched on a stool. Steve hadn't arrived yet. She ordered a vodka and slimline tonic. She looked down at her legs. Was this dress too short? Were fishnet stockings going a bit too far? Yep. She spied a hole a few inches above the knee.

Never mind. She took another sip of her drink then tugged at the hem of her skirt to cover the hole. It didn't do much good. Thank God for dim lighting.

The place was filling up. Despite their efforts at fancy dress, she recognized a few hoteliers. Jim Sadler, the financial director of a big hotel group, was dressed as a rabbit. A colleague – or it could have been his wife – was dressed as Alice in Wonderland complete with a blue dress and an Alice band on her head. The dress was low-cut, the skirt short. Honey frowned. She couldn't remember Alice ever having such a deep cleavage or wearing white stockings held up by frilly garters. Oh, well!

She heard laughter that wouldn't have been out of place on a hyena. She saw Stella Broadbent draped over a large player from the Bath Rugby team. He didn't look comfortable with Stella's attention, but Stella didn't seem to notice. She was sozzled and sprawled over the thick thighs that formed his lap.

The Samoan rugby player stood up. He was built like a battleship. Stella slid off him like a bundle of wet seaweed.

'Hey, big boy! You off already.' Her voice was slurred.

The rugby player stomped off, chairs and tables scraping the floor as he sidled through them. Stella's gutted look followed his progress. That was how their eyes chanced to meet.

Shit, she was coming over.

Honey took a sip of her drink and averted her eyes. Hopefully Stella's vision was on the wobble and she wouldn't see her as long as she kept her head down.

'You,' she shouted and pointed a bejewelled finger. 'You! Honey bloody Driver!'

Too late.

Stella staggered across with far less agility than the rugby player. A chair or two toppled over and one or two of the patrons she bumped into ended up wearing their beer instead of drinking it. They shouted at her to watch out. She totally ignored them.

'I want a word with you.' She spat the words. At the same time she attempted to scramble on to the next stool. Her scrambling attracted some attention. Her skirt, a really nice silky brocade number – definitely designer – rode halfway up her thighs. The height of the stool proved too much. She ended up resting her arms on it, buttocks prominently jutting behind her.

Her smudged make-up was the good stuff. Her earrings were gold, the size of toadstools and matched her necklace. Her eyes were narrowed, like a sharpshooter taking aim.

'You've been slandering both my good name and that of my establishment,' she said, making a wobbly attempt at being sober.

This was new. Slandering the woman?

'Slandering you? A woman of your expertise? No, certainly not. You're quite capable of doing that for yourself.'

Stella's brain wasn't quite in gear. She looked puzzled – vaguely aware that something profound had been said, though not quite understanding what it was.

She finally seemed to cotton on. Her look darkened. 'You've been spreading rumours that I married a man I met on safari.'

Honey picked up her drink, swirling the liquid so that the ice clinked against the glass. 'No, I was told this.'

Stella's brows beetled over her nose. 'So who told you?'

Sheer envy that this woman had a hotel with a car park made her relish the moment and take her time answering. Slowly she set her drink down. Slowly she twirled the lemon round with her finger. 'Your husband. At least, he said he was your husband.'

Stella's indignation was like a spluttering firecracker fizzing all over the place. 'He is *not* my husband!'

She said it emphatically. She said it loudly. Heads turned. Whispers passed from one curious ear to another.

Honey was relishing this. 'Are you sure? I hear these safaris are great fun – and full of plenty of booze, of course.' The colour running down Stella's throat matched her rouged cheeks. 'I did not sodding marry anyone! Someone put him up to it. You probably!'

'Not me!' Honey shook her head emphatically.

A whole sentence of nothing but expletives issued from Stella's mouth. A hushed gasp ran amongst those who'd heard.

'OK,' said Honey, indicating the crowd with a toss of her head. 'Now everybody knows.'

Stella was livid. Suddenly her anger got too much for her body. Clutching the handle of her Lacroix handbag, she swung it through the air aiming it at Honey's head. Honey ducked. The backswing of the handbag took Stella with it. She overbalanced, landing flat on her rear, legs in the air.

Honey gasped. So did a lot of other people. Some sniggered. Stella's secret was out. Beneath the designer facade, she was wearing 'fat' knickers, the firm sort designed to keep everything under control.

Accompanied by subdued sniggers, a couple of off-duty hotel managers helped her to her feet. The manager of the Zodiac also appeared, his expression as flat as a frying pan.

'I won't have trouble,' he said. His mouth clacked shut like a spring-loaded letterbox. He nodded in the direction of Clint and one of the other doormen. The latter was dressed like Russell Crowe in *Gladiator*. He didn't look like Russell

Crowe; more like a very blond Brad Pitt but giant economy size.

Cruelly self-satisfied, Honey ordered another drink and watched as Stella was carried out through the door that opened on to North Parade Gardens. The public entrance to the gardens was locked at this time of night, but there was a seat just outside the Zodiac's private exit.

Honey imagined her out there all alone – Stella the hostess with the mostest! She chuckled and raised her drink in a silent toast. Poor Stella. Sitting out there in her designer outfit until she'd sobered up.

The club got stickier as the crowd increased. A bunch of fairies complete with pink tutus, fairy wands and five o'clock shadows, trouped through to rousing applause. One of them was wearing a pair of riggers boots. Judging by the dust and dirt clinging to the soles, his day job involved getting dirty.

Faces she recognized flitted past. Some acknowledged her. Some were too drunk or too wrapped up in the people they were with.

She glanced at her watch. Steve was late. He'd phoned earlier to say he might be held up. The job was taking its toll. He'd been on duty too long. When she looked up she saw him pressing his way to the bar.

'I forgot where I left my phone,' he explained. 'Had to find it.'

She ordered him a drink and slid it beneath his hand. He looked floppy and worn out. If she'd had a heart or been twenty years younger she might have offered to firm him up a little. As it was it was getting late and she had lots to do in the morning.

'OK. Tell me all about it.'

He yawned. 'No luck with Jones the seven foot Masai warrior.'

'Don't exaggerate. He was only six three I think.'

'Big enough.'

He sounded grumpy. She reckoned it was due to the fact that he wasn't much above five eight himself. But nicely put together.

'Never mind,' she said, patting his hand. 'Big isn't everything.'

'Somebody must know where he is.'

She'd expected a more sexual riposte, but Steve blew hot and cold. She liked the hot best. His gaze wandered to the fairies, the Roman soldiers and the Jane Austen lookalikes. The latter in particular held his gaze. She could see why. Would Jane's bosom have ballooned out of a 36D cup?

Her mind ticked over as her eyes followed the swirl of crazy outfits.

She pushed her drink away. 'OK, we know the Masai warrior wasn't for real, but he must have got that costume from somewhere. It may have looked slung together, but it wasn't. So that means he must have hired it.'

Steve glanced at the mix of people and outfits. 'You could be right. I suggest you check it out. Women and clothes go together.'

She gave him a look before she accepted the mission.

'How many fancy-dress outfitters are there in Bath?' he asked her.

'One I think, and a few more in Bristol.'

'That shouldn't take you long then.'

'I kind of wanted him to be real,' Honey said.

Steve yawned again.

'You're tired.' She rubbed his shoulders. Usually he would have taken advantage of that, suggested they find a private place where she could rub him some more. Instead he lowered his eyes. Something was wrong.

'What is it?'

'I need another talk with your chef. I'll be there just before lunch. By the way. You dropped this.'

His tired bloodshot eyes glittered wickedly as he brought the conical brassiere out of the carrier bag he was carrying.

She grabbed it and shoved it into her bag.

'They're not mine – I mean I don't wear that size.'

Steve grinned. 'I know. I've noticed.'

She caught herself blushing. It was kind of nice knowing he noticed as much about her as she had about him.

Still, she mustn't lose sight of the professional side of their relationship, especially when it referred to business. Something *was* up. Had Smudger lied about where he was? Her stomach churned. She wouldn't ask him whether he had. For now, until Steve arrived tomorrow, she'd have to let sleeping dogs lie.

Stella Broadbent's eyes flickered, fluttered and flitted between shutting and opening. The world was presently a bleary place and there was no one to talk to. Why wasn't she in bed, she wondered. She couldn't remember getting ready to go out but knew she was out. She was just a bit unsure of where.

It was night time; that much was certain. The sky was black like the inside of a coal lid. The lights up on the road didn't seem as bright as usual and the facades of Regency buildings wobbled as though they were made of rubber.

'I need a drink,' she slurred.

No one brought her one. Didn't they hear? Had everyone gone home?

Her eyes flickered one more time and then shut. Unfortunately the buildings were still there wobbling around behind her eyelids. She was unaware of the stealthy footsteps, the figure emerging from the shadows. Her eyes popped open when a hand was clamped across her mouth. Her voice was stifled by another hand around her throat. She tried to scream.

Moist breath seeped into her ear. 'No talking to the police, Stella.'

She tried to say that she hadn't been talking to the police.

'Or anyone involved with the police.' It was as if her thoughts had been read. 'Leave the sauce alone and keep your mouth shut.'

The tips of iron-hard fingers dug into her throat. She felt the breath being choked out of her body, the world blackening around her.

She fought for air and, at the same time, emptied her bladder.

Just as suddenly as they'd arrived, the hands were gone. She could breathe. She coughed and spluttered taking great gasps as she tried to refill her lungs.

Huge tears erupted from the corners of her eyes taking her make-up with them. Ashamed and soiled, she struggled to her feet, terror following like a snarling dog at her heels. She ran through the passageway that bypassed the bar and went straight to the exit.

The doorman asked her if she wanted a taxi.

'I've got my car.'

She didn't see him frown. Neither did she hear him remark that she really shouldn't be driving. She had to drive. She had to get away.

Fourteen

Sleep had weighed heavily on Honey's mind – and on her eyelids. She struggled from bed at around eight, wriggling her toes into her slippers before making her way to the shower.

Water cascading on her face helped clear her head. That was when she looked down at her feet and realized her head hadn't been clear enough. She was still wearing her slippers.

Slippers in bin, body in clothes, she made her way to Reception. Smudger wasn't due in until ten.

She phoned her mother. 'Are you up?'

'Of course I am.'

Her mother sounded indignant.

'How did things go last night?'

'Not too good actually. Roland got called away on a matter of business. Someone called him from the warehouse. He had to go.'

Honey offered her sympathy though secretly thought it the best thing that could have happened. It was nothing to do with jealousy, she told herself. She was just looking after her mother's welfare.

'He's making it up to me. He's taking me for a drive in the Cotswolds.'

Honey's attention clicked in. The Cotswolds. That's where Sylvester Pardoe lived.

'Today's Wednesday. I thought Wednesday was your day for Second-hand Rose.'

Second-hand Rose was a dress shop her mother ran in conjunction with a few other well-heeled, fashionable women. Dresses and other items bought for a fortune were brought in by women who'd tired of them. The items they brought in were sold at a knock-down price, the sum received divided between the shop and the customer. Her mother never missed a Wednesday in the shop where gossip sparkled as brightly as sequins on a cocktail dress.

'I changed shifts,' she explained.

'Mother, don't you think you're getting a bit too involved . . . ?'

'Mind your own business.'

The phone went dead.

This was worrying. The dead chefs were worrying. She forced herself to concentrate and figured she was doing pretty well.

Although not quite up to speed, things were chugging along well enough – or so it seemed. Wake-up time was bound to come and it did. She had just made up a bill for a three-night stay for two Canadian guests.

The retired accountant perused his bill and raised his eyebrows. 'Hell, am I paying for gold taps in that room?'

Not quite getting the implication, Honey eyed him through narrowed, burning eyes. 'Sir, we don't have gold taps.'

'Why such an expensive bill?' he asked, pointing to the four-figure total.

Honey apologized profusely as she scribbled over the extra nought that had appeared from out of the blue.

Seeing her mother being a dunderhead, Lindsey muscled in. 'Let me do that. Why don't you go and have a lie-down.'

'I can't.'

'Try.'

They exchanged the mother–daughter look of understanding, the old warmth wrapping around the words.

She headed for the door marked private that led out to the path leading to her private quarters in the coach house. Just as she reached out to open the door, she heard that old familiar hiss; similar to the sound of a gas leak.

'Psst!'

She looked round. A dismembered head was hissing at her. The rest of the body was behind the tapestry screen dividing her private door from the main reception area.

A pair of blue eyes sparkled through layers of fine wrinkles.

'I need to speak to you,' said Mary Jane in a hoarse whisper.

A long, thin finger beckoned her to follow.

That was it. The quick nap wouldn't happen. She smiled at Mary Jane and followed her crooked finger into the lounge.

Mary Jane was tall and gaunt, favoured wearing pink and had decided she was living for ever. She'd lived in California in the hippy years and still had the pink 1963 Cadillac to prove it. The car had been shipped over just after she'd decided she was moving to England on a permanent basis. Driving on the left-hand side of the road in a left-hand drive car had proved a bit of a problem at first, but eventually both Mary Jane – and the City of Bath – had got used to it.

The conservatory was empty of other guests, but still Mary Jane's voice dropped to an octave above a whisper. 'Polly came to my room last night, hammering on my door like a demented banshee.'

Honey frowned. Did she have a member of staff named Polly? Casual perhaps? She started to apologize. 'Oh, I'm so sorry, Mary Jane. I'll look into it.'

Mary Jane's wrinkles disappeared in a look of amazement.

'Hell, no, Honey, darling! Isn't that what I came here for? Having my friends from the other side cross over to visit me? Polly's never quite got the hang of walking through walls. She still thinks she's alive and can't do any of that stuff.'

The penny dropped. Pennies dropped a lot with Mary Jane seeing as she mostly lived in another world.

The 'crossing over' she referred to had nothing to do with flying across the Atlantic. She was talking about the dearly departed who seemed inclined to drop in to see her on a regular basis.

'I'm sorry, I thought you were referring to one of the chambermaids,' said Honey as Mary Jane pressed her into a chair.

'I was referring to a maid!' exclaimed Mary Jane, her bright eyes aglow, her expression animated. 'Apparently she was a gypsy child left on the doorstep and Sir Cedric's wife took her in. And before you ask me which wife, it was his second. You know how it was with Sir Cedric.'

Honey adopted the most serious expression she possessed and nodded. Of course she knew how it was. According to Mary Jane, Sir Cedric, a man of means who'd died round about 1750, had married three times and seemed to have chased anything wearing a skirt. Mary Jane claimed to be his direct descendent.

'I see,' she said as though she'd just been told that next door's cat had got run over.

For the umpteenth time since Mary Jane had first descended on the Green River Hotel, she asked herself why she was listening to this drivel. But she kept listening; eyes wide open. Sir Cedric was their resident ghost, though not the only one it seemed. Ghosts were for ever asking Mary Jane's opinion on where they'd gone wrong in their lives. 'Sometimes I'm kind of an agony aunt,' Mary Jane had explained. 'And sometimes I'm just someone they want to impress.'

'Of course.'

It wasn't inarguable or irrefutable, just plain unbelievable. But Mary Jane was nice and she didn't want to upset her.

'Anyway,' Mary Jane went on. 'Polly is adamant that she has second sight and can read the cards and what have you. Whether that makes her a bona fide gypsy or not I don't know.'

Neither did Honey. A dead gypsy, yes, but she was saying nothing.

'Anyway, she tends to materialize in the rose garden just beside the sundial.'

Now this was something new.

'We don't have a sundial – or a rose garden for that matter.'

'You don't *now*,' said Mary Jane, her wrinkled hand patting Honey's as though she hadn't long started school. 'But back when she worked here there was a rose garden and a sundial.' She looked up at the ceiling, a normal aspect of her thought-collecting process. 'Now what was I saying? Ah, yes! She's made a prediction that someone who used to be married but isn't any longer is about to come to a sticky end. She says they're to be wary of travelling in a carriage especially if there are no horses pulling it.'

Honey blinked. 'A horseless carriage. A car.'

Mary Jane closed one eye and took a few seconds to think about it. 'A car. Yeah. I see your point.'

'Do we know the name of this person?' Honey asked her.

'She'll appear just as we say . . .'

Mary Jane's sentence was cut off mid-stream. The door swung open and Gloria Cross, Honey's mother, made her grand entrance.

She floated in accompanied by the clicking of her kitten-heel shoes. She was dressed in a light lavender outfit liberally sprinkled with hand-sewn silver rosebuds around the hem.

Honey threw Mary Jane an ominous look. Mary Jane threw one right back.

Her mother did a twirl between them and the French doors.

'Guess what? Roland is taking me to a Freemasons' lunch at Grover Park.' She paused for effect, hands together, her eyes bright with enthusiasm. 'In his Rolls Royce!'

Honey and Mary Jane exchanged more startled glances. When it came to getting divorced, her mother was a prime contender for Mary Jane's prophesy.

'You can't!' exclaimed Mary Jane.

'Do you have to?' Honey's scepticism was reflected in her tone. She didn't want to believe Mary Jane's warning, but still, you couldn't be too careful.

Her mother looked alarmed. 'Have you any idea how long it's been since I rode in a real Rolls Royce with a handsome, attentive man?'

In her mind, Honey was telling herself that Mary Jane's ghosts were just figments of her imagination. And so were their prophesies. Weren't they?

This would be a balancing act. Much as she had no wish to upset her long-term guest, she recognized her own cowardice. 'OK, OK. Enjoy yourself. What do I care about the way he might drive? What do I care if he careers along at ninety and you hit the back of a bus and—'

'Hey there! Just hold on.' Her mother looked horrified.

'It was Polly,' explained Mary Jane, her glittering eyes unblinking, her expression tense. 'She's Sir Cedric's maid – or rather his wife's maid – and she said . . .'

Gloria pulled herself up to her full five feet four inches. 'Mary Jane Jefferies, you are out of your skull! Get a life! Get real! Get a man!'

She marched off, got as far as the door and turned round. 'And you,' she said, pointing her finger at her daughter, 'are just plain jealous. You'd have liked Roland's attention yourself. God knows you've had enough opportunities with some really suitable men I've put your way. But you've blown them all. You're just like your father. He never listened to me either. But never mind. I've got my man. And you have not!'

The door slammed.

'I'm sorry,' said Mary Jane once the echo had died away. She was biting her bottom lip, the corners of her eyes down-turned.

Coupled with her wrinkles, it made her look like a very sad bloodhound.

Honey didn't remark on the fact that her mother's efforts at matchmaking were insufferable and that the men she'd found for her daughter were as interesting as a garden full of limp lettuce. She shook her head.

'No need. You know my mother. She pleases herself.'

Mary Jane was holding her head to one side as though she were listening for something. Her eyes had a glazed I'm-not-in-this-world kind of look.

She frowned. 'Polly tells me to take a rain check on this. She reckons the accident may already have happened and that the person may have already crossed over.'

She nodded sagely, like some big-time newspaper editor who picks and chooses what stuff he's going to print.

'Right you are, Polly. You think she may already be there – and close too.'

She looked surprised; then more of the tilted head, the eyes gazing at the ceiling.

'Polly asks if perhaps there's someone else you know who happens to be divorced . . .'

'My father's dead.'

'I know.'

'So why doesn't he come visiting?'

Mary Jane shrugged. 'Ain't got no need to? Besides, your mother's here. He might not want to rekindle her acquaintance.'

'When did Polly tell you about the accident?'

Her frown was deep and she bit her lip quite hard. 'It was late last night when she told me about it. She always comes just when I'm drinking my primrose tea beneath the moonlight out in the garden.'

'Well, let's hope she's wrong.' Honey made her excuses and left her there. 'I'll get someone to bring you some herbal tea.'

Mary Jane nodded. She looked crestfallen. Honey arranged the tea.

'With or without a teaspoon of medicine,' asked Lindsey.

'With,' Honey replied.

Lindsey added a dash of gin to the raspberry-flavoured tea. Mary Jane would never admit to it, but herbal tea without a dash of gin stayed in the cup. With it, it was gone in seconds.

The sound of saucepans clattering came from the kitchen. Smudger had arrived. Honey pushed open the swing door.

Smudger was already in his whites. His voice filled the kitchen. 'Okra, mangetout, squash and Jersey Royals.'

A trainee chef scuttled out to the vegetable store to fetch what was required. One of his commis chefs was already slicing up the mis en place – a salad selection for lunch-time use.

Her head chef looked surprised to see her. 'Is it Monday? Are we changing the menu?'

Entering his kitchen without a pre-scheduled arrangement was never something to be taken lightly.

'I need to speak to you.'

A certain something about his face caused her to look and look again. Normally clean-shaven, a few days' worth of stubble now shadowed his chin.

'Fine,' he said, whilst slicing an eighteen-inch cucumber at breakneck speed.

'In private.'

His eyes met hers. He didn't say anything, but followed her out into the hallway.

She cleared her throat and folded her arms. 'Steve Doherty wants to ask you some more questions. He's coming in just after lunch.'

He turned promptly away. 'Not a good time.'

'Mark!'

It wasn't often that she called him by his real name. When she did he knew he was in big trouble.

'Did you lie about that night?'

His expression hardened. He shook his head. 'No.'

Honey did an in-depth evaluation of his expression. Mouth defiant, nostrils narrowed, chin firm; no direct giveaway, but there was something about the look in his eyes.

'Is there anything else you want to tell me?'

He shook his head again. 'No.'

Again the abrupt turn. It made her angry, so much so that she had an urge to say something truly shocking to make him stay – something erudite but plucked out of thin air.

The best she could come up with was, 'What do you know about the Grande Epicure?'

Had she plucked the words from nowhere? No. Surely

someone had mentioned it. Richard Carmelli? Whatever. They were enough to stop him in his tracks.

His hand had been holding the door open. Now he let it go. 'Who told you?'

Her heart raced. Smudger didn't usually frighten her. 'I . . . um . . . think it was . . .' She shook her head. 'Never mind. Tell me what you know.'

He looked down at the floor when he nodded as though he were remembering something and trying to get things clear in his head. 'OK, I will. After lunch? When our pet copper arrives?'

She agreed. The door to the kitchen swung shut and he was gone. She heard shouted orders. Once more Smudger was lord of his own domain.

Honey wandered through Reception, into the lounge and out into the conservatory. She was again the model hotelier, nodding and smiling at her guests. In her head she was thinking of the two dead chefs. She'd seen Smudger's dislike of Oliver Stafford. She hadn't asked him about Sylvester Pardoe. She turned on her heel meaning to do just that. Lindsey blocked her path.

'I thought you were going for a lie-down.'

It seemed daft that she had to excuse herself to her daughter, but that was exactly how she felt.

'I'm fine now.' She beamed brightly.

Lindsey's smile was weak; thoughtful. 'You look fine. And we're both fine – aren't we?'

Honey looked out at the garden. Invigorated by her infusion of herbal tea and Gordon's gin, Mary Jane was practising her t'ai chi, her long arms moving like a willow in a breeze.

Honey smiled. Her thoughts were most definitely with Lindsey. Just a short time ago – not long after she'd taken on this crime-liaison nonsense, she'd pressured Lindsey to forego chamber music concerts and go nightclubbing. 'Be a bit footloose and fancy free,' she'd said. And now that her daughter had kicked over the traces, who was she to condemn? It was just that Oliver Stafford had been married. If she cared to admit it, the generation gap was showing. People rarely stayed in the same relationship all their lives nowadays. She hadn't. Neither had her mother. They'd been the early birds breaking the trend.

She shrugged as she smiled. 'Just one of those things.'

Lindsey's dark eyes brightened. 'So I'm your beautiful girl again?'

Honey hugged her and kissed her on the cheek. 'You'll always be that.'

Steve Doherty rang her to say he'd be late. 'Should be closer to three.'

'I look forward to it.'

'I always do.'

She could imagine the cheeky grin. He was very tempting. But not yet, she told herself. Not just yet. There was plenty of time.

Her mother wouldn't agree, of course. Gloria Cross never tired of telling her that she'd be left on the shelf. 'You'll end up a dried-up old spinster,' she'd warned Honey many times.

Pointing out that she had been married, produced a daughter and that spinsters were usually virgins had cut no ice. In fact she'd been told to wash her mouth out. Deep down her mother was a dyed-in-the-wool romantic. The pile of Mills and Boon books with titles like *The Italian's Virgin Bride* and *Taming the Lady Angela* on her bedside table was testament to that.

Over a quiet cup of coffee and a pile of unpaid bills, she asked herself why 'it' hadn't happened between her and Steve yet. Time had a lot to do with it. When he wasn't involved in a big investigation, she was busy arranging next year's advertising or interviewing yet another batch of 'wannabe' chefs or waiters or a prospective bride and groom wanting perfect arrangements for their perfect day. And when a crime involved tourism and the hospitality trade in general, they were both strapped for time.

'Life's a bitch,' she muttered to herself.

The door opened. A draught of air sent paperwork fluttering in a white wave over the desk.

'Honey! Have you heard?'

Few people dared barge into her office unannounced and without knocking. But Casper St John Gervais considered the foibles and preferences of mere mortals didn't apply to him.

White suit, panama hat, black shirt and carrying his signature silver-topped cane, he waved the offer of tea or coffee aside with a grandiose flourish of a white gloved hand.

'Have you heard?'

She flipped her own hand dismissively and made a face. *No comprende!*

Casper sank on to the sofa, hat and cane gripped with both hands, knees tightly together.

'Bling Broadbent. Speeding along the road on her way home, lost control and hit a wall.'

'Is she hurt?'

'Very, my dear girl. She's dead.'

A cold chill swept over her as she put down her coffee cup.

Casper prattled on. 'Her car was smashed flat and so was she. Cutting equipment was brought in and the car was dismantled into manageable bits. I suppose Stella was too. How dreadful!' He sighed. 'Still, that's life – or rather death – such as it is. They say she was pickled last night. Some friends of mine saw her at the Zodiac.'

Honey remembered her encounter with Stella the previous night.

It wasn't a case of getting over the shock when she invited Casper to stay for lunch; she did it automatically, feeling a need to do something ordinary, everyday, a basic pleasure of life. Being alive and having no car park was preferable to being dead and having the best hotel car park in Bath. And an imposing hotel. And a chef (though recently deceased) who'd won the BITE competition.

Casper declined her offer. He explained that he was selling a few items at auction left to him by his father when he received the news. 'My father collected train sets,' he said in an off-hand manner. 'Not my cup of tea at all.'

'I see,' said Honey. She did see. It explained a lot about Casper. It explained something about Mary Jane too or at least about the ghostly Polly's prediction. She debated whether to tell her mother or not. She decided not.

Steve Doherty came at around three as promised. She hadn't phoned him, guessing he'd tell her everything then.

She was still plodding her way through a pile of invoices when he arrived. She asked him whether he'd heard about Stella Broadbent.

'Traffic told me they had to scrape her car off the road.'

She presumed they'd had to do the same for poor Stella.

She sighed and sat further back in her chair. 'I saw her last night at the Zodiac. She was very drunk. Very drunk,' she repeated, fixing him with an intensity meant to emphasize the point.

She went on to give him a blow-by-blow description of what had happened. Ordinarily she would have laughed and mentioned what Stella wore beneath her expensive designer-label clothes. But this was neither the time nor the place. Her expression doubtless betrayed her feelings.

'There's nothing for you to feel guilty about.'

'I didn't know she'd driven home. I could have stopped her.'

'Could you?'

She forced herself to nod an affirmation. Rubbish. Nothing could have stopped Stella from doing exactly as she liked. A bit like herself really. The realization made her blood run cold.

'Poor Stella. Squashed flat like that.'

'Not entirely.'

When something was interesting, Steve's tone of voice altered. She looked at him with narrowed eyes. He was pensive, as though sifting through his thoughts.

'Her lower body was badly injured, but from the waist upwards . . .'

There! That thoughtful tone again. And she could see something in his eyes.

'What is it?'

'Well, it's not confirmed on paper yet, but the pathologist isn't happy about some marks around her neck. They look like finger marks.'

Honey pushed aside the thought that she'd once considered strangling Stella. This was for real.

'And?'

He shrugged. 'We'll see. Now!' he said, slapping his thighs as he got to his feet. 'Where's this bloody chef of yours?'

The kitchen was cleared of lunchtime debris and readied for the evening shift. Sometimes a chef who wasn't working that evening would stay on to do the prep. Today no one had stayed on.

Steve stood in the centre of the kitchen and spread his arms. 'So where is he?'

'He must have forgotten.' She plotted murder in her mind.

She'd promised Steve that Smudger would be there. He'd let her down.

'You did tell him?'

She gave him one of her hardest looks. 'I stressed the fact.'

Her eyes were suddenly drawn to a dirty knife left hanging over the edge of the sink in the washing up area. The blade was smeared with something red.

'What are you doing,' Steve asked as she swilled the knife off in running water.

'Washing up.'

He tried to grab the knife. 'Is that blood?'

'No!' She ran her finger along the blade and licked it. 'It's jam,' she said with an air of light relief. 'Just jam.'

To her great relief, it *was* jam, but that didn't explain why it had apparently been flung aside unwashed. Smudger was a stickler for cleanliness and everything being in its place and if no one was staying on, he was usually the last to leave. Something had happened to make him rush off. She'd tick him off about it later. So would Steve judging by the look on his face.

Fifteen

S teve Doherty finally tracked Smudger down after the evening shift and asked him what time he'd left the pub the night Oliver Stafford was killed. They were rechecking because someone had mislaid the original statements. Smudger told him he couldn't remember but the barmaid would. Steve said he would check.

'And where were you the night Brian Brodie was killed?'

'With a friend.'

'A girlfriend?'

Whoever the girlfriend was seemed to check out.

'And the Grande Epicure?' she'd asked once Steve had left. 'You were going to tell me about it.'

He avoided her eyes. 'It's a cookery competition in Paris.'

Smudger had worked for a five-star hotel before coming to work for her. She'd sometimes asked herself why. The prestige of a five-star always outranked a four in a chef's estimation. It looked good on the CV just in case they got to open their own restaurant or end up with their own television programme.

He'd admitted that Oliver Stafford, Brian Brodie and Sylvester Pardoe were there too.

'Who won?'

He'd shrugged. 'I don't remember.'

He was lying. She knew it deep in her deepest whatever, that he was lying. Of course he knew. And she told him so. He shrugged and turned away seeming to prefer the sizzling of a hot pan to facing further questions.

Ever since he'd worked for her she'd never known him lie. But he was lying now. She was sure of it.

The following morning she kept her promise to Steve regarding the fancy-dress outfitters. The shop in Batheaston was her first stop; she hoped it would prove fruitful.

Rumour had it that the woman who ran Fancy Pants and Fantasies had once been a stunt woman in Hollywood. Whether it was true or not was the last thing on Honey's mind. She was still concerned about the change in Smudger's behaviour. He gave no real clue as to why he'd rushed out without keeping his appointment. His explanation was plausible enough – that he'd had a headache – except that she couldn't recall him ever having a headache – even after a few pints of extra strong pulled from a large oak barrel.

Batheaston seemed an odd place to have a fancy-dress shop. Situated three miles to the east of Bath, a steep hill swept down towards Bathford and the old route to Bradford on Avon and the A4 on to Chippenham. Narrow pavements divided old stone buildings from the road. What shops there were had blank frontages. Although the road wasn't so busy since the opening of the new bypass, it was still difficult to park.

To her left, steep lanes sloped up into a cul-de-sac and the village of Northend. She shot up the second one and found a parking space, not too much of a problem at this time of day when most folks were at work.

It was a fair walk back from there to the main road. The road was fairly empty of cars and the pavements of people.

A man stamping his feet at the bus stop was the only person in sight. He nodded a brief good morning. 'Bloody buses. None at all or three all at once.'

'That's the way it is,' she replied. She glanced up at the gold and green sign saying Fancy Pants and Fantasies.

'That used to be a pub,' said the man at the bus stop. He shook his head glumly. 'Nothing's the same as it used to be.'

He sounded like Marvin the paranoid android in *The Hitchhiker's Guide to the Galaxy*. Feeling bad about Stella, the last thing she wanted was some misery bending her ear and making her feel worse. She pretended she didn't hear and pushed her shoulder against the shop door. There was a rushing of air from the rubber surround as it sucked itself open.

Madame le Proprietor was sitting behind a green plastic counter. Rumour had it that Andrea Andover had doubled for the likes of Carrie Fisher and Demi Moore in some of their trickiest stunts. The only thing she'd doubled since then was her size.

Andrea Andover wobbled. She had three chins and her

breasts were big enough to use as a bookshelf and likely to come into sight around a corner before she did.

She appeared to be rummaging up the rear of a bright yellow chicken costume. She looked up on hearing the door open.

'Can I help you?'

Honey eyed the chicken. 'Are you stuffing that?'

Judging by her deadpan expression, Andrea Andover had never been asked to double humour.

'I'm sewing its tail back on,' she replied in a voice that matched her expression. 'People do strange things when they're in costume. I blame television myself.'

Honey cocked a surprised eyebrow. Coming from someone who had worked in Hollywood that was a bit rich, but she wasn't here to debate the fact.

As she sewed and stuffed, Andrea Andover's flinty eyes stayed fixed on Honey's face. Disconcerting was an understatement; she found herself searching her memory, just in case she'd hired and broken a chicken costume without being fully aware that she had.

Reason overcame her.

'I'm looking for a man who might have hired an African costume from you. A Masai costume in fact, you know, animal skin, red wool and brightly coloured beads.'

'Yeah.'

'He's about six feet three, African and well-spoken. He told me his name was Obediah.'

The chicken outfit ceased heaving as Andrea Andover stopped what she was doing, closed one eye, and fixed Honey with the other one.

'I told the daft sod not to do it. It was too serious pretending to be someone's husband they married when they were drunk. Different if it was a party or something. Everyone knows it's just a giggle. But what he took on was not meant that way. I told him, "Francis, that man that's paying you is up to no good." It was a wicked hoax. The woman had a problem and the guy who paid Francis all that money did it out of malice not fun.'

So Obediah's real name was Francis. And someone had paid him to dress up in that stupid costume. The question sprung to mind of how much had embarrassment paid in Stella's last booze-up and a speeding car to infinity?

'How much was he paid?'

'Five hundred pounds plus expenses. I only charged him seventy-five for the costume – it ain't much of a costume anyway – just a bit of animal skin, necklaces, bracelets and what have you.' She cocked her head to the side, one eye closed again, the other looking thoughtful and all alone.

'It was a laugh and it wasn't a laugh; that was the way it was meant to be. Something was funny, but something was sad.' She shrugged and picked up the costume again. 'That's the way I saw it.'

'Francis. Do you know where he lives?'

Andrea nodded. 'Sure I do. I've got his card.'

Shoving the chicken outfit aside, she tugged out a small Rolodex with her podgy hands and handed a plain card with block black writing on it: Francis Trent. Actor, impersonator, kissograms a speciality.

Sixteen

Before leaving Batheaston, she tapped in the numbers on her phone. There was no answer from the telephone number on the card. Was Francis Trent away on holiday or out acting, impersonating or embarrassing some unfortunate whose friends thought it might be fun to make them squirm?

She phoned Steve and told him about it.

'We'll want to speak to him. This could be serious.'

'I can understand that.' She told him she'd see him later. Nothing to do but go home.

After parking her car in a nearby car park, she headed for the exit. A sudden whirring sound made her look up. The light on a security camera blinked red. Had there been a security camera at the Beau Brummell Hotel? Pictures of the building clicked through her mind like the pages of a stiff-paged Filofax. No camera? Wasn't that a little odd? Most good sized car parks had them – even small ones like doctor's or vet's surgeries. She presumed Steve had checked it out.

She strolled back into the Green River Hotel through the lunchtime crowds. A short cloudburst had sweetened the air and, like the buds of spring flowers, people were emerging from shop doorways and arcades loaded with stuff they wouldn't have bought if it hadn't rained.

The sun warmed the pavements and the water turned to steam.

A horse-drawn carriage was coming towards her. They were regulars on the sightseeing circuit; ten pounds and you got the slow ride round Bath allowing a bit more time to take in the sights or be lulled to sleep by the gentle motion and the running commentary of the tourist guide. Picturesque and practical in a city built for sedan chairs.

The grey horse tossed its head as it came to a stop.

'Hannah! Hannah!'

Her jaw dropped. Her mother wasn't the type to do the tourist thing unless you counted going first class on a cruise liner. She was in the company of Roland Mead. They both looked happy. So much for the trip to the Cotswolds. Roland Mead had let her mother down again. Didn't she just know that would happen?

A sudden pang of something she couldn't quite identify hit her. Was it jealousy? No way. She still couldn't forget that Roland had made a pass at her.

Her mother beamed at her as Roland helped her down from the carriage. She was sharply dressed in a navy-blue suit edged with white piping.

'Hannah, we've had such a wonderful morning. Roland and I are off to lunch now.'

Honey noted the adoration in her mother's eyes.

Roland was wearing an expensive suede jacket. A gold sovereign dangled from a thick chain around his neck. The man had money but no taste.

On top of bad taste, he followed bad form daring to grab Honey's shoulders and kiss her on both cheeks.

She barely controlled the urge to wipe them off.

What he did next was also unacceptable.

'How about your little girl joining us?' He was addressing her mother almost as though Honey wasn't there.

'Ask me,' she said, visibly grinding her teeth.

'Ask her,' said Gloria. She didn't look too pleased about the deal.

The smile barely flickered. 'OK. How about it?'

Honey flinched. The last thing she wanted was to spend a precious lunchtime with her mother and her boyfriend – though boy was hardly the right word. The most boyish thing about him was the toupee, perhaps scalped from a childhood friend.

A sweet smile was called for. 'I wouldn't want to impose. I've got a business to run.' She glanced tellingly at her watch.

'Business! Yes! That's just what I'd like to talk to you about,' said Roland.

Honey eyed the arm protectively draped around her mother's shoulders. 'Me and your mother being so close, stands to reason I can give you a real good meat deal,' said Roland.

It pained her teeth, but she held on to the sweet smile. 'I

wouldn't want to ruin your lunch. I think mother would prefer to have you to herself.'

Roland's white teeth flashed like a toothpaste advert. Were they real?

'A proper business date perhaps?' he suggested with a fixed, wide-mouth smile. Flash, flash, flash!

Her mother jumped in feet first.

'Two's company, three's a crowd,' she said, tightening her grip around Roland's waist, smiling up at him like a lovesick teenager. 'We don't need kids out with us adults.'

'Well.' He glanced swiftly at mother then daughter. 'Another time perhaps.'

Although it hurt her jaw, Honey pasted on what passed for a sincere smile. 'Definitely another time.' *When hell freezes over.*

They sauntered off, her mother giving a cute little wave over her shoulder and calling out, 'By the way, your chef's not being very sensible. You need to have a word with him.'

Now what did that mean? Her stomach felt as though she'd been swallowing scrap iron as worst-case scenarios flashed through her mind like streaks of lightning. Please God she hasn't upset Smudger. Her footsteps quickened.

Her mother was walking out with a master butcher and her meddling was affecting the business. But there was something else.

Was it possible that she was missing her mother's spurious attempts at matchmaking? Never mind. Her first priority was her chef. Why was Smudger upset? Worse still what part had her mother played in his unhappiness?

She caught Smudger reading the newspaper when she got back and prayed it wasn't the employment section.

'Everything OK?' she asked breezily and crossed her fingers behind her back. *Don't mention anything until he does.*

He turned his head slowly and fixed her with an accusing eye. Nightmare situations flashed through her mind. Advertising for a new chef; interviewing; new menus; old customers' muted response to new blood . . . the list was endless. Her blood ran cold.

'What have I done?'

His jaw shifted from side to side as he chewed over his thoughts, prolonging the agony. 'I'm not in favour of changing butchers.'

She was taken aback. 'Who told you we were changing? No! Wait. Don't answer that. My mother.'

She sat down next to him. 'Smudger. Whose hotel is this?'

'Yours.'

'Not my mother's. Mine. What did she say to you?'

He hesitated.

Honey's stomach churned. This could be bad.

'She said that if Mead became part of the family then we'd be switching to him.'

Marriage? Mother was talking about marriage? Had she taken leave of her senses?

'Over my dead body! Now listen to me. I value your judgement. Choice of supplier lies ultimately with you. OK?'

The rigid shoulders relaxed as the tension left him. 'OK.'

Honey gave a big sigh of relief.

'Right,' she said, getting to her feet. 'It's Lindsey's night off and mine too, so how about you cook us a delicious meal. We'll have it in the coach house. OK?'

She didn't add that it was a kind of making-up celebration between her and Lindsey.

'I'll rustle you up something special. Coquilles St Jaques?'

'Just the ticket!'

Feeling as though her feet were floating six inches off the ground, she sauntered off. Her mother's meddling had been fixed again.

Everything in the garden was lovely – for a while – until Lindsey disappointed her. Surprise, surprise, she had a date.

'Sorry, Mum.'

She went on to say that she was going to a nightclub with a group of friends including a guy she was quite keen on.

'Fine.'

But it wasn't fine, though it should be. What was happening here? For some time she'd been encouraging her daughter to let her hair down; now she was doing exactly that, so why the peevishness? Lindsey had male company. So did her mother. *And there's the rub . . .* Her daughter and her mother both had dates and she didn't.

Petulant, peeved and feeling left out, she slumped off to the coach house, making for the bathroom.

Have a long, luxurious soak. Do your nails. Do your hair. Pamper yourself.

Yes, a nice soak would do the trick. After stripping off she eyed her naked self in a full-length mirror. Did she look good naked? The lighting was good, the mirror sharp. The truth was nebulous.

'The jury's out on that one,' she muttered to herself, when suddenly something happened to make things better. The hot water was still tumbling into the tub, the steam misting the mirror and blurring her image. A great improvement!

Now could she scoff two portions of Coquilles St Jacques with all the trimmings and a bottle of Chardonnay all by herself? The prospect was far from daunting. Comfort eating had kicked in

She eased herself down into the warm water, her head resting on the roll top. The bath was Victorian, with lion's claw feet and was big enough for two. Her spirits rose.

Being alone this evening wasn't very appealing though. Neither was telling Smudger that the special meal was off. His ego was still fragile. She didn't want to upset him.

Her eyes slid sidelong to her mobile phone. She picked it up and punched in Steve Doherty's number. Two murders. He was busy, but surely he could fit in a lovely meal and an available woman?

'I'm all alone tonight and my chef's cooking a special meal for two.'

'I'll be round at ten.'

Whooping for joy, she ducked beneath the surface. Mission accomplished.

Seventeen

He was leaning on the door post when she opened the door, one hand flopped over his forehead, a blue tie hanging loose around his neck. Surprise, surprise, he hadn't shaved for days judging by his stubble. He drew a hand across his chin. The stubble made a rasping sound; audio testosterone. Honey's legs turned to jelly.

He looked tired, but his mouth lifted in a lopsided smile. 'You didn't say whether it was a black-tie event, but I managed a blue one.'

She'd warmed to that smile shortly after she'd met him. Given half the chance she'd get a lot warmer, quite hot in fact. So far the right time hadn't materialized. But it would. Shortly.

The table was laid and the food was ready.

As she set out the first dish, Honey told Steve in more detail about her visit to the fancy-dress shop in Batheaston. Steve listened as he dealt with the wine.

'But no reply when you phoned him,' he managed between yawns.

'No.'

They clinked glasses. 'I was also going to ask you whether there were any security cameras at the Beau Brummell Hotel.'

He nodded. 'There are but they're well hidden. The trailing geraniums play a starring role.'

She took a taste of wine. 'Not the variegated ivy?'

He grinned. 'That too. We've got the tapes down at the station. The security bloke isn't sure they were working that night, but we're going to check them anyway. He mentioned something about maintenance.'

They sat down to their meal.

'The owner and the dead chef were definitely the victims of a hate campaign,' said Steve, gently cradling a glass of wine in his hands. 'A couple of months ago Stella Broadbent's car was the victim of a spray job from someone who wasn't too hot on spelling.'

Honey saw the amusement on his face and sensed she was about to be enlightened.

'Fucking – without a C – cow written in purple and green. Similar thing happened to the chef's car; some of the customers' cars had punctures, coach parties had been misdirected – though that could have been accidental – but the rat in the pantry and the cockroaches in the rice sack were a bit suspect.'

Honey made a face. 'Killing the chef was a bit drastic. One hatred too many. And what about Brian Brodie?'

Steve frowned and gulped back his wine in frustration. 'Now there's the rub, as that bloke Shakespeare once said. Are we looking at two separate crimes? The murders of the chefs were done by the same person. Forensic are pretty set on that. But is the hate campaign connected to the murders?'

Honey sat down and sipped at the wine he handed her. 'Right. Let's take it that they are unconnected, in which case my money would be on a past employee or someone she'd crossed in business.'

'Did she cross many people in business?'

She almost choked on the wine before answering. 'This is Stella Broadbent we're talking about. Flasher of everything she's got; rub it into the wounds extraordinaire! She *made* people cross that was for sure.'

He grinned. 'Like you for instance.'

Honey made little mewing noises of discomfort and heaved her shoulders.

'I was envious of her car park, I admit. Of her hotel too come to that. She's got more rooms than me and they're pretty swanky by all accounts. She told everyone how much better they were than anything her competitors could offer. She told them to their face. The cow loved winding people up. Dracula drank blood. Stella thrived on envy. She loved rubbing your nose in it.'

She noticed Steve's attention wandering between her eyes and her lips. She imagined he liked the colour of her eyes. She sensed him forcing himself back to the subject in hand.

'It's worth pursuing. We questioned the staff, but not rivals in business.'

Honey eyed him speculatively. She felt a task coming on when he smiled at her like that.

Steve held her eyes with his own. 'I'm sure you'd be better at that. You know which hoteliers she wound up the most. There may be something, or there may be nothing, but do it for me, eh? Just in case there is some connection.'

She narrowed her eyes. 'You're loading me up with a lot of work, Doherty. Do you know how many hotels there are in Bath? And don't think I don't know what you're playing at.'

He smiled in that boyish, rakish way of his; Colin Firth as Mr Darcy but without the thigh-hugging breeches. On the other hand, he didn't need the tight trousers. His jeans hinted at what was on offer. She could go with that. She also accepted that other hoteliers were more likely to confide in her than in Steve. She knew the game. After a few words with Casper – who knew everything about everyone in the hospitality trade – she would know which hoteliers to question.

As she considered who might come top of the list, she assessed the calorie count of the scallops before heaping salad on to her plate.

A thought suddenly came to her. 'Something funny, something sad. That's what Andrea Andover said about the guy who booked the deal. Annoying that he didn't give her his name. She reckons Francis Trent– Obediah – our pseudo Masai warrior knows. I've asked Andrea to let Francis know that I want a word with him.'

Steve perked up. 'The stuntwoman. I hear she used to double for a load of Hollywood stars. Did she look anything like Demi Moore?'

Honey grimaced at Steve's shallow moment. She threw him a disapproving look, shook her head and swallowed a new potato. 'No. More like Bruce Willis after a year of living on doughnuts.'

He pulled a face. 'Grim! Mind you,' he said, his look flowing over the area of body between her neck and her knees, 'present company makes up for the disappointment.'

She felt herself getting hot – and it was nothing to do with the weather.

'Cheese?'

She left him with a wedge of St Augur and a box of crackers sat in front of him. No need to present food that well with

Steve. He knew what he liked. No need for trimmings. He'd probably like her the same way, she mused.

Whilst he spread cheese and chomped crackers, she went to the bathroom.

The eyes she saw in the cabinet mirror were looking a little wild tonight – and it wasn't just due to the wine.

'Right,' she said taking a deep breath and tousling her hair. 'It's now or never.'

Granted that their professional relationship was something of a barrier to their personal one, but once that was put aside it was no holds barred. Getting better physically acquainted was like a spectre at the feast; the feast they never quite got round to.

Her bosoms surged against her neckline as she took a deep breath. Tonight could be the night. They were both tired, but also relaxed. Time to take the plunge.

Besides making sure the bedroom was tidy and the sheets fresh, she squirted extra perfume behind her ears, down her cleavage and up her skirt. Who knows where things could lead?

Recalling her naked self in the wickedly honest full-length mirror, she turned down the lighting and recalled the saying that less is more. In this case she hoped that less lighting equalled less bumpy bits and dimpled thighs. Before leaving the bedroom she tugged off the knee-length controlling under-garment and slipped on a black lace thong. The bulges that had been smoothed bubbled against her dress. Never mind, Steve had sunk two glasses of wine and eaten well. And rule one was in operation; the lighting was low.

She studied her reflection. Cleavage? Not enough but easily rectified. She undid the top button. Cheeks? Flushed. The wine was responsible for that. Shoes? Drat! Why hadn't she noticed earlier that she was wearing her flat black ballerina shoes? She swapped them for a pair of four inch heels that she couldn't stand upright on for longer than fifteen minutes. Fifteen minutes should be enough.

Right! One last look in the mirror, and hey presto! She was sex on legs. Fabulous! Totally irresistible.

Sashay in. That was the thing. She stopped just before the door. Would sashaying in be sexy enough to tempt him. Perhaps not. She tossed her head. Be a bit more alluring. Use everything you've got.

She ran her hands down over her ribs and her waist care-fully avoiding the 'love handle' areas. Well, the legs were good. Good enough for a dancer, a very sexy alluring dancer.

Smiling she hitched up her skirt. If this didn't impress him, nothing would.

'Da, da, da, de, da, da, da . . .'

Accompanied by her off tune rendition of 'The Stripper' she slowly extended one near-naked leg, then curved it around the door.

She'd expected some response like 'Holy Cow' or 'Wow'.

Nothing. She told herself he was dumbstruck.

Gradually, she eased her body round ending up posed provocatively against the door post.

And there was Steve. He was lying full-stretch on the settee, eyes closed, mouth open.

'Steve?'

Even an outright rejection would have been better than his sudden resounding snore.

There was only one thing left to do. The dishes were waiting. She gathered them up and took them to the kitchen.

Eighteen

The day could have started better. The dishwasher was having one of its away days, thus the kitchen resembled a Turkish steam room.

'The rotation arm's not turning,' shouted the kitchen porter, his head emerging from the machine in a sweaty, hot haze.

Honey resigned herself to ringing the repair man. His answer phone gurgled into life telling her that he was away on a cruise around the Mediterranean and wouldn't be back until the 16th.

She swore at the phone as she slammed it down. People could be so selfish. On holiday! Did he have no idea of her dishwasher's fickle temperament?

A lever arch file of useful contacts left by the previous owner was her next port of call. As thick and heavy as a volume of *Encyclopaedia Britannica*, she heaved it up on to the desk.

'I need to enter all this stuff on our database,' she murmured with a sideways glance at Lindsey. Her daughter's face was lit up by the computer screen.

'That's impossible,' said Lindsey.

'Why?'

'You don't know how to.'

Lindsey had a point.

'By the way,' her daughter added. 'What's the decoration hanging from the ceiling fan?'

Honey glanced over her shoulder at the closed door to her private office. She remembered the huge brassiere she'd flung into the air on her return from the kitchen last night. She'd left her bag on her desk in the office behind Reception. As she'd grabbed it the contents had spilled on to the floor. The 'brazier' had been amongst them. Irritated by Steve's snoring and now this, she'd thrown them skywards. More aerodynamically designed than she'd thought, it had flown higher than she'd envisaged and had landed on the ceiling fan.

She searched for and found an unbelievable excuse. 'Those things have multiple uses don't you know. Lampshades. Trendy don't you think?'

After sorting out a repair man for the dishwasher, she rang Francis Trent – Obediah the Masai warrior. There was no response. Shame. He was the only person who knew the identity of the bloke who'd hired him.

The ridiculous hiring of a kissogram actor was over the top but also a flaw in the perpetrator's thinking. Francis had to have a name. Sylvester Pardoe fitted into this somewhere, but she hadn't figured out where. Neither had Steve Doherty. He'd told her that over toast and coffee this morning – that was after apologizing for falling asleep the night before. She'd made him suffer a bit, showing her displeasure, though not letting on about the floor show he'd missed. It could be a while before she was that keen again.

Totally out of the blue, Roland Mead turned up to talk business and sent the morning into a nosedive. Thinking crime was not threatening. Talking business with a supplier that her chef so obviously disliked was close to suicide of the financial sort. She didn't want this.

Remembering he was a touchy-feely person, she was quick to put the reception desk between her and him.

'Am I expecting you?'

'Of course you are. And you'll be glad I came. I'm going to make you an offer you can't refuse.'

He was big, bluff and over-confident. Too 'in the face' for her taste. What did her mother see in him?

'My regular butcher rings to make an appointment if he wants to see me.'

Roland shook his head and made a hissing, disapproving sound. 'Strike whilst the iron's hot. That's my motto. And anyway, Hannah, I'm not a *regular* butcher. I'm a wholesaler with a wide range stored in a cold store at Avonmouth. I can supply you cheaper than your *regular* butcher.'

His familiarity with her name put her back up. She couldn't help snapping. 'My name's Mrs Driver. Only my mother calls me Hannah.'

His smile remained the same, like that on the face of a rag

doll, the stitches showing around the edge; too ragged to be real.

He eyed her appraisingly, drawing himself up to his full height in an effort to impress her. 'A woman who sticks to business. I like that. That's why I know you'll be glad I came. No one can touch me for price. It stands to reason. You can't afford not to try me. I know you're tempted,' he said, clicking his teeth and tipping her the wink. 'Go on. Admit it.'

The double entendre was obvious. She knew damn well he wasn't just referring to meat. And this man was chasing her mother's tail?

'I'm afraid I *can* resist you,' she said, her tone meant to leave him in no doubt that she'd sooner be sunbathing in a ditch full of snakes.

His eyes flickered and fell to her bosoms.

She drew a deep breath and deftly buttoned up the blouse button that had come undone. 'I leave the choosing of suppliers to my chef and he's very happy with the Davis brothers,' she snarled.

Roland guffawed as though she'd just cracked a huge joke. 'They're past their sell by date.'

'Their meat isn't.'

Roland's eyes, which had strayed momentarily to her cleavage, hardened and fixed on her face. Leaning forward, he dared to place his beefy palm on the open lever arch file. His fingertips edged towards hers.

'Let me remind you, sweetheart, that you employ that chef of yours, not t'other way round. Get on top of 'im darling, before he gets on top of you. Take my advice.'

'Take mine, Mr Mead. Remove your hand from mine.'

He grinned. His hand remained.

Her fingers were already over the paper punch. She clobbered his knuckles. The rag-doll smile hung on by a few loose stitches.

She purposely turned her back on him. 'Now, if you'll excuse me, I need to attend to my website.'

Lindsey had got up from her chair to use the photocopier. She looked back in horror as her mother took her place.

Roland lingered.

Honey pressed a few keys. A string of gobbledygook raced across the screen.

Roland leaned as close as he dared none too sure of what she was likely to do with the computer screen if he got too close. 'Think on it and give me a call when you're not too busy. You know it makes sense.'

'Will you tell Grandma that he was making a pass at you?' asked Lindsey after he'd left.

'Was it that obvious?'

'Dead right it was. Are you going to tell Grandma? Come on. You have to do something surely.'

Honey thought about it. What would be gained by telling her mother that Roland Mead was a creep? The answers were easy-peasy. There was a fair chance that her mother wouldn't believe her and, besides, her pride would be damaged, her ego pinched like a pair of tight shoes. And if she did believe her, there was an equally fair chance that she'd chuck him and revert back to finding a new man for her widowed daughter.

'I think I'll let sleeping pigs lie,' said Honey, making a face as she nodded her head.

'Don't you mean sleeping dogs?' asked Lindsey.

'No. The man's a pig. Sleeping pigs sounds about right.'

Nineteen

A party of doctors from the city hospital had booked in for a birthday celebration. 'Work hard, play hard' was a saying they lived up to. By the time they'd been shoe-horned up to their rooms, they'd polished off far more than the monthly alcoholic limit per head as recommended by the National Health Service. Not bad for a four-hour session.

Giving a hand with the clearing up was more of a necessity than an option; mainly because someone had to be in charge of operations and those that should have been could not. Highly appreciative of the food, wine and service, the chef and head waiter had been invited to join the merry throng – one of whom was wearing his wife's high heels by the end of the evening. Hence Smudger and a few of his crew were sleeping it off on the settees in the bar and the boss was left with debris, a mop and a bucket.

Those left exchanged their concerns about ever ending up in the operating theatre with one of that lot holding a scalpel.

'Might cut out the wrong thing,' said Doris, their casual and very plump breakfast cook. 'I knows I got a lot of flesh, but I don't want to lose any by misadventure.'

It briefly crossed Honey's mind that Doris could do with a bit of flesh reduction. Couldn't say so of course.

By one o'clock Honey was left to lay the tables for the morning. The hotel was quiet, the building creaking as the day's heat seeped from its walls.

She was lost in thought when someone banged on the bar door at around two.

'We're closed,' she called out once she'd settled back in her skin.

Whoever it was banged again.

In no mood to be pleasant, she adopted her I'm-going-to-punch-your-lights-out kind of voice.

'Go away. You'll wake my guests and I won't be happy. If you keep it up, I promise you, I'll call the police.'

No more knocking.

The mop and bucket were finally finished with. It was approaching three o'clock by the time she tumbled into bed, face unwashed, limbs aching with weariness and clothes thrown into a heap on the floor.

A church clock chimed three. As if she needed to be reminded. Instantly roused from a moment of truly deep sleep, she blinked her eyes open as the clock struck its last note. She frowned. Why had she woken up so abruptly? She was used to the clock. It didn't normally disturb her. It swiftly entered her head that she had heard something else. A tap, tap, tapping at her door.

Feeling puzzled rather than nervy, she got up on one elbow. 'Lindsey?'

Lindsey was sleeping over at a friend's in Bradford on Avon, but it was possible that she'd changed her mind and come home.

Her tired brain flipped a mental coin. Heads it was Lindsey, tails it couldn't be Lindsey. Lindsey would have answered if it was.

She reached for her silk dressing gown then glanced down at herself. Naked. Silk dressing gown was not a good idea. She pulled on a scruffy pair of leggings and a 'comfort' sweater; big and baggy and hiding a multitude of sins.

Looking like an egg with legs, she crept out to the hallway grabbing what she thought was a walking stick on her way.

'Who's there?' Her voice wasn't much more than a loud whisper. 'This is my home. The hotel entrance is round at the front,' she said, suddenly deciding that it must be a hotel guest who'd gone astray, not beyond the bounds of possibility. Perhaps one of the surgeons had gone walkabouts. Thinking about it, at this moment in time they'd be hard pressed to find their way back to the hospital unassisted.

This is my home! The thought was profound, like possession being nine-tenths of the law but no one quite knowing what it really meant. An Englishman's, or woman's, home was her castle seemed to fit the bill. She had a right to protect it, though it helped if you were bigger than the other guy.

'I am armed,' she said, a little too shakily. She raised the walking stick, which promptly attacked her. Her hair was caught on fine metal spokes. She'd picked up an umbrella by mistake and had pressed the button!

Judging by the length of shadow falling through the glass half of the front door, this guy was big! Really big! His shadow was all height and no breadth – a bit like a telegraph pole.

'Hello? Mrs Driver? I'm talking softly so I don't wake your guests. It's Francis Trent. I heard you wanted to speak to me.'

He was here? At gone three in the morning? What sort of excuse did he have? She asked him.

'I've just flown into Gatwick at eight o'clock tonight. Things took longer than they should have done because they lost my luggage.'

A good one.

After disentangling herself from the umbrella spokes, she opened the door. Her hair stuck out at one side in a tangled mess. A good match with the outfit, she thought on catching a glimpse of her reflection.

Looking up at Francis Trent took some doing.

'Andrea said you wanted to speak to me.'

He was dressed to kill – though this time his outfit was more suitable for a nightclub.

'My day wear,' he said on seeing her eyes sweep over him.

Once they were both cradling cups of coffee and sitting comfortably, she asked him what she wanted to know.

'Who hired you?'

'A chef.'

The most obvious contender – the one she knew best – immediately sprang to mind.

Her stomach cleaved to her spine. 'Do you know his name?'

'Sure I do. So do you.'

The worse case scenario entered her mind. Smudger serving time in the modern-day equivalent to Devil's Island; hopefully he'd get an en-suite room. He wasn't very sociable at the best of times, but terrible in confined spaces.

She heard herself asking for confirmation in a squeaky, unfamiliar and very nervous voice. 'Who?' and 'What was his name?' Her voice sounded far away.

Please don't let it be Smudger. Please, please, please!

Francis carried on, all youthful confidence and lust for living glowing in his big brown eyes. 'That young chef feller

– Richard. I wasn't going to do it at first. It was a bit too heavy to be a fun thing. But I could see he was suffering. That's what makes people do over the top things. Had no time for that boss of his, none at all.

Well, that was OK! As long as Smudger was out of the picture. She sighed with relief and was sure her blood pressure chose that moment to take a nose dive. Great. She'd spotted a custard slice in the fridge back at the hotel. And a tub of Cornish clotted cream and a piece of overripe Stilton. This was cause for celebration. No need to advertise for a new chef.

'So why didn't you tell us the truth?'

'I didn't mention it to you and that Casper because it weren't what mattered. I heard the argument and thought I should tell. Anyway, I thought I should give Richard his money's worth. Fair's fair.'

'Very naughty all the same,' said Honey, shaking her head like a disapproving aged aunt.

'Well . . .' He looked contrite and made a so-so movement with his hand. 'I just felt sorry for that guy. Mind you,' he said, his face brightening, 'I enjoyed wearing the costume – I especially liked the spear.'

Honey eyed him from beneath darkening brows – like Gandalf in *The Lord of the Rings* – though without the bushiness – or the greyness. Thank goodness for eyebrow pencils. 'The police did want to examine it. Something very sharp was used to cut Stafford's throat.'

Francis grinned. 'Not my spear.' He sighed. 'Anyway,' he said, 'I needed the money. I had a bit of a problem – I won't go into what kind of problem, but let's just say I was in need of cash. It seemed a great idea at the time.' He stopped smiling and bit his bottom lip. 'Fact is my wife – my pretend wife that is – was a tart and her chef was a shit. They suited each other.'

He confirmed what she was thinking; yes, he had been telling the truth about the argument and Stella threatening to kill him.

'I think someone was hustling her for money, if you know what I mean.'

'Blackmail?'

'No. Sex. She paid him for it. That Oliver bloke. That's what Richard told me and judging by that argument . . .'

Clocking Honey's dumbstruck expression, he proceeded to explain.

'It was like this,' he said, using his hands as an extension to his voice, waving them up and down in line with cadence. 'According to Richard she paid this guy Oliver Stafford far more than he was worth. Mind you it's rumoured Oliver had a lot of stamina. Did you know him?'

His question took her unawares. 'Uh, no . . . no, I didn't.'

Honey was no longer concentrating on Francis's long drawn out explanation. At last they had a suspect. Richard Carmelli. *What had Stella and Oliver done to him to make him that mad? Mad enough to kill?*

Deep in thought, she didn't immediately notice that Francis was eyeing her over the rim of his cup. Alarm bells rang.

'You're a nice-looking woman. Have you got a husband?' he asked.

'No. I'm a widow.'

'Do you want another one?'

'No,' she said, adamantly shaking her head. 'I've got someone in mind.'

It was almost the truth; just that Steve was too tired to read the signals. But he would. In time he would.

The phone rang just as Richard Carmelli got out of the bath. Typical. Night off and someone couldn't wait until he'd finished. No matter.

He picked up the phone. 'Hi there.'

Nobody answered. His jaw tightened. 'I know it's you. Stop mucking about.'

Still no response and yet he knew – *definitely* knew someone was there.

'Sod off!'

He slammed the phone down. His heart hammered in his chest. The game was over. He had to get away. He picked up the phone and dialled the only person he knew he could trust.

'Mark? I need to lie low for a while . . . no, not at your place. I'm going to camp out. Can you give me a lift to my lock-up?'

Twenty

This thing between her mother and Mead was annoying Honey no end. It bugged her when she was doing paperwork, and it bugged her when she was at the hairdresser's, and it bugged her now on her way to see Richard Carmelli. Was the randy butcher after her mother's body or the hotel's meat order? If the latter, would he drop her mother now she'd made it clear that chef was in charge of ordering supplies?

She called round to her mother's flat on the pretext of delivering a slab of Smudger's home-made fruit cake and a box of Earl Grey. Her mother answered the door wearing a face mask and a dressing gown. Her legs were smeared in something similar to the stuff on her face.

Honey eyed her up and down. 'This looks like a serious beauty treatment session.'

'It is. I've got a hot date tonight.' Her mother's lips stayed in a straight line. 'I can't move my lips too much. It'll crack the face mask.'

'Right.' Honey followed her mother into the palatial flat with views across the city. 'Anyone I know?' It was a stupid question. Of course she knew.

Her mother stood in the middle of the room doing windmills with her arms.

'Roland of course. Excuse me whilst I do my exercises. I can't sit down. I've got moisturiser on my legs. It's new stuff, guaranteed to exfoliate and moisturize all at the same time. You know how much I love labour-saving beauty products.'

'Don't tell me the price,' said Honey, waving one hand dismissively after putting the cake and tea out in the kitchen.

Slim hope! Gloria Cross set great store by big prices. She had to tell.

'Less than a hundred.'

Honey rolled her eyes and shook her head. A pot of Nivea

cream was the closest she ever got to serious moisturizing. Her mother was a sucker for brand names, preferably French.

Hair, pedicure, manicure and shrink-wrap fat removal; her mother's annual expenditure on beauty treatments and clothes was mind-boggling. But today was not the time to be criticizing her expenditure. Should she say what was on her mind or not?

Despite the mud pack, the look on Gloria's face said it all. Her eyes sparkled. Romance wasn't dead. Yet.

Honey pushed a furry orang-utan, a pink elephant and a doe-eyed Eeyore further along the sofa so she could sit down.

She felt a bit like a school-teacher as she folded her hands and gathered her thoughts.

'Mother, I think we need to talk.'

'Hurry up, dear. These days it takes me a wee bit longer to achieve perfection. I don't want to keep my darling Roland waiting.'

Honey fixed her gaze on a gilt-framed still life hanging on the opposite wall; plums piled high and purple grapes falling from a silver salver. Right! Her mother was a plum ripe for the plucking, and Roland Mead was plum rotten – she knew it! She knew it in her bones, but how best to broach the subject?'

'I think Roland Mead is a creep!'

Hardly subtle. Hardly what she'd had in mind at all. It just fell off her tongue.

Her mother was surprisingly reticent. 'Now, now, dear. You're turning quite green.'

Honey was almost – though not quite – speechless. 'Jealous? Me?'

'Yes, dear. I'm seeing the green-eyed monster flashing in your eyes.'

'That's eye shadow, Mother. You've smeared it across your eye ball instead of your eyelid.'

Her mother eyed her sidelong. 'Get out of my space, Miss Busybody.'

Get out of my space?

Honey slapped her thighs as she got to her feet. 'OK! I'm going. But don't say I didn't warn you.'

Cool as a cucumber, her mother began spreading scarlet varnish over her fingernails.

'No need to warn me, Hannah darling. I know what he is.'

'You do?'

'Sure. He's a red-blooded man and after my body.'

Honey grimaced. 'He's also a wholesale butcher and just as likely to be after my meat order!'

Enough was enough. She took her leave and headed for sanity – if chasing after a disgruntled chef could be called that. Never mind. It beat being told she was jealous and hadn't got any romance in her life.

She swung into the car park of the Beau Brummell Hotel. The place was being run by a manager, who told her that Richard Carmelli hadn't been there for days. He gave her his home address.

'And if you find him, tell him he's fired.'

Fair enough!

She rang Casper to ask him if he knew of anyone in particular that Stella might have upset.

'I will have a list ready for you, though it may fall well short of the true total. Our darling deceased Stella made a habit of upsetting people.'

Honey then scooted over to the other side of town, almost enjoying the ease with which the black Volkswagen Beetle nosed through the traffic. Not too much traffic at this time of day and surprise, surprise, a parking space outside the Old Dispensary.

Detached and elegantly imposing, the building from which dubious cures for common and uncommon ailments had been dispensed from in years gone by was now converted for multiple occupations. Buses, cars and Lycra-clad cyclists brushed past the miniature Roman temples garnishing each end of the bridge. At least they looked like Roman temples though were little more than toll booths with Roman-style pediments and Doric columns, a product of early nineteenth-century imperial pretensions. They definitely weren't Roman.

One of the booths had a sign outside saying aromatherapy oils for sale. The others were craft shops this week. By next week they could be something entirely different. That was the way it was in Bath; quick profits and fun for all; that was what everybody was looking for. Who was it that had said that? Beau Brummell himself probably, that Regency rake with an eye for the main chance (and the ladies) and the ear of the Prince Regent.

'*Whatever you want, sir, I will endeavour to get.*'

As she eyed the bridge, a head popped out between the Doric columns and waved. She squinted. Clint had acquired another little sideline. She waved back. What was he selling? Artwork . . . herbal remedies . . . or something else? She blanked the possibility that it might be something illegal. Clint was a dab hand with the dishwasher and the kitchen mop. She had to give him some slack.

She sent a text to Steve: *Richard Carmelli hired the warrior. Am off to find him.* Well, that should make him shift his butt! There was no evidence to support Carmelli being the murderer, but she had to make a start with or without Doherty.

Richard Carmelli lived on the second floor of the Old Dispensary. His name was written in green felt tip beside his buzzer.

Once, twice, three times; there was no answer.

She pressed the one above that. A woman answered.

'I'm looking for Richard Carmelli. I'm not getting any reply when I press his buzzer.'

'So?'

Not the helpful type.

'Has he gone away?'

'I hope so,' the voice snarled. 'And taken his bloody drum kit with him!'

No welcome mat outside *her* door.

She pressed the one below. An old voice crackled in response. Honey asked her about Richard Carmelli.

'Can you speak up a bit, dearie?'

She said it louder.

'Who?'

Louder again. She strained to hear the old woman.

'Oh, you mean the young man from upstairs.'

'That's right. The one who played the drums.'

'Did he?'

That deaf.

'Do you know anything about him?'

She was sure her voice was carrying to the other side of the road. Despite the noise of the traffic, people were looking in her direction.

'Of course I do. Come on in. I'll make you a cup of tea.'

The kettle was already on by the time she was inside the front door and that of the ground-floor flat.

Miss Meadows was small and thin as a bird. The hands that poured hot water into the pot were like sparrow's claws, tiny and fine; they'd be featherweight in the hand, Honey guessed.

She was shown into a pale green living room. The carpet was green, the furniture was green and the walls were that old Georgian green eggshell surface. Thankfully, the ceiling was white otherwise she would have felt she'd been swallowed by the Jolly Green Giant.

With a fragile, fluttering wave, Miss Meadows gestured that she sit down. She chose an old settee with squashy cushions, then wished she hadn't. The cushions almost swallowed her. She swapped to an upright chair.

White china cups decorated with ivy leaves – green of course – sat on a silver tray. The teapot, sugar bowl and milk jug matched the cups and saucers. The tray was covered with a green tray cloth edged with a red cross-stitch design. Silver edging betrayed the tray's quality.

'He's gone away,' said Miss Meadows once she'd gone through her own version of the tea ceremony. This consisted of using a real tea strainer, real tea leaves, sugar dispensed with silver tongs and milk poured from a silver-lidded jug. It was necessary to shake one's head emphatically in order to emphasize that she did not want sugar. Miss Meadows was more than a bit deaf.

'When did he go?'

Her shout seemed to bounce off the high ceiling and come crashing around them. Miss Meadows looked vague. 'What was that you said?'

'When did he go? Him from upstairs,' she shouted, pointing at the ceiling.

She could tell from the old dear's expression that she still hadn't heard what she'd said. She wondered if she could lip read.

She repeated herself, louder this time and exaggerated her lip movements, moving them like melting rubber.

'Hold on, dear,' said Miss Meadows.

A high-pitched squeal followed as the fragile fingers fiddled with something in her pocket. A hearing aid.

'That's better,' she said at last. 'I try not to use my hearing aid too much to save batteries. But sometimes one needs to know what is being said.'

With what she considered the patience of a saint, Honey repeated the same question. 'I was asking about Richard Carmelli.'

Miss Meadows winced and adjusted her hearing aid. 'No need to shout, dear.'

That awful squeak again.

Honey took a sip of tea and counted to ten.

'Such a nice young man,' said Miss Meadows, her tiny head tilted to one side, peering at her like a short sighted sparrow. 'He played the drums, you know.'

'Yes, I know.' Honey curbed her impatience with another sip of tea. She refrained from saying, '*Yes. It was me that told you that.*'

'Biscuit?'

Miss Meadows pushed forward a plate containing four garibaldi biscuits.

'No, thank you. I'm trying to lose weight.'

'I've never had that problem,' said Miss Meadows, and tucked in.

'So he went away – Richard Carmelli – your neighbour?'

Miss Meadows nodded, swallowed her biscuit and took a loud slurp of tea.

'Lovely biscuits.' She picked up another one. 'He left with a friend. I watched them from the window. He didn't take all his things. Certainly not his drum kit. Just one article of luggage. One of those soft things. Not a suitcase.'

'A holdall?'

'Is that what they call them?'

'Yes. They fold up easily. What did the friend look like?'

Miss Meadows chewed and sucked on her biscuit. At the same time she looked up at the ceiling with dark eyes. In contrast her hair was snowy white. In her youth she might have been pretty – like a dormouse – not taking up much room.

'Fair. Corn-coloured hair I think. About five feet ten and wearing a black leather jacket with a white line down each sleeve.'

Honey felt the colour draining from her face. She knew

that jacket very well. Its owner worked for her. Smudger Smith!

'Are you sure about that?'

She nodded. 'Oh, yes.' And took another garibaldi. 'His car was parked right outside. It was very small. No room for a drum kit.' She shook her head, her expression conveying that small cars with no room for a drum kit were an affront to good taste.

The description of the car was going to confirm her worse fears. The jacket was bad enough. Her stomach muscles tightened. She knew; she just *knew* what Miss Meadows was going to say next.

'The car was green with shiny wheels and a black hood. The hood was down of course. The day was clement. They drove off. But they have been back of course. To collect the post,' she explained, in answer to Honey's questioning look. 'Sometimes it's that nice young Richard, and sometimes it's his friend, the nice young man who collected him that day. The girl used to come too, but not for a while.'

Honey remembered the one and only shift Smudger had taken off sick. At the time paranoia had swept in with a vengeance. What if he was really ill and couldn't work any more? she'd thought. Or worse still, what if he'd really been for a job interview? Now she knew the truth. He'd been lying.

Just at that moment, a four-wheel drive Mercedes pulled out of one of the parking spaces outside. Another car rolling along with the morning traffic stopped, indicated and pulled into the empty space. A green sports car. The driver got out.

Honey stood up. 'Thank you for the tea, Miss Meadows.'

'Do come again. What did you say your name was?'

'Driver. Hannah Driver. My friends call me Honey.'

'How sweet.'

The door to the ground-floor flat shut behind her at the very same moment as Smudger turned the key. He stopped in his tracks when he saw her.

'I'm parked along the end,' she said. 'You didn't see me.'

'Christ!' he murmured and closed his eyes.

'I think you've got some explaining to do.'

He nodded. 'Yeah. I suppose so.'

'Where is he?'

Smudger grimaced. 'At my place.'

'I'll follow you.'

After they'd parked their respective vehicles, she made her way to Smudger's flat. He got there before her, and was now looking disconsolate, standing in the doorway.

'He's gone.'

'Are you lying?'

'Scout's honour.' He made a cross sign on his chest.

She pushed past him, her jaw grimly set for action – or at least a bloody good argument. 'I doubt whether you ever were a bloody scout.'

The living room was typically lad culture. No pictures on the walls, no ornaments and magazines and newspapers stacked in handy heaps. A few beer cans formed a tight pyramid in front of the large bay window.

'So where's he gone? The bedroom?'

She peeked into the bedroom. No one. Next the bathroom. No one there either.

When she got back into the living room, Smudger was standing in front of the window, hands in pockets. He was staring out at the road outside in that vague way that meant he was seeing nothing.

All of a sudden she was angry.

'What the bloody hell do you think you're playing at?'

Throat tight with a whole dictionary of insults and expletives, she stood with fists tight on hips; a bit like Widow Twankey in *Aladdin*, though not so ugly she hoped. And she wasn't carrying quite so much weight on the hips. It couldn't be exercise. Sleuthing must burn calories.

'He's a mate. I had to help him out.'

Honey slumped into a chair. 'Mark, he could well be a murderer.'

It wasn't often she called him by his first name. It was usually either Smudger or Chef. But serious crime calls for serious measures.

Smudger stood looking his usual square-faced self; non-committal, convinced he was right.

'Well?' she said, once she'd pushed open a few more doors and found nothing more unnerving than a pile of dirty laundry and a hijacked road sign saying 'Access Only'.

Smudger gave her one of his challenging looks, the sort he

used when they were having a tussle over whether to use mangetout or French beans.

'Fire me if you like!'

There it was; the first salvo in a battle of nerves.

Her blood ran cold. 'Did I say I was going to fire you?'

She tried not to show just how much the comment unnerved her. There again, depending on what these two had been up to, she might lose her chef anyway. Nervous tension sucked in her stomach muscles. In consequence she felt half an inch of slack in her waistband. A good thing, but a fat waistline was preferable to losing a good chef.

It was no good. This was serious. A girl had to do what a girl had to do. 'I have to tell Steve Doherty. You know that, don't you?'

He shrugged and gestured with his hands. 'Yeah.'

Feeling like a fink but telling herself she had no choice, she pulled out her phone.

Steve answered on the third ring. 'Hi there, stranger!'

'It's me.'

'I know. I saw your number.'

Of course he did. She explained about Richard Carmelli.

'Come into the station,' he said. 'And bring Smith with you. Our meeting's a bit overdue.'

Twenty-One

'Oliver Stafford deserved to die.'

Glancing at Smudger's expression, Honey could see that he meant it. 'I don't think you should say that in the vicinity of Manvers Street Police Station.'

The rain was belting down. Even the thrashing backwards and forwards of the windscreen wipers failed to make much impact. Visibility was minimum and spasmodic. And she hadn't brought a coat.

She made a face at the rain. 'I'm not walking all the way from the car park.'

'Your choice.'

Smudger offered up another of his 'not bothered' shrugs. She threw him a withering look. 'We wouldn't be here at all if you'd told the truth from the start.'

'It's a grown man's prerogative.'

'Well, aren't you fun company today. You're right there! Thirty-six and going on ten years old.'

Fun he was not.

'This is the police station car park,' he said sounding surprised as the Volkswagen did a swift right and mounted the curb.

'Clever boy.'

'They won't like you parking here. See?' he pointed. 'Patrol vehicles and staff cars only.'

'I'm almost staff.'

Smudger looked bemused. He snorted. 'In your dreams. That copper only tolerates you 'cos he wants to get 'is leg over.'

'Chef!' She felt herself blushing. 'That's no way to talk to your boss!'

He grinned. Smudger knew he had her over a barrel. He was a good chef and knew it. He was a loyal employee and knew how to play her. The last item was a little short of a problem. But she found his mix of bluntness and insight incredibly refreshing.

She eased herself out of the car butt first and proceeded to strip the seat cover from off the driver's seat.

Smudger looked bemused. 'You don't need to vandalize your own car. Leave it in a side street long enough and someone will do it for you.'

She ignored him. 'This is an emergency. I paid good money for this hairdo.'

The seat cover was made of stretchy grey material trimmed with a red racing stripe. It wasn't much protection against the rain, but the head rest bit fitted neatly over her head, the rest did a little to shield her shoulders.

The rain began trickling down her neck. She made the obvious conclusion. Made in China, in an area where it doesn't rain that often. By the time they were in out of the rain, her hair was flat and sticking to her skull.

'I've just had this done,' Honey muttered. 'Now look!'

Her bouncy hair was now plastered to her head like a shiny wimple. She tried dissecting it with her fingers, plumping it out so that it looked reasonably presentable.

Steve met them in the foyer. Sensibly, he was wearing a rain-proof jacket with a hood.

'We're going for coffee,' Doherty said.

'We can't. It's raining. Look at my hair.'

She could see he was looking, but not really *seeing* it.

'I thought the wet look was fashionable.'

'Only if you're a sea lion!'

Doherty herded them out of the door and nodded at the desk sergeant on the way out.

He grabbed Smudger's shoulder. 'What the hell are you playing at? Aiding and abetting a murder suspect.'

Honey leapt to his defence. 'He didn't do it.'

Smudger was adamant. 'I didn't do it.'

So was Steve. 'You've been mucking me around.'

Smudger was taller and heavier, so Honey's eyes boggled when Steve caught hold of his collar and spun him round so they were snarling into each other's faces.

'Only the evidence matters, not your bloody opinion. Now where is he?'

As Smudger shook his head, the look in his eyes hardened and his hands clenched into sizeable fists. Honey held her breath. She could feel the hostility sizzling between these two.

Recognizing he was in a no-win situation, it was Smudger who gave in. His voice was surprisingly even when he answered. 'I don't know. I honestly don't know.'

Something about his expression seemed to hit a chord with Doherty. Perhaps it was threat, perhaps plain belief that her chef was telling the truth. His hands loosened.

'OK. I believe you, but ring me if you hear from him. Clear?'

Smudger nodded. 'Clear.'

Charmy Down was deserted. Three miles or so from the centre of Bath, no one disturbed the battered buildings or the weeds pushing through the concrete here. Sometimes a heavy plant firm parked unused earthmovers. Apart from them, the place had a neglected air, and yet the old buildings were visible from the main road, stuck like a lighthouse at the top of an incline. The buildings had been built for the RAF back in the Second World War and as such were flat roofed and uninteresting. Back then practical usage had been more important than aesthetics.

Richard Carmelli parked his car where it could not be seen from either the road or the fields, shielded by an old building on one side and a bulldozer on the other. He knew this place from the days when he'd come here camping with his stepfather. He knew how to light a fire without it being seen, how it felt to snuggle down inside a thick sleeping bag. Just like a boy scout, he'd come prepared. He was always prepared, always planning ahead for any eventuality.

He tipped the contents of his holdall on to the floor. Beans, beans and sausages, tinned soups, tinned meats; he could survive for days on this. He'd also brought Coronation Chicken. A lot of Coronation Chicken.

He got out his phone and selected a familiar name from the phonebook listing. A female voice answered.

'It's me,' he said softly.

'Where are you?'

He smiled. 'I'm a fighter pilot.'

'I see.'

Of course she did. Saying he was a fighter pilot to anyone else wouldn't make much sense, but it did to her. She knew this place as well as he did. They'd camped here when they were children and played amongst the tumbling ruins. That was in the days before the heavy plant was left here. It had been all wild flowers and tall grass back then, a fun place for kids with a view of the valley.

'Don't worry about me.'

'Richard, you don't need to do this. I'm fine. I'm happy.'

'I understand that, but there's other things happening. Oliver had dangerous friends.'

'Richard, be careful.'

'I've got to get it out of my system. I'm rattling a few cages that's for sure. Calling in favours too.' He decided to terminate the call. 'I'll be in touch.'

She didn't argue. He hadn't explained all his reasons for doing what he was doing. It was too complicated and much too dangerous. He hadn't even told Smudger everything he should have.

He felt bad letting Smudger Smith down, but he'd had no choice. He hoped he would understand. He had to hide until things calmed down. No one ever came here. No one else would know he was here.

Twenty-Two

S teve collared Mark for a second time at the Green River Hotel. Smudger swore and rolled his eyes when he heard the news.

'What the f—?'

'Chef!' Honey's tone brought him up sharp. 'It has to be done. It won't take long,' she went on.

Without a word Zak, his commis chef, and Freda, his trainee, took over the chores he'd been doing, heads down, pretending they hadn't heard.

Few and far between were the times when she'd seen Smudger looking worried, but he was now.

She squeezed his arm affectionately. 'Don't worry. It's just questions.'

Over coffee Honey and Steve listened and learned about what had happened to make Richard plot revenge.

A subdued Smudger warmed his hands around the coffee mug as he swigged at it.

'It was three years ago in France at this competition – the Grande Epicure.' He raised his eyes to Honey's face. 'Before I worked for you. Young Richard had already won God knows how many 'Young Chef of the Year' competitions. But this was the big banana and he was tipped to win. Richard's a great chef.'

'Greater than you?' Honey asked.

His expression darkened, then lightened again. 'He had great potential.'

Honey took that as a yes.

'The competition consisted of three parts: starter, main course and dessert. Richard was good at all of it, but particularly at desserts. I won the starter course, Oliver second. Oliver won the main course, Richard second. Richard was expected to win the dessert course but he didn't. Someone substituted salt for sugar. We all knew who.'

'So Oliver won?'

'Yep! Trouble was Richard was such a sensitive lad. He took it to heart. Took to drugs after that so I hear. I hadn't even heard he was working with Oliver. I didn't hear anything from him until he phoned me just after Oliver got well and truly roasted.'

Honey frowned as she thought things through. 'That's a bit strange, isn't it? I presume he hated Oliver, so why go to work with him at the Beau Brummell?'

A wicked grin lightened Smudger's face. 'To get his own back. Oliver hated practical jokes. They wound 'im right up.'

Steve had stepped into his ultra-serious mode. 'But why involve Stella Broadbent? I presume your friend Richard was responsible for Francis Trent?'

That grin again. 'I don't know whether that was anything to do with 'im, though it might have something to do with Sunday nights.'

Honey raised a single puzzled eyebrow.

Steve's look was steadfast, almost unblinking, as though he was loath to miss anything.

'This is what happened, right? Oliver and her organized the weekly menus on Sunday nights and they went up to the honeymoon suite to do it.'

A mental picture of Stella's office flashed into Honey's mind; large desk, thick carpet, comfortable chairs, ideal surroundings for office work. She couldn't be sure, because she'd never been in the room, but no doubt the honeymoon suite on the other hand had more varied and intimate prospects.

'They used to get in the bath together. Richard said he could hear the swishing about from outside.'

'Menus tend to go soggy in the bath,' said Honey. She shot a swift look at Steve. 'Not that I've had experience of that.'

Smudger nodded. 'Correct. Richard used to go outside for a smoke behind the shed. They didn't know it, but he could hear them from there splashing about and all that.'

Steve had let his coffee go cold. Honey could tell by his grim expression that he wasn't letting up on Smudger that easily. And she'd told Smudger that everything in the garden would be lovely.

'He didn't confront them?' Steve asked.

Smudger, who thankfully was far from being his volatile self, shook his head. 'Nope. Richard had a quirky sense of humour.'

'Hence the Masai warrior. It's a well-known fact that Stella gets drunk as a skunk when she's letting her hair down. She wouldn't know whether she'd got married or flown to the moon as far as that goes.' Honey narrowed her eyes as a thought suddenly struck her. 'But the joke would have cost money.'

Smudger grinned. 'And chefs ain't exactly overpaid – unless they end up with their own restaurant in the West End of London complete with their own TV show. Perhaps if I swore a lot more . . .'

She knew which TV chef he was referring to. 'You swear plenty enough!'

Steve had put on his serious hat. 'So where is he?'

Smudger was emphatic. 'I've already told you, I don't bloody know. He had a phone call and shot off, and before you ask, he didn't tell me who it was and where he was going.'

Steve's expression remained hard. 'And Brian Brodie. What's the connection?'

Smudger shrugged. 'No idea. All I know is that he was at the Grande Epicure at the same time as the rest of us.'

They left the chef and kitchen to each other.

Steve studied the floor as they walked back to Reception.

'Do you think Carmelli did it?' she asked him.

'I don't know. He had a grievance and he had been playing silly devils. I can't stand practical jokes. They can backfire badly. A friend of mine told all his family and friends that he'd won the lottery. His wife took him at his word and immediately claimed half of the winnings. Unfortunately it didn't end there. She said that the moment the money came in she would take her half and shove off with his brother. Apparently they'd been having an affair for years.'

They reached Reception, both quiet, both thoughtful.

'So where do we go from here?' she asked.

Steve sighed. 'How about a walk?'

Things were quiet so she chanced it. They walked down Great Pulteney Street towards the bridge, the abbey and the heart of the city. A guy dressed as a clown was handing out flyers for a new restaurant. Despite the fact he was wearing clown make-up, the spider's cobweb tattoo and the nose rings gave Clint away.

She took one of his flyers. 'Clint. Nice day.'

She sensed the white face turned whiter. 'Crikey, Mrs Driver. I didn't recognize you.'

She thought about saying that *he* was the one in the make-up and supposedly unrecognizable.

'Clint, if you take on any more jobs the tax man's going to have a field day.'

'Don't say things like that, Mrs Driver. I won't be able to sleep at night.'

He spotted Steve Doherty. 'Nice day, Mr Doherty, sir.'

He did a quick salute – two fingers at the side of the head – something between Boy Scout and downright rude. Then he was gone.

Steve smiled and shook his head in pretend despair. 'I reckon I could arrest that bloke on a whole portfolio of charges.'

'That's a big word,' said Honey.

Clint was always working. She doubted he slept. Perhaps he was just naturally hyperactive, or perhaps it was something else.

One of Roland Mead's delivery vans drove past. Honey eyed it dispassionately.

It took her by surprise when Steve said, 'Mead's vans are everywhere.'

'He's courting my mother.'

'That's an old-fashioned term.'

'My mother's an old-fashioned girl.'

They were like two tourists out for a stroll. She was enjoying this; the day was warm and a band across the road in Parade Gardens was playing everyone's favourite bit from Dvorak's 'New World Symphony'. Never mind crime, never mind murder; something about designer stubble turned a girl on. She wondered whether the look was due to laziness or intentional. Or did he have a weak chin. She sneaked a quick glance. No. Strong chin. Strong jaw. Both prerequisites for the man of the moment.

By the time they were strolling around Parade Gardens, their elbows were brushing. Funny how erotic that could be; just touching, just brushing.

'I've been thinking,' he said.

She popped the thoughts she'd been thinking and adopted a deadpan expression, the one that said *I'm in professional mode; wouldn't dream of being anything else.*

'And?'

'I've been wondering when we're going to get round to going to bed together.'

The deadpan expression went down the toilet.

'Um . . . well, I've been kind of busy . . . and you have too . . . so . . .'

Her voice trailed away. There was no way she was going to admit he'd fallen asleep and missed his chance. What if he had been awake? Wow, we could have been an item by now.

She breathed in; yes, he did smell nice, and that stubble would feel so . . . She drew back from going there. She hadn't answered his question.

They were still walking along, Steve looking unperturbed, almost as though all he'd made was a comment about the weather.

'It would have happened by now if we worked more regularly together. Why don't you join the police force? You'd look good in a uniform.'

He sneaked the kind of smile conveying he was thinking of what lay *beneath* the uniform.

'I don't want to. I like what I'm doing. I like meeting people.'

'I meet people too,' said Steve. 'OK, I admit some of them are scum.'

Honey raised her eyebrows. 'In Bath? Don't let Casper hear you say that. He swears that this city is God's little acre.'

Steve grimaced. 'He's biased. Never mind that, you still haven't answered my question.'

She shook her head in a lazy manner. 'Well . . . you have to ask yourself whether getting close might have a detrimental impact on our professional relationship.'

He looked at her. 'Was that English?'

'Of course it was.'

Emptying her mind of what was possible between them left room for other thoughts to creep in.

Falling into silence, they walked on. Steve was first to break the silence, returning to the former subject.

'I suppose it means that we should take a rain check.'

The word fell out of her mouth before she could stop it. 'Yes.'

She wanted to kick herself. Her mouth was not voicing what she really wanted to say. *OK, I want to jump your bones. Let's set a date.*

It was too late. She couldn't go back on it and say, 'OK, let's do it.' She had her pride.

Steve did a kind of hunching thing with his shoulders – something between a reluctant shrug and a stretch.

'You're right and I'm tired. No point in going off half cock is there?'

She smiled. *No point at all.*

Twenty-Three

S teve Doherty sifted the pieces of paper on his desk, moving them around like so many playing cards. He told his team what Smudger Smith had told him about the cooking competition and Richard Carmelli. Honey had been invited to sit in. As she listened she took notes from which she could compile a report for Casper.

Steve was well into his stride. His voice was strong. He sounded committed.

'Richard Carmelli is the only person we've come across with a motive. Possibly strong enough to commit murder, but possibly not. Oliver Stafford was none too popular, but Carmelli had been playing practical jokes on him for weeks knowing full well that he hated them.'

A detective interrupted. 'What sort of jokes, boss?'

Steve looked to Honey to fill in the details.

'Misdirected post, girlfriends' phones being redirected to his phone – and his wife at home. And a so-called pregnant woman turning up at his work place. She actually had a pillow stuffed up her dress.'

The pregnant woman had been a friend of Richard's and hadn't charged for her services. The bloke with the leopard skin around his neck had cost good money.

Steve thanked her and carried on. 'There are a few questions we still need to ask – when we find him.'

So far Steve had been looking down at the pieces of paper. Everyone in the room was slouching, taking it in but leisurely. Steve flicked his gaze from paper to the detectives sprawled and slouched in front of him. One or two had one eye on him and one on their computer. He had no doubt they were playing Spider Solitaire. In the past he'd done the same when he was bored, frustrated or both. Well, he'd soon put pay to that.

It came full pelt from his diaphragm. 'Wake up, people!'

There followed a general readjustment of bodies and eyes.

Steve could flick his eyes into fast-forward when he wanted, searching each face in turn and adding a little warning; *Don't go to sleep on me. Listen to what I am saying.*

'There has to be a link between Oliver Stafford and Brian Brodie besides this cooking contest they entered in France. Apparently, Richard Carmelli only had it in for Oliver Stafford so why Brian Brodie?'

Honey frowned. 'Why Stella?'

A mix of admiring and hostile eyes turned in her direction. The men were admiring. The women looked as though they would like to execute her on the spot. Steve brought out the beast in uniformed women.

Steve's frown matched hers. 'Maybe this isn't about the chefs. Maybe this is about her.'

'Another question,' said Honey, attracting silent glares from the girls in blue. 'What about the marks around Stella's throat?'

Steve threw her a grateful nod. 'That's a good point. Pathology confirms that these were inflicted prior to her demise and that the car crash killed her. However, we have to ask ourselves, did someone frighten Stella Broadbent, bearing in mind that she was already drunk? A lethal cocktail; fear and alcohol. If one doesn't get you, the other will, and both together are lethal.'

Twenty-Four

It had been a pleasant day before her mother and Roland turned up. The moment her mother was out of earshot, Roland Mead leapt forward, his breath falling over her.

'You'll regret not doing business with me. No one can touch me for price.'

'The Davis brothers supply quality.'

'Profit!' said Roland. 'That's what this game's all about, lass. Profit. You can stuff quality up your shirt!'

Not for the first time she wondered what it was her mother saw in the man. She managed to mutter, 'Up your shirt,' before her mother came back.

He'd tried to curry favour with her chef, now he was trying it on with her – again.

Her mother had brought him in for coffee and ordered a tray with three cups.

'Hannah, darling, do join us. We'd love you to, wouldn't we, Roland?'

Roland said something in agreement.

'I'm too busy, Mother.'

'Don't disappoint us,' Gloria mewed. She adopted the classic Cocker Spaniel look; no other dog could look so mournful. Her mother could. She looked up into Roland's rustic face. 'This is the problem when you get older, Roland. The young are too busy to bother with you.'

Roland turned all bluff and hearty. He patted the empty space in the chair immediately opposite him. 'Come on, girl. Take the weight off your feet.'

She glanced back at the reception desk. Mary Jane was standing there, a splash of colour in a psychedelic pink and pistachio kaftan with matching trousers.

'I'm sorry, Mother. Mary Jane is waiting at Reception.'

Ever helpful, Mary Jane overheard and decided to help out.

She'd taken to waitressing on tables since she'd moved into the hotel, lock, stock and barrel. Her assistance was mostly confined to clearing the dishes. No one had objected. Most restaurant diners and hotel guests had been shocked into silence. Black and white was the usual uniform for waitresses, most of whom were young and agile. A tall octogenarian dressed in pink, took some getting used to.

'I only want brochures. I know where they're kept,' Mary Jane called out. Ignoring the notice banning guests from going behind the reception desk, she did just that and helped herself. The phone began to ring whilst she was there. Honey got up.

Mary Jane got there first. 'I got it. You stay there with your mother and enjoy your coffee.'

'There you are,' said her mother. 'Sit down.'

'You and I should get to know each other better,' said Roland, his smile as watery as his eyes.

Honey kept one ear on Mary Jane.

'You're calling from La Jolla? Hey, that's where I'm from.'

Honey groaned. Whoever was phoning merely wanted to book a room and would want to know the price. By the time they got off the line from Mary Jane, their phone bill would pay for three nights' accommodation.

She told Roland the same as she had before; her chef chose suppliers and so far she'd not found any reason not to continue that policy.

Her mother passed her a coffee. She put it down on the table.

Mary Jane was still in full flow. 'Well, if you're coming to England, then you have to visit Bath, and if you're coming to Bath there's nowhere else better to stay than the Green River Hotel. Would you believe it's even got a resident ghost? Not that he'll bother you unless you're a relative. Sir Cedric and I are intimately acquainted because, do you know what? I *am* a relative!'

Honey groaned inwardly. Now the caller would think that everyone at the hotel – and possibly in the whole city of Bath – was as batty as Mary Jane.

By mid-morning she had it in her mind to go for a drive.

The edge of the reception desk was digging into her behind

and her arms were folded. Lindsey was sitting in front of the computer screen.

'I need to talk to Sylvester Pardoe,' she said thoughtfully.

'Haven't the police spoken to him?'

Honey shook her head. 'He's too lightweight a contender to figure in their inquiries. But I've got a feeling in my water . . .'

'Then go for it – but plan things, Mother. I know you like to fly by the seat of your pants, but let's take this one step at a time.'

Feeling suitably chastised, Honey raised questioning eyebrows. 'Lead on, Sherlock. What do I do?'

Lindsey tapped a few keys. 'Bullet point the reasons you need to speak to him.'

Honey paused, her emotions stirred by the sight of her daughter's face bathed in computer-generated light.

'Right! Number one. He attended the Grande Epicure in France three years ago along with the two dead chefs and our own, dear Smudge.'

'OK.' More tapping of keys. 'And what's the significance of that?'

'I don't know. I think the dead men did. It's just finding someone they might have mentioned it to.'

They both fell silent as their eyes met. This was telepathy of the mundane variety.

'He never mentioned it,' said Lindsey, referring to Oliver Stafford, and looked away.

Honey forced herself back on track. 'Right. Number two, he opted out of judging the competition at the last minute. Why was that?'

Lindsey typed it in. 'Did you think of phoning him again?'

'He won't speak to me. I'll have to go up there.'

Lindsey sat back in her chair. She had that elderly look that belongs with someone over forty.

'You remember that Smudge had an affair with Oliver's wife?'

Honey had forgotten that piece of information.

Lindsey pulled a face. 'Oliver Stafford had a very open view of marriage. He expected his wife to have the same. Smudger said she found it hard to have carte blanche. Said it made her feel sick.'

'But Smudger still went ahead?' Honey couldn't believe it.

'Not so much sexually as supportive. I think things got quite serious, almost to the stage of setting up home together.'

'So why didn't they go through with it?'

'Oliver got murdered. She's free now.'

Honey threw back her head as the truth hit her like a stone-age cudgel.

'Oh my God. No wonder he's been so offhand. He got involved and got dumped. She used him as a crutch.'

'Cow,' muttered Lindsey. 'Poor Smudger.'

Leaving with a list of questions, Honey retrieved her car from the underground car park where it usually sat and gunned it for the A46 and the Cotswolds. Green, yellow and corn-gold fields fell like blankets to either side of the road. Once past Westonbirt Arboretum, honey-gold cottages clustered around village greens and village pubs. Grander houses became more frequent, the latter glowing with Virginia creeper showing signs of changing to red.

Judging by its exterior of mullion windows and iron-tie rods shaped like horseshoes in its walls, the Haywain was once just an ordinary pub. Long before the Chelsea tractors and Mercedes sports cars, drovers on their way to market and ploughmen congregated beneath its smoke-blackened beams to drink cider and eat their bread and cheese.

Now the building boasted two Michelin stars. In years long past, the cost of just one item from its menu would have kept a ploughman or drover for nigh on a year.

The slate floor was grey and shiny, the oak beams ancient and a foot wide. Suffused with the vision of how many people had passed under its mass, Honey reached up and touched it.

'It's real. Not plastic,' said the young waiter, white cloth over his arm, silver tray clutched like a breastplate to his body.

He had an open face and his smile was helpful.

'Hello. I would like to speak to Sylvester Pardoe.'

'And the name of your company?'

She couldn't believe her luck. The waiter had assumed she was a sales rep. It was on the tip of her tongue to set the guy right, but her crafty side kicked in. Telling the truth would probably result in her being shown the door.

'Liaisons L'Escargots,' she said. Heaven knows where the

name came from, but it sounded good. 'Fat little snails from the best fields in the West Country.'

She flashed him a confident smile. 'Better than the French produce,' she added.

He asked her if she had a card. She acted out the pretence of looking for one.

'No,' she said, shaking her head sadly. She went on to explain that she'd had her handbag stolen the day before and was waiting for a new batch.

'That's a shame,' said the waiter. 'Never mind. What did you say your name was?'

'Mary Jane Jefferies!'

The tall American's name was once again the first that came into her head. It was something to do with the paranormal bit – as though Mary Jane's ectoplasm was whispering in her ear.

The waiter went off. She watched his tight rear and tighter trousers until he'd disappeared, then had a look round whilst she waited.

Glasses were being collected. The last of the lunchtime diners were paying their bills, sauntering off to use the cloak-rooms before leaving.

The walls were painted off-white; the mullion windows were intact and tapestries rather than modern artwork comple-mented furnishings that could have been made just after the Puritan Oliver Cromwell had hacked off the head of King Charles the First. The oak furniture and old-style artefacts pleased her. To his credit Sylvester Pardoe had resisted the urge to follow fashion trends and make the old place plain and modern.

A young couple came in making enquiries about a wedding. 'I think you need to see Mr Pardoe himself,' she told them. 'I think we could be going in the same direction.'

The waiter came back. This time it was his face that was tight. She had a feeling what was coming.

'He says you should have made an appointment first, but that he can spare you five minutes.'

'Thanks for your efforts. I appreciate it.'

He shrugged and managed a nervous smile. 'It was nothing.'

She guessed it was far from nothing. If she guessed right, his ear had been well and truly chewed if Pardoe's attitude on the phone was anything to go by.

Mentally girding up her loins, she followed where he led.

She heard Pardoe before she saw him and winced at the bad language. She reminded herself that he was a chef not just a restaurant owner.

Another F-word rocked the eardrums of everyone within shouting distance. My word, Smudger's vocabulary was reserved compared to this!

Pardoe was verbally wiping the floor with a diminutive commis chef. It was something to do with making Coq au Vin with red wine instead of white. The words he used to describe what he'd do if it ever happened again were best censored.

'Now get out of here!'

The poor creature, head bowed, scurried off like a hamster in search of a wheel.

A man with a pony tail and a heavy shock of fringe falling over his face swivelled round to face her.

Unsmiling, he glanced at his watch.

'You've got five minutes.'

Pardoe was not immediately aware of the couple following her.

'I'm not selling snails. I've come to talk about murder. These people behind me have come to talk about a wedding. Perhaps you'd like to deal with them first.'

For a moment Pardoe looked shell-shocked, his expression flitting from arrogance to discomfort and closely followed by gushing familiarity.

Teeth flashing, he addressed the young couple. 'My profound apologies. Mr Greg and Miss Sommer.'

He arranged for them to have coffee and a complimentary glass of champagne in the lounge whilst perusing menus and table arrangements.

'I'll be right with you after I've dealt with this lady,' he said, his smile not quite reaching his eyes.

Mr Happy Face closed the door. Mr Bloody Angry turned to face her. 'What the bloody hell . . . ?'

'Don't shout at me, Sylvester bloody Pardoe!'

He couldn't have looked more surprised if she'd slapped him in the face with a pound of cod.

She kept the initiative. 'I am Hannah Driver.' She swiftly flashed her wallet full of credit cards and suchlike. The one from Bath Library complete with her picture looked the most officious. And she'd specifically used her true name.

'I'm liaising with the police regarding the murder of Oliver Stafford and Brian Brodie on behalf of Bath Hotels' Association. I need to ask you some questions.'

She groped in her bag for a notebook and a pen. The former came to hand. The latter did not. Deeper and deeper she went. By virtue of their shape and weight, pens always seemed to worm their way to the bottom.

The tips of her fingers touched one. At the same time her sleeve snagged on something. When she pulled her arm out the 'something' came too.

'Bugger,' she said, her face already reddening. 'They built them to last back then,' she said apologetically, as she tried to untangle herself from the metal fasteners on the outsize bra. Why did it always happen to her? And why now, just when she'd adopted the role and tone of authority?

She looked at Pardoe. His jaw was slack and his mouth open. She actually saw a twinkle dance in his eyes. Well, that was a turn up!

First the corners of his mouth twitched. The twitch became a wider movement and ultimately a wide grin.

'What the f—?'

Honey regained her composure. 'I am of the opinion that bad language is a last resort of a total moron.'

She could have said do you mind not using bad language, but sensed too many had already gone down that road. Sylvester Pardoe didn't pardon himself for anyone.

'They're nothing to do with you,' she added, pushing the offending item – which she would for ever and a day refer to as a 'brazier' back into her bag. 'Now. Shall we make a start?'

'Crack on,' he said, a half smile wavering on his face as he settled himself into a chair.

Honey did the same, pulling a chair forward so she could rest her notepad on the corner of the very trendy blue metal desk. In her mind she blessed whoever had shoved the giant undergarment into her bag. Pardoe's mood might never have lifted but for them.

Honey composed herself. 'Right. First off . . .'

'Hold it right there. I've changed my mind. I'll tell you what I do know, such as that bloody witch Broadbent was

screwing her chef. Mind you, he'd screw anything anyway
depending on the stakes. This could be about sex or it could
be about money.'

Honey pounced on the money angle. 'You mean stakes as
in money, cut of the action, valuables . . . ?'

He dropped his head in a curt nod. 'That sort. And before
you ask, no, I don't know what kind of wedge we're talking
about here. Something valuable. Something that would keep
my old *friend* Oliver in the lifestyle he easily became used
to. And, yes, my referring to him as an old friend is facetious.
I hated the b—'

'Was that why you opted out of judging the BITE competition?' Honey interrupted.

'I hated him.'

'And you knew Brian Brodie. Were he and Oliver close
friends?'

'In a way. Brian limped along in his shadow.'

'Who tipped you off?'

'A friend.'

'Who?'

'A friend.'

She frowned. 'I understand you met Stafford and Brodie at
the Grande Epicure some time ago. Did they do something
there that formed your opinion of them?'

'That's my business.'

Honey eyed the hard features, the firm chin, the lips set in
a straight thin line. The soft look in his eyes was at odds with
all that. Sylvester Pardoe was burning inside, but why and
with what?

She sensed he wasn't going to give any more, unless perhaps
she rescheduled her questioning to a more personal level?

'My chef, Mark Smith, attended the Grande Epicure. Did
you hate him too?

She held her breath as she awaited his answer.

Sylvester Pardoe shook his head and smiled sadly. 'Poor
Smudger. He's a good egg and a good chef, but when he gets
on the beer . . .'

Smiling, Honey nodded her head knowingly. Four pints and
her chef was sound asleep. Any more than that and he was
comatose. 'Vulnerable to pressure,' she said winningly.

'Aren't we all?'

'I find family pressures are worse than business pressures,' she said without thinking, without expecting Pardoe's reaction.

He didn't meet her look so didn't see her watching his knuckles turning white. He was clenching his fists fit to burst. Sylvester Pardoe was quick-tempered, arrogant and a damn sight more. But there was something else beneath the surface, something she couldn't quite put her finger on.

Suddenly the door opened. 'Sylvester, Mr Greg and Miss . . . oh. Hello.' The woman who had entered the room was slim and dark. Her smile was winning and her face beautiful – or at least half of it. Her right cheek was badly scarred.

She turned to Pardoe. 'I'm sorry, Sylvester. I didn't know you were busy.'

Pardoe got to his feet. 'She's just leaving.'

Honey was in no doubt she was being shown the door. The interview was at an end.

The lovely young woman looked a little disconcerted, arching one eyebrow at Pardoe as though she required an explanation. None was forthcoming.

Honey blurted an explanation. 'I was trying to sell your husband some snails.' A split second later it came to her what she'd just said. Just a hunch as they say, but she'd mentally assumed that this woman was Sylvester Pardoe's wife. Judging by the young woman's response, the smile and the arched eyebrow levelling out, she was right.

'We use local ones. Are yours local?' asked Mrs Pardoe.

'Yes. Sort of. From Cornwall.'

Mrs Pardoe nodded. 'I see.'

Sylvester Pardoe came out from behind his desk. 'I'll see you out,' he said to Honey, then turned to his wife. 'Tell the young couple I'll be with them shortly.' All trace of the loud-mouthed lout was gone. This, she guessed, was the better half that hovered beneath the surface.

Honey allowed him to cup her elbow and escort her out.

'Thank you for that,' he said, once they were outside.

'For owning up to being a snail salesman? I quite like snails.'

'They taste OK,' he said.

Again there was that look in his eyes; a mix of tenderness and concern.

'I didn't want her to know why you were here.'

'May I ask you why?'

'No.'

She turned away from him, wresting her elbow out of his grasp. 'Do I have to go back in and ask your wife?'

He caught her elbow.

'No. Please.' He looked pained.

She wondered how many times in a day, in a week, in his whole life had he used the word 'please'.

Folding her arms, she stood in front of him, looking grimly and directly into his face. She saw his discomfort. There was no need to ask questions now. He had to tell it as it was. He had no choice.

He looked away towards the road, gathered his thoughts, and looked back at her.

'You saw her face?'

She had a horrible feeling where this was going to go. 'Yes. She was scalded?'

'Yes. Hot fat.'

The day was cool, and yet in that instant imagining how it had felt, the air turned warm then hot.

She didn't ask because she knew he preferred to tell. And he did.

'My wife is also a chef. She too had been entered for the Grande Epicure. That's where we met. We clicked straight-away. Stafford was jealous. He wanted what I had. Gina didn't want to know and I thought we were safe. We weren't. Stafford made advances. She refused them, made a fool of him in front of everyone when she accused him of stealing pasta she'd made herself that morning. He denied it. She proved it. The bowl she'd stored it in was marked on the bottom. He was furious. He lost his temper and said it was an accident. It was difficult to prove any different. Brian Brodie was also there.'

Not once had he looked at her as he related this. He paused now and seemed deep in thought.

She dug her hands in her pockets and waited. The hot feeling had surfed over her. A cold chill remained.

He took a deep breath. 'I wanted to kill Stafford.'

'Did you?'

Eyeing her sidelong, he shook his head slowly and method-ically, almost as though he was measuring the distance between his own thoughts and wondering what her response might be.

The softness in his eyes was obliterated with outright hatred.

'Gina is Italian?'

He nodded and looked away. She studied his profile, thinking what a fine Heathcliff he made to Gina's Cathy. Thinking of Cathy's looks, her pulse began to race. She'd seen those features, that profile, before.

'What was your wife's maiden name?'

She waited impatiently, wondering if he would answer and confirm her suspicion, or lie and leave her to check at the records office.

'She was Gina Carmelli before we were married.'

And then she knew and was suddenly overcome with a great feeling of foreboding. Richard Carmelli had had more than one axe to grind.

Twenty-Five

B efore starting the car, she phoned the hotel and asked for Lindsey. Mary Jane answered.

'Hi there. This is the Green River Hotel. What can we do for you?'

Honey frowned. 'Where's Lindsey?'

'A nice young man phoned. He wanted to speak to you, but Lindsey told him you weren't here. He said it was vital he talked to someone. I expect he had information about the murders for you.'

'What did he tell her?'

'No idea. He hasn't told her yet. At least I don't think so. She only left ten minutes ago.'

Talking to Mary Jane was sometimes like pushing a large jelly bean uphill; it didn't go straight and kept rolling in odd directions.

'So she isn't there?'

'No. She's gone out. The young guy insisted. She's quite safe Smudger says; he knows the guy and swears he's trust-worthy.'

'Let me speak to Smudger.'

'Hold on. I'll just press this here button . . .'

The line went dead. Honey shouted down the phone. No response. The line was dead. She dialled again.

'Is that you, Honey?'

Honey rolled her eyes. 'You should have said this is the Green River Hotel. It might not have been me.'

'Of course it was you. I knew it was you.'

Communicating with older folk was often difficult; some-thing to do with the different plains of life. With Mary Jane it was like dealing with life on another planet.

There again, perhaps she *had* known it was her. After all, this was a doctor of the paranormal.

Smudger came on the line. "'Lo.' Amazing how he could shorten 'hello' to one syllable.

'You didn't say that Sylvester Pardoe was married to Richard Carmelli's sister.'

'Hmm.'

'Stop grunting. Grunts are not words. Why didn't you tell me?'

'You're the private dick. Work it out for yourself.'

Honey sighed and rolled her eyes. 'He has a motive.' But does Richard Carmelli have an alibi, she asked herself. Come to that, how about Sylvester Pardoe?

'My daughter's gone to meet a possible murderer. Why is that?'

'Ask Mary Jane. She took the message. Must say I was surprised though. Why would he ask Lindsey to meet him? Why not you?' Smudger sounded puzzled, as though he really couldn't understand it himself.

A cold chill sent Honey chanting her fears. 'Oliver Stafford and Brian Brodie were involved in Gina's disfigurement. Stella was having an affair with Oliver. Perhaps our murderer is out of control and out to kill anyone who had anything to do with Oliver.'

'He wouldn't do that. Not Lindsey.' Smudger didn't sound totally convinced.

'Where were they meeting?' Honey asked, her throat suddenly dry.

'I don't know. Mary Jane took the call and passed on the details.'

'Put me on to her. *Now!*'

He didn't waste a minute.

'Hi there, Honey!'

Judging by Mary Jane's chirpy voice, she had no idea of what she'd done.

It was difficult, but Honey forced herself to moderate her tone, telling herself it was just an age thing and she too would be old one day.

'Think carefully, Mary Jane. Where did the young man ask Lindsey to meet him?'

'The young man?'

'The young man who phoned. You passed the message on to Lindsey.'

'Oh.' There followed a pause. Honey imagined her with one finger on her cheek, her misty eyes studying the ceiling. 'Yes. He said to meet him at . . . Oh my! Now where was it?'

'Mary Jane! Think! For goodness sake think!' Moderating her tone slipped a bit. She couldn't help it. If it was possible to *will* someone to remember via a telephone, Honey was doing that now.

'Come on, come on, come on,' she muttered under her breath.

Whether any of her urgings was doing any good was another matter. She even drifted away when you were speaking to her. Like now. So not much hope between taking the earlier phone call and this one.

Fearing for her daughter's safety, Honey hit the panic button and the moderation went flying out of the window. 'Mary Jane, *think*!'

She heard a whine of worry on the other end of the line. 'Oh, dear. I don't remember,' said Mary Jane.

Honey closed her eyes, tried deep breathing and counted to ten. Nothing alleviated her concern for Lindsey's safety.

'Put Smudger back on,' she managed to say, still taking deep breaths, still trying to squash the panic that made her blood race.

She explained the situation. 'Mary Jane hasn't a clue where Lindsey's got to. I'm afraid for her, Smudge. Richard may be your mate, but he's got an axe to grind and he may not have finished grinding it yet. Get on to Steve. Ask him to keep a lookout for her.'

After she'd said it, she realized how worthless it was. How could Steve keep a lookout? No one knew where Lindsey was.

She punched in Lindsey's number on her mobile. '*The person you have contacted is not available . . .*' Then she phoned Steve.

She rushed outside, turned the car key and gunned the engine.

The journey from Oxford to Bath passed in a blur. Never mind the seventy miles per hour speed limit; she was flying low.

Each mile covered seemed four times as long as it should be. Damn the yellow lines, damn the traffic wardens, she parked where she could promising herself she wouldn't be a minute, just long enough to check with Steve.

He was on his way out. They bumped together in the foyer. 'Easy,' he said, grabbing hold of her arms.

'I'm not flapping,' she said giving an impatient shrug. 'I promise I'm not flapping.'

He gave her a sidelong, disbelieving kind of look. Normally such a look would have made her rip at his clothes – her own too. But not now.

'Have you found her?'

'Let me get you home.' He began guiding her towards the car.

She shrugged his hands off her arms. 'Don't patronize me. I asked if you'd found her.'

Bad temper had no effect on either his manner or the firmness of the hands that pushed her into the front passenger seat. He pulled up outside the Green River Hotel. 'You go in. I'll park it for you.'

She didn't need him to say it twice. Like a greyhound she sprang out of the car and through the hotel doors.

Anna was on Reception. Mary Jane was nowhere to be seen.

Honey glanced at an incredibly beautiful floral display that hadn't been there when she'd left that morning. If she'd had time she would have questioned where they'd come from. As it was, blooming bouquets were the last thing on her mind.

Anna smiled. 'Hello, Mrs Driver.'

'Any news?'

Anna frowned. 'Of what, Mrs Driver?'

'Lindsey. My daughter.'

The corners of Anna's wide mouth stiffened as she frowned. 'Lindsey? Lindsey is in the conservatory with a nice-looking man.'

Honey stared at her. Was it possible that Richard Carmelli was actually here?

She headed through the lounge and into the conservatory, a light and airy place of woven rattan with pale coloured upholstery. Overhead fans provided the air conditioning and tall palms in terracotta pots provided the shade.

Lindsey looked up when she saw her. 'My mother,' Honey heard her say.

The man sitting opposite her pushed back his chair, stood up and held out his hand.

He was slim, about forty, with light-coloured hair and hazel eyes. The colour of his eyes matched his suit.

The first thought that crossed her mind was that this was not the sort of guy Lindsey usually went for. He was too neat, too conservative. Ragged jeans and careless designer were more her cup of tea. The second thought was relief that it wasn't Richard Carmelli.

'Slade,' said the man offering his hand. 'Warren Slade.'

They shook hands. Honey tried to work out where she'd seen him before.

'I'm sorry. I've a terrible memory for names, but I feel I should know you.'

Lindsey was doing charades behind his back and silently mouthing the clues.

Charades had never been Honey's favourite party game. Postman's Knock had been her game of choice. Much more fun. No guessing, just kissing and minor fumbling – usually in a broom cupboard.

'I was staying here a while back.' A red blush didn't just spread over his cheeks; it exploded! 'I was a wee bit naughty. Got my fingers burned. But you and your daughter were very discreet. I brought these back.'

He indicated the shoes and clothes neatly stacked on a spare chair. A chef's hat sat beside it all.

'The hat was your daughter's idea,' he said as if reading her mind. 'I told my mother that I'd been to a fancy-dress party dressed as a chef.'

'Of course!' She remembered the naked man tied to the bed. Overwhelmed by the relief of finding Lindsey was safe she made the most obvious faux pas. 'I'm sorry,' she said in an exuberant rush, 'but I didn't recognize you with your clothes on.'

Lindsey pulled a face.

Warren Slade stammered, 'Um, yes . . . um . . .'

Swift action was called for.

Honey took a deep breath. 'Marvellous, really marvellous. I'm so glad to see you. To see you both,' she exclaimed, hugging Lindsey tightly.

Warren Slade's blush intensified. 'I brought you flowers,' he said. 'As a thank you.'

Honey nodded profusely. 'I saw them. They're lovely.' she

said. ' She sensed his acute embarrassment. 'It's not often we're thanked so wonderfully. So really, really wonderfully.'

She couldn't help the wide, stupid smile or the gushing oratory. She couldn't help sounding as though the return of a chef's outfit was the most wonderful thing in the world. She didn't care how she sounded or how she looked. Lindsey was safe and Richard Carmelli was nowhere in sight.

Honey breathed a sigh of relief. Mary Jane had got it all wrong.

Twenty-Six

U nder cover of darkness, Richard Carmelli made his way through Larkhall to the lock-up garage where he kept his motorcycle. He reasoned that a motorcycle could give him a better edge than the car.

A streetlight behind him glinted on the black fairing and chrome bodywork. He checked the fuel tank. Plenty. Got his helmet from where he usually left it on the workbench at the rear of the garage and put it on.

Once he'd donned his leather gloves, he rolled the bike out, sat astride and turned the key. The powerful Kawasaki engine purred into life. Sliding his visor down over his eyes, he turned the throttle. The sound changed from a purr to a roar. He set off back the way he came, speeding along the M4 then branching off on to the M5 and finally the Avonmouth turnoff.

During the day the motorways were chock-a-block with traffic. At this time in the morning his route was unobstructed. The wheels ate up the empty miles. Flat-roofed units dealing in car tyres, hydraulic hoses and second-hand office furniture lined St Andrew's Way. Only the watered-down orange of sodium streetlights lit his progress, them and the lights of a twenty-four-hour garage; lighthouses in a city asleep.

He took a turning off towards the docks and passed blank metal walls of prefabricated warehouses. There was a truck ahead of him with a Czech Republic number plate. He glanced up even though he guessed what it was carrying and where it was going; the same place as he.

There had to be somewhere to hide his bike. To his right was a privet hedge and tough railings around an electrical substation. To his left was an empty yard in front of a darkened building – empty that is except for two waste skips. The property, like most of those on the industrial estate, had been built in the sixties or early seventies and was being renovated.

Sliding off to his left, he drove in between the two metal skips. The haulage truck had swung across the road, its unit nosing into the gate of the next property, its rig running at a right angle.

Keeping low, Richard crept towards the side wall of the warehouse. Like others around, it was constructed of metal sheets, a modern building designed to be maintenance free. The sound of the truck braking and stopping mixed with that of the cooling units above his head.

Still keeping low he squeezed through a gap in the railings. The truck cab was only feet away. He saw the driver get out of the left-hand door. Not a British truck then, where the steering wheel was on the right.

He got out his phone and took a quick shot of the printing on the side of the truck. It said R.W. Mead, International Meat Packers and Warehousing. He added the text, 'Check this out,' and sent it to Smudger. He trusted the chef to understand its significance, then asked himself why he'd done it. Why couldn't he check it out himself?

Creeping along with the railings against his back, he kept low and listened. Two men came out of the warehouse. There was conversation going back and forth, mostly in English. He strained to hear what was being said and chanced getting closer.

Not looking where he was going, he stepped on a sheet of bent iron. The upright end clanged against the railings.

A voice rang out. 'Who's there?'

Richard fled, squeezing himself back through the gap in the fence. He heard running feet, the sound of a car starting up. He ran faster slithering to a halt next to the waste skips. He considered lying low. No. Not a good idea, he decided. He leapt into the saddle. The motorcycle burst into life and he was gone.

Empty roads meant he could get up speed, but then so could the car that was following him.

He sped back towards the motorway, frequently glancing over his shoulder. There were headlights. No details. He didn't have time for details.

There was some traffic on the motorway. Weaving his way through he kept up the pressure until Junction Eighteen and the A46, accelerating the last two hundred feet to the slip road.

The traffic lights at the exit stayed green until the very last minute when they flashed amber. He was through! He almost whooped with joy. The lights had changed to red. Whoever was pursuing him would have to stop.

He didn't bother to take the Kawasaki back to the garage in Larkhall but headed for Charmy Down. It was where he felt safe.

Relieved to be back, he took off his helmet and wiped his sweating brow. Carefully, he peered out at the road from between the two bulldozers. Nothing. Not a car in sight. He smiled. Thank God for the traffic lights.

Letting out a whoop of joy, he headed inside for his sleeping bag and the comparative safety of his tumbledown haven.

Ripping off his crash helmet, he sighed with relief and wiped the sweat from his forehead. His stomach chose that moment to rumble. He was hungry. Perhaps there were a few crumbs of Coronation Chicken left in the plastic box. He grinned. Coronation Chicken. That was a laugh. Chicken it most certainly was not.

Richard hadn't noticed that a rear light was burning on one of the bulldozers and that it was falling on to the chromium plating at the rear of the bike. But the driver of the car that had jumped the red light did see it. It had been a helter-skelter of a ride. He'd driven fast, and then slow, and now he stopped and spoke into his phone.

'Boss? I know where he is.'

Twenty-Seven

M ary Jane kept a low profile until the time came when she'd forgotten that she'd muddled up a message and sent Honey diving into despair. A few hours later she was practising her t'ai chi movements out in the garden.

On coming back from parking the car, Steve had been amused at Warren Slade's plight but relieved for Honey that Lindsey was safe.

'He asked me out,' said Lindsey, referring to Warren Slade. A wicked smile played around her mouth.

Honey thought twice about asking the obvious question, but couldn't help herself.

'Tell me you turned him down.' She felt her temperature plummet as she said it. The fact that she'd seen Slade in the nude would wash over her – as long as Lindsey didn't date him.

'He's interested in medieval tapestries.'

This was bad.

'But I turned him down. I told him I've got a reaction to dust mites in carpets; tapestries come under a similar heading.'

Honey breathed a sigh of relief and invited Steve down to the coach house to discuss progress in the case. 'I need to relax,' she said, by way of an excuse. 'Is that OK with you Lindsey? Can you cope?'

Lindsey was still smiling, amused that she'd managed to wind her mother up, but her face softened when her mother asked her. 'You don't need to get my approval. Hurry along there, Mother dear, or I'll take him there myself, gorgeous dish as he is.'

Steve grinned. 'Thanks, Lindsey. It's nice for an old man to feel wanted.'

Once in her private accommodation, she poured them a glass of chilled Chardonnay, sat herself down and kicked off her shoes.

'I never want another day like today.' She swigged at the glass and raised it. 'Here's to Warren Slade and his leather jockstrap. Far preferable to Richard Carmelli and his very sharp knife!'

'We're still looking for him,' he said. 'No luck so far.'

'Have you asked Mrs Pardoe? She's his sister. It's all to do with her, more so her than anything else I think, so it stands to reason they're close,' said Honey looking worriedly up into his face.

Sighing he plunged his finger into his whisky and began swirling it around.

'We've asked her. She says she doesn't know. I'm not sure that she's telling the truth. I suspect she's been in touch with him, but her husband sticks around. I get the impression he doesn't want her to trip over her words and tell us something that would crack this case.'

Cradling her drink with both hands, Honey nodded. 'Her husband is extra protective.'

'You can say that again.'

They both fell silent, absorbed in their thoughts.

Then Honey began voicing her opinion. 'Judging by attitude alone, Pardoe is as much a suspect as Carmelli. Remember, they had a fight according to Harold.'

'I take it you mean your man in the tricornered hat and satin britches.'

'The sedan-chair bearer.'

He smirked. 'Strikes me there's too many people wearing fancy dress in this city.' He swigged back his drink. 'We need a break. We need something to happen that might point us in the right direction. Time I was going.' He got to his feet.

'Can't you stay a bit longer?'

There it was, her neediness burst out of her mouth before she could put the brakes on.

'Duty calls,' he said, setting his glass back down on the table.

'Oh, well.'

She swooped on the empty glasses and headed for the kitchen. Steve followed her.

'I could do with a kiss before I go.'

She put the glasses down, turned and looked at him. Who gave a toss about the dirty dishes in the sink? They could wait. Her neediness couldn't. Steve Doherty was here and close and about to give her the snog of her life.

It all went according to plan; hot lips, hot bodies and breast pressing against breast. This was as close as bodies could get, her rear flattened against the kitchen sink and everything else flattened by him.

'That was good,' he said breathlessly as they came apart.

Honey took a big gulp of air. 'One more,' she said, her lips diving forward and instantly connecting with his.

Unfortunately, they kind of collided with each other, nose to nose, mouth to mouth though not with resuscitation in mind. On impact they both sprang back. The pocket of Honey's jeans caught on a drawer handle. The stitching parted with the cloth. There was a loud ripping sound.

'Did I do that?' he said, his palm lingering over the ripped pocket and the rounded flesh beneath it.

'I'll wear it with pride,' she said.

He smiled. 'I'd better go before I'm tempted to carry out an in depth inspection.'

'I'll keep them just as they are. You can do one another time.'

Twenty-Eight

S mudger poked his head around the door to Reception. 'Anyone seen my phone?'

Nobody had. He disappeared and the Reception phone began to ring. 'Hannah, darling, I need to get over to Roland's place.'

Honey ground her teeth in response. Up until now Roland had picked her mother up from her flat in Cavendish Crescent in his Rolls Royce.

'Mom, I am busy.'

Her mother's sigh sounded down the phone like a small hurricane. 'It's not often I ask you for favours, darling.'

In response to the old guilt surge that her mother was so good at stirring up, her stomach threatened to throw up on the carpet.

Lindsey distracted her, choosing that moment to wander by, a picture dressed in a white tracksuit trimmed with pink.

'Perhaps Lindsey . . .'

Her daughter's alarm was instant, obvious and written all over her face. 'I'm off to the gym. I'm meeting people.'

Honey thought about using that old guilt trick on her own daughter. No. Certain things in one's genes were best bred out of existence.

'So where are you?' she asked her mother after wishing her daughter a good time.

'Here. Look.' She was on the other side of the reception doors waving her mobile phone in the air. 'I've got myself a new phone. A load of different coloured covers came with it so I can coordinate with my outfit.

The main door swung open. If *Vogue* ever did a style magazine for the over sixty-fives, then her mother would have been in it. Colour coordination figured high on her mother's agenda. Even her dusters and dishcloths were colour coordinated – not that she used them. She had a 'daily' who came in to indulge in domestic tasks.

Mary Jane was 'helping out'. Honey had asked her to replenish the brochure rack and generally tidy it up. It kept her out of the restaurant and from hogging the phone.

Honey smoothed down her skirt and straightened her blouse. Her mother had that effect on her. She noticed a smear of something prawn-coloured on her sleeve. She swivelled it around so that it didn't show.

'So where's Prince Charming?' she asked her mother.

'His Rolls is in the garage having something done to its big end or something – something mechanical anyway,' she said, dismissively waving her hands. 'So we decided to have a night off.' Her mother's eyes twinkled and her lips, presently coloured with 'Perfect Peach' lipstick and liner, spread in a conspiratorial smile. 'But I thought I would go over anyway and surprise him. Look, I'm all prepared.' She brought out a bottle of champagne, a tin of caviar and a packet of luxury crackers from a carrier bag. 'Aren't Marks and Spencer wonderful?'

Honey wasn't thinking of the contents of the carrier bag. Alarm bells were ringing.

'Mother, do you want to reconsider that idea?'

A face carefully made up with only top-flight foundation, crumpled and a suspicious look came to her eyes.

'Why?'

She couldn't bring herself to say what she was thinking, that perhaps Roland was trying to let her down gently. Perhaps Lindsey was right and he'd really been after the meat order. Butchering was literally a cut-throat business. But it was no good. She couldn't bring herself to say that.

She shrugged. 'Well, Roland might want a night off. You know, to wash his hair or something.'

Honey cringed. It was a pretty lame excuse.

'I'll wash it for him. I like toying with men's hair.' Gloria winked and made a little clicking sound at the side of her mouth.

The permutations of that particular comment were endless. Honey resigned herself to the fact that her mother's hormones had not yet gone walkabouts. There was no getting out of this.

'OK. I'll get Anna to take over Reception.'

Mary Jane who had finished sorting out the brochure racks and was all ears collared her before she could escape.

'I've got a table-tapping session with the Psychic Development lot down at the college. Can I cadge a lift?'

'How can I refuse?'

As she drove, the two senior citizens chatted in the back, mostly about men, although true to form Mary Jane did bring the less physical sort into the conversation.

'I expect Sir Cedric and your darling departed have made acquaintance on the other side,' said Mary Jane. 'I expect they're meeting on common ground.'

Gloria fixed her with a jaundiced eye. 'Common tarts more like! That's how my ex-husband died; on top of a tart.'

'Mother, he married her.' Honey knew her reminder cut no ice.

'You always defend him,' Gloria snarled, accusation burning in her eyes.

'He was my father. And she was his wife – eventually.'

'Yeah. Eventually is the word! There she was all in white when he'd been bonking her for months. Trooping down the aisle like a born-again virgin.'

Mary Jane patted Gloria's hand as she got out. 'Life's too short to be bitter, Gloria. You must have cared for the man once.'

Gloria made her angry bulldog sound.

Undeterred, Mary Jane patted her shoulder. 'Never mind, gal. What say you I try to get Herman to rock my table? What would you like me to tell him?'

Gloria's scowl was as dark as Bodmin Moor in winter. 'Tell him that rocking your table is about as close as he's ever got to making the earth move for me.'

Gloria's mood had lightened the moment there was no one to remind her that her husband had walked out for a bimbo with a Barbie-doll figure. The past was dead and buried. Her mother was not.

'Roland will be surprised,' she said as they headed up towards the Royal Crescent. Lowering her head, she peered out and up at the elegant facade of perfect houses set in a perfect crescent. Even a one-bedroom flat here could cost close on half a million. To own a whole house would cost a fortune. 'I wonder whether he's furnished his place with antiques,' she said.

Honey sensed refurbishment plans were being made, though something else was more pertinent. 'So you've never been inside his place?'

Her mother smirked in a manner far too salacious for a woman of her age. 'Not yet. We're kind of building up to it. There's a great deal of mutual respect between us. We're not the kind that jump in the sack and jump out again. We're looking at long-term commitment here. And once I'm married and happy as Larry . . .' She patted her daughter's arm. 'I can get our home the way I want it, and then I can turn my attention to finding a nice man for you.'

Honey suppressed a shiver. 'Don't rush into things, Mother. There's a lot to be said for a long engagement.' She felt like a coward and a killjoy and, last but not least, a woman who wanted to run her own life.

The sun was setting in a rosy glow and throwing long shadows. During the day the crescent had soaked up the sun. Now, at sunset, those same stones released the trapped warmth. It made you want to cuddle up and lay your cheek against the warm walls.

Overall there was grandeur. To Honey's mind, Bath's Royal Crescent resembled a grand tiara raised slightly above the city. For the most part, traffic was banned from trundling over the cobbled road. She spotted the blue sedan chair of earlier acquaintance at one end of the crescent. Another sedan chair and two more bearers were at the other end. The four looked as if they were glaring at each other.

Honey drove around the back and found a parking space. 'Do you know which number it is?'

Her mother angled her slim legs out of the car. 'Of course I do.' This evening she'd donned a little black dress, real pearl earrings, a matching necklace and bracelet. Her heels were high and Honey noticed the fishnet stockings and red shoes.

Her mother straightened her skirt and lifted her head. 'Do I look good?'

Fishnet stockings and red shoes might have screamed, 'I'm a tart and I'm dirt cheap,' on some women. On her mother they looked fabulous. Age had nothing to do with it; she had the knack of throwing the right things together.

'You look great.' Honey meant it. There were times when her mother made her feel proud. There were other times she made her shrink to two inches tall and want to drown herself in a puddle.

Her mother smiled then looked her up and down. 'We'll have to do something about those jeans, Hannah. They've seen better days.'

The puddle had followed the proud moment. Honey managed a tight smile. 'Yeah.'

She didn't go into detail about them having seen some action and Steve Doherty ripping them. Things would get too complicated.

Honey handed her mother the carrier bag of goodies. 'Do you want me to come with you?'

Her mother glared. 'Certainly not. This party's strictly for grown-ups.'

Her mother tottered off. She lingered, strolling into the crescent and heading for the two carriage bearers she knew.

'How's business?'

The guy she'd met in the park tried to put on a happy face. 'OK.'

His partner, on the other hand, had the expression of a squashed walnut. 'Foul. There's nothing but couples.'

The solution seemed simple. 'Why don't you team up with those two? They can take one, and you can take one. That makes two.'

'We can count,' the dour bearer said. 'It's a matter of principle. We started first and they copied us.'

'Does that matter? I mean, if my place is full and I've got people wanting rooms, I send them on to other hotels. It works both ways. When they're full, they send them on to me.' Honey thought she sounded pretty eloquent, even wise. What she said was quite true. She'd send on business to anyone who might need it and the favour was often reciprocated. Hoteliers were basically generous people. Except for Stella Broadbent. That cow had never been known to pass anything on except perhaps a cold or a severe case of influenza.

She smiled sweetly. 'So how about you guys burying the

hatchet and forming a cooperative? United we stand. Strength in numbers and all that.'

The reasoning seemed to work – at least with one half of the business.

Her friend from the park jerked up his britches and looked at his partner. 'Eric, I reckon we should try and come to some arrangement with Aubrey and Brett.'

Eric glared at him. 'Harold! You traitor.'

Harold sighed and shook his head. 'Eric, I've got to earn some money.' He paused as if churning things over in his mind. 'If I don't earn anything, then I'm going to have to relinquish our business partnership and get a proper job.'

Eric's head swivelled round in double quick time. 'You wouldn't!'

'I've got no choice.' There was nothing threatening in Harold's tone; he laid it on the line flat and without embellishment.

Eric's expression turned from downright stubbornness to outright shock. Laid-back Harold stood his ground.

'Well,' said Eric. 'Well . . .'

It might have been fun in seeing how the forthcoming amalgamation of two separate businesses would come about; their crises meeting was over. Hers was about to begin.

Heels tip-tapping like an out of control metronome, her mother was heading her way apace, far quicker than when she'd been going in the other direction. Humiliation coloured her Estée Lauder foundation. Something was wrong! Badly wrong.

Her mother came to a halt. Her face was like stone. Her bottom lip trembled. 'He doesn't live there.'

Best not to force it, thought Honey. All in good time. She peered into her mother's face with what she thought was a sympathetic expression.

'He told me he lived there.'

'But you never went in. Did you see him go in?'

Her mother turned angry eyes on her. 'I'm not that senile.'

She took hold of her mother's arm. 'Let's go for a coffee.'

Her mother shook her off. 'Don't patronize me.'

'I'm sorry.'

Honey looked over her mother's head to Harold and Eric. They looked concerned.

'Is there a problem,' asked Harold.

'My mother was calling on a friend. It doesn't look as though he's at home.'

In all honesty, she didn't know whether she'd got the wrong end of the stick, but her mother wasn't being very forthcoming. She looked livid, she looked shell-shocked; she looked small.

'A woman answered the door,' growled her mother. She looked up suddenly. Honey's gaze travelled in the same direction.

A tall woman, in her late forties with Latin looks and swaying hips was striding towards them. A black patent belt cinched in the waistline of a red, wrap-around dress. If sex really did come on legs, then she was it.

She came level, an amused smile playing around her lips. She stopped but wasn't completely stationary; her curves just wouldn't stay still. Except that they didn't wobble. Ouch! How did she do that? One slinky leg rested provocatively against the other in classic seductive pose.

'My apologies, signora. Are you all right?'

Gloria Cross's red lips compressed in a tight straight line. She nodded brusquely.

'If I offended you in any way . . .' The woman's voice was as languorous as her looks.

Jaw stiff as iron, her mother nodded again, mouth tightly buttoned.

Honey said nothing as she attempted to size the situation up.

The glamour puss departed with a final smile of bright red lips and a huskily whispered, '*Ciao.*'

The eyes of the sedan-chair bearers followed the rolling rump until it was out of sight.

Honey waited for an explanation. It was slow in coming and hissed through tightly clenched teeth. 'She thought I was Roland's mother.'

'And I don't suppose she was the housekeeper.'

Her mother scowled. 'Depends what you mean by keeping house.'

'That woman had the same effect on me last time,' said Harold, pushing his hat further back so he could mop the sweat that had broken out on his brow.

There was something about his tone of voice that made Honey curious.

'Do you see her often?'

He smirked and winked at her. 'Not as often as I like. That one's as fiery as they come. Latin I bet. Hot-blooded like, you know, in the right department. Though there's something about someone shouting and swearing at you in a foreign language or with a foreign accent. It's passionate, ain't it? Know what I mean?'

Honey's curiosity intensified. The instinct of a hotelier is sharper than that of lesser mortals; it has to be. Judging a book by its cover was right out of the window. You had to be able to get to the first page if nothing else.

'Sounds as though you've seen her sound off in a passionate manner.'

'That I have.'

'Must have been some scene.'

Her mother was almost spinning on the spot, wanting to go. 'Passionate? Fishwife more like!'

Honey ignored her.

Harold made a clicking noise at the side of his mouth. 'That chef went knocking at that door. Gave 'im 'ell, she did.'

'Which chef?'

'One of them I 'ad fighting in my pub.'

'Pardoe?'

He nodded. 'That's right. Sylvester Pardoe.'

Twenty-Nine

It was dark out, but cosy and warm inside the old building at Charmy Down. Richard Carmelli spread his last portion of Coronation Chicken on to a hunk of wholemeal bread. He eyed it cautiously before taking a bite, telling himself that he should make it last and not eat this much all at once. He washed it down with a can of Coke.

A wind got up. The trees on the other side of the fence began to rustle and creak. Most of the glass was missing from the windows and the doors were ill-fitting. Richard tucked himself into his sleeping bag. No point in staying up. No point in sitting and freezing his butt off.

He dozed off.

He didn't know how long he'd slept, but he woke up aware that the walls around him were shaking. Bits of loose plaster trembled and fell to the floor. Even the floor itself was vibrating beneath him.

The wall at his head shook as something clanged against it. He blinked himself to wakefulness. His logic kicked in. Someone had started up one of the machines outside. Kids probably, joy riders wanting a change from nicking motors; heavy plant machines were far more exciting. You could knock a building down with one of the buckets on those machines.

'Oi!'

He shouted as he struggled out of his sleeping bag. Clang! Another hit. Old bricks were dislodged and old plaster crumbled to dust. He dragged open the door and swore beneath his breath. The bucket of the earthmoving machine was hanging in mid-air. The air was thick with diesel fumes.

He shouted and waved at the windscreen of the cab. Someone had to be in there, but he couldn't see them. Again the bucket hit the side of the building.

'Oi! Knock it off! D'you hear me? Knock it off.'

The bucket seemed to tremble. The engine accelerated. The air was filled with exhaust fumes, stinging his eyes, filling his lungs. There was barely time to see the bucket swing, barely time to get out of its way.

Accompanied by a cloud of diesel smoke, it swung again, stopped above him, then dropped.

Ernie Kemp rented a transport yard down near the motorway interchange where the passing traffic sounded like a rushing wind and the hedgerows were thick with dirt and discarded crisp bags. The yard was surrounded by high-wire fences and filled with oily black puddles. Great big tipper trucks – with motorway maintenance written across the back – were parked side by side like a load of snub-nosed triceratops. But there were some trucks he didn't have room for; that was why today he was off up Charmy Down to make room for one that wasn't being used at present. It just meant moving the other truck already up there. He muttered under his breath as he drove over the rutted track leading to the old yard.

'Fred Foster, can't you park your bloody plant a bit bloody better than that?'

Bloody was his favourite swear word; it had been ever since he'd married Pauline and she'd balked at his vast itinerary of unmentionable words that rough men in rough company tended to use. And he needed to use rough words; Fred Foster never parked any of his machines very tidily.

Ernie came to a stop, shut off the engine of his sleek silver Mercedes and got out. He frowned when he saw the car parked between the buildings.

'Fred?' he shouted.

He looked at the car again. No! An old Ford? Fred was careful, but not that careful. A Ford, yes, but not an old one, and he'd definitely choose top of the range if he did. And whose motorbike was that? Surely something way beyond old Fred's capabilities?

He called out again. A few rooks took off from the nearby trees. The sound of a tractor filtered up from the valley. A host of squalling seagulls followed the machine as it trekked backwards and forwards.

He headed for the nearest machine. Its tail end was sticking out into the yard. Its heavy metal bucket was lowered between the two buildings.

What he saw next made him stop in his tracks. Two legs – two human legs – plus the lower part of a torso stuck out from beneath the bucket.

Shaking from his head to his boots, he pulled out a small container of tablets from his pocket. His heart was hammering against his rib cage, his blood rushing into his ears.

Poor old Fred. He should have been more careful. I told him to be more careful.

That's what he thought. Poor old Fred. And then he heard a car, turned and saw the familiar black Land Rover Discovery pull into the yard.

He recognized the face behind the wheel.

'Fred!' he shouted, running forward on shaking legs. 'Fred. Call the police! And an ambulance, and . . . everybody!'

Thirty

'I like scraping Jersey Royals,' said Honey in answer to her chef's searching look. 'Have you found your phone?'

'No.'

'It'll turn up.'

She'd phoned Steve telling him about Sylvester Pardoe's visit to the address in the Royal Crescent. Roland Mead's address. Why had he gone there?

Steve said he would investigate. Once that was done she'd headed for the relative safety of the kitchen. Her mother had stayed overnight, in too much of a state to go back to her own place. Murder most foul was definitely on the menu. Gloria Cross was vengeful and didn't care who knew it.

The Jersey potatoes were small, covered in flaky skins and a devil to scrape, but she had to take her annoyance out on something – or somebody.

Smudger Smith was having none of it. He stood looking at her, waiting for the rest of the reason.

'And I'm out here avoiding my mother.'

He nodded in mute understanding and got on with what he was doing.

The woman scorned had nothing on her mother. When treated kindly she could sometimes be a pain in the neck. Make her look a fool and things could get deadly.

Mary Jane, bless her, was doing her best to make her mother feel better. 'Now, come on, Gloria honey, pull yourself together.'

Mary Jane had managed to persuade her to have a Tarot reading. Her mood hadn't improved much even when Mary Jane had explained that the fool suspended upside down didn't mean what she thought it did. There was no placating her.

'I know,' said Mary Jane. 'Take a snifter of my tonic. I guarantee it'll make you feel better.'

The last Honey had seen of the pair of them, was her mother taking more than a snifter of Mary Jane's tonic and Mary Jane telling her that she had plenty more in her room.

She'd whispered her thanks to Mary Jane before scooting away.

'You carry on, Honey,' said Mary Jane. 'Me and your mother will be just fine.'

'I wouldn't want a sip of that stuff,' said Smudger, when she told him.

Honey attacked a potato. 'It looked like syrup of figs. Smelled like rubber sports shoes.'

Smudger dipped his finger into the roux he was making. 'Hmm. Not quite haute cuisine then?'

'No. More like eye of newt and leg of frog . . . Still, if it does the trick. I don't want her to go on till her dying day about what she'd like to do to him. I warned her, didn't I?'

Smudger grimaced. 'The bloke's on a roll. He thinks he can do as he likes.'

Honey nodded and attacked a particularly evasive blemish in a small potato. 'I won't hear the last of this for a while. She's sworn revenge; breach of promise even.'

'Breach of what?'

'It's an old law. I told her it was no longer on the statutes, but she didn't care. She wants his ass!'

Chuckles and sly grins ran around the kitchen, but didn't last. Today was a very important day. Everyone fell to silence and carried on with the tasks allotted to them.

Honey adjusted her very white hat and brushed an imagined smut from her very white overall.

She glanced up at the clock.

'He's late.'

Smudger threw his head back and closed his eyes. 'Prolonging the agony. Typical!'

The phone burbled.

Like a pack of wary meerkats, everyone turned to face it. No one rushed to pick it up until Smudger made a dash, sliding the last few feet.

'OK.' He looked at Honey. 'Mr Westlake. Look busy,' he added. The last order was directed at the kitchen staff. Heads down, they laboured on with their work as though the Environmental Health Officer was no big deal. If only!

Adopting her best welcoming smile, Honey met him at the door. He was a while appearing, but at last there he was. 'Mr Westlake, how nice to see you. Do come in.'

Mr Westlake had never shown any signs of having a nervous disposition – until now. There was a haunted look in his eyes, and he seemed almost relieved when the kitchen door was safely closed behind him.

'Right. Shall we start,' said Honey in the most sugary tone she could muster.

His hands shook as he arranged his official forms on his clipboard. His pen was fastened by Velcro to the clipboard, but still he managed to drop it.

'I'm retiring, you know.' He said it vaguely, as though the fact had suddenly hit him and come as a great surprise. 'I think it's time,' he added, his bald head gleaming like a freckled bowling ball beneath the stark lighting.

Face full of concern, Honey asked him if he was feeling all right.

He looked back at her blankly. 'You're not usually in the kitchen when I call.'

He said it in a strangely searching way, as though he were seeking a kindred spirit who was also suffering the same kind of haunting as himself.

There was no way she was going to say that she was hiding away from her mother. She began fabricating a convincing lie. 'I just thought I'd help out . . .'

He interrupted, his voice shaking. 'Your mother's been telling me about some problems she's been having.'

The truth was out. She did her best to paper over the cracks. 'Well, she is going through a bit of a crisis.'

'With a man,' said Mr Westlake. 'She told me all about it.'

Honey groaned. Smudger rolled his eyes. The rest of the kitchen did their level best to stifle their giggles, though the young assistant commis chef laughed so much she had to run for the ladies' room. The kitchen porter hid his head inside the dishwasher, his shoulders shaking with mirth.

Honey apologized. Mr Westlake, who was usually such a stickler for getting stuck into the job of rooting out unsafe hygiene procedures, appeared severely unsettled at having landed the job of agony aunt.

Honey broke the cardinal rule and offered him a cup of tea.

Mr Westlake broke his own cardinal rule and accepted. Fearing he might collapse then and there, she offered to accompany him out into the courtyard where he could sit in the sun. She looked askance at her head chef. He looked askance right back. Was it really possible that her mother wittering on about her love life had worn down the inbred contrariness of an Environmental Health Officer? If the skill could be bottled, the catering industry would be queuing up to buy it!

Honey sat down with him on the wooden benches set beside a nice wooden table.

'Nice,' he said, looking around him.

'Yes. Nice.'

Later it might sound trite, but at this moment in time Honey was feeling nice. Nice seemed a . . . well . . . nice word. Usually she was on edge when Mr Westlake called. Today, well . . .

Perhaps it was the calming surroundings, perhaps the cup of tea, perhaps the home-made oat biscuits with real almonds, or perhaps having escaped her mother's browbeating oratory, but whatever it was due to, Mr Westlake began to unwind.

'I retire at the end of this week and when one is retiring, dear lady, one tends to better evaluate good kitchen practice.'

Her heart sank. He wasn't going to give her kitchen a good going over once he'd drunk his tea, was he? She closed her eyes and prayed. Mr Westlake carried on with his assessment of the rules and regulations, especially with regard to meat.

'I particularly condone separate fridges for cooked and uncooked meats, and in the case of uncooked, I would even go so far as to divide meat further; i.e. poultry in one, pork in another, beef another and so on.'

She wondered about game, but wasn't going to ask.

He carried on. 'Ground meat is a problem. Ground pork and ground chicken look very much the same. Tons of cheap ground meat is coming in from Europe. Unfortunately, it is not always quite what it seems. Chicken and pork all ground up together. Very worrying if you happen to be Jewish or of the Islamic faith. Are you of either of those faiths?' he asked suddenly.

'No.'

He picked up his clipboard, nervous fingers fiddling with the pen.

She glimpsed the reflection of her face in the window opposite. Flummoxed was the only word to describe it. What did any of this have to do with his inspection? Nothing.

'I'd better carry on.'

He got to his feet and tottered back into the kitchen. His inspection was fast and furious. She could barely keep up with him. At the end of it, everything was in order.

Unseen by Mr Westlake, Smudger mouthed a silent 'Phew,' and swiped the back of his hand across his forehead.

'Just one thing, dear lady,' said Mr Westlake as she guided him towards the door. 'Is there a rear entrance I can use?'

She smiled. 'Of course there is. Follow me.'

She'd fully expected the whole of the catering team to be clapping wildly when she went back in. Instead Smudger was looking grim.

'Don't tell me my mother's made it up with Roland?'

Her head chef was standing with his hands on his hips. He looked down at the floor when he shook his head.

'Steve Doherty wants to see us. Richard Carmelli is dead. And it weren't an accident.'

Thirty-One

The bar door was closed to the public so a good place to talk. The lights were off. It was a cool, green place that had a hollow emptiness about it when it was empty of paying guests. Staff wouldn't come in until it was open and neither would her mother. Gloria Cross didn't approve of drinking. Her third husband had approved – too much as it turned out.

Steve and a uniformed colleague were swift in movement, sweeping into the bar, declining to sit down and looking impatient to go.

Honey noticed he was having trouble meeting her eyes. His questioning was directed at her head chef.

'We're busying ourselves questioning suspects and witnesses. You're one of them. Tell us all you know about Richard Carmelli. Where you met, what form the relationship took and whether you'd want to kill him.'

Smudger was unruffled. 'He was a mate. Mates don't kill each other.'

Honey held her breath.

'Oh, yes, they do,' he snapped. 'Depends on whether one or both of them have got a bit of a temper.'

Gone was the sexy Steve of the other evening. This was serious.

Honey felt her mouth growing dry. 'He couldn't have done it. He was here when it happened,' she blurted.

'When what happened?'

'When everything happened.'

Steve's serious expression stayed in situ, though his eyes twinkled when he looked at her. There were a few interesting observations in that look, and none of them had anything to do with crime.

He turned back to Smudger. 'We'll need to take samples

from your hands and beneath your fingernails. Do you know how to drive an excavator or any other item of heavy plant?'

'I could learn,' he said with a grin.

'This isn't a joke.' Steve's look hardened.

Honey noticed.

Smudger noticed too. His attitude shifted ninety degrees. 'No. Never needed to. There's not much of a call for driving heavy plant in a hotel kitchen.' He frowned. 'How did Richard die?'

Steve stated the facts without too much description of the gore. 'Someone brought a half ton bucket down on his head up at the old RAF place at Charmy Down.'

Honey felt the blood drain from her face and pool somewhere around knee level.

The gathering fell to silence, their faces bathed in reflected thoughts. Even Smudger's country-boy cheeks paled to rice-pudding white.

Each was picturing Richard Carmelli's demise; legs sticking out from beneath an iron bucket, head smashed like an over-ripe strawberry.

The situation called for an inappropriate intrusion; someone to say or do something smart or funny, anything to break the stony silence.

Can anyone do cartwheels, Honey wondered. They were all on pause and needing to move on.

Suddenly there was a sound. Someone was mumbling. They all looked at each other.

'I didn't catch that,' Steve said to her.

'I didn't say anything.'

She looked at Smudger. He shrugged. 'Not me.'

'The bum! The low-down, snake-in-the-grass, rat-assed bum!' The voice was slurred, but still recognizable.

Honey felt her face reddening and saw trickling amusement widening Steve Doherty's mouth.

Fingers thick with diamond rings appeared on the bar top – first one hand, then the other.

All eyes were on the bar except for Smudger who was still distracted, still in shock. He was shaking his head. 'Whoever did it is a low-down . . .'

'Bum!' said a voice from behind the bar.

Steve gave a nod of acknowledgement. 'I couldn't have put it better myself.'

'Roland Mead is a bum!' Gloria Cross's blurry vision travelled around the room. Recognizing a captive audience when she saw it, she smiled.

Honey sensed a performance coming on, groaned and hid her face in her hands. Without looking at her, she knew that her mother's face was lighting up; first there'd be a joke in the worst possible taste.

'Bum!' Gloria Cross's reverberant voice rang around the dimly lit bar. 'What do you call a dwarf or a butcher with short legs? A low-down bum!'

Honey peered through her fingers. Steve's serious expression had fractured into a grin. 'Your mother isn't too hot on the politically correct front.'

Honey reeled off a number of totally rubbish excuses. 'She doesn't know the meaning of the term. She's old! And she's not usually in the bar. She doesn't drink.'

'She does now.'

Her mother's shoulders came into view, then her chest.

Oh, Christ!

The room went goggle-eyed. Steve Doherty's jaw dropped. His uniformed colleague sniggered but was silenced with a warning glare from his boss.

Honey groaned. She'd discovered where Lindsey had put the brassiere. Her mother had found the pair down behind the bar – and had tried them on. As for the alcohol . . . ?

Her mother's face was blearily happy, soft like kiddies' building clay. 'Mary Jane gave me a strong tonic.' She hiccupped. 'It was *very* strong, but it's done me the power of good.' Wobbling slightly, she looked down at her chest with a slightly surprised but accepting look. 'My! I was always a 36B. Do you think the tonic did that?'

Thirty-Two

It was two days later when Steve dropped in and brought her the result of his inquiries regarding Sylvester Pardoe.

'He's covered with alibis,' he said, resting his elbows on his knees as he ran his fingers through his hair.

Honey could feel his frustration.

'But why did he call on Roland Mead?'

'He said it was a while ago. He was looking for Stafford.'

She was about to ask him why Pardoe would ask Mead for the chef's whereabouts, but Steve pre-empted her question.

'He said he'd come down to look up old pals and it was Carmelli who pointed him in that direction.'

Honey frowned. 'Friends? So that was just amiable fisticuffs in Eric's pub?' She shook her head. 'No. Don't believe it. Friends don't try to punch each other's lights out.'

Steve sighed and rubbed at the corners of his eyes with two fingers.

'I've just told you, he's got an alibi for each of the murder times. He was shocked at the last murder though.'

'He would be. Richard Carmelli was his brother-in-law. Did anyone question Gina Carmelli?'

Steve sighed again, though deeper this time. 'She confirmed her husband's story – or stories.' He lay back against the soft comfort of the creamy coloured Knole settee – an expensive little number she'd picked up at auction and had recovered; even more expense. 'Christ, I'm knackered,' he muttered, closing his eyes.

'You could do with going to bed.'

One eye reopened and eyed her with expectant hope. 'Are you offering?'

She slapped his shoulder. 'I thought you were tired.'

'I am. Could you pour me another coffee, please?'

She did so at the same time suggesting he needed some time off.

He mumbled an agreement and yawned. It didn't take him long to come to an attractive suggestion.

'How about dinner tomorrow night? My place.' He smiled seductively, his eyelids as heavy with innuendo as they were with tiredness.

She smiled right back. 'That's nice. It'll be the first time.' She said it meaningfully.

His eyebrows arched. 'Really?'

She shook her head. 'The first time I've been invited to your place, Steve. My God, you are tired.'

He drained the black coffee and offered his cup. 'Another, please. I've got to keep going. I'm under too much pressure. I've got the chief constable giving me hassle.'

Honey pulled a face. 'It could be worse. I've got a broken-hearted senior citizen being a continual pain in the backside.'

His expression would have been a mirror image of hers except for the smile hovering around his mouth.

'Point taken. How is your mother?'

'In purdah. She's telling everyone that she's had a virus and is out of circulation until she gets over it. Perhaps in a day or two she'll make her golf morning or her duties at Second-hand Rose. It's a dress shop,' she added, in response to his questioning look.

He put down his empty coffee cup. 'Tomato juice, egg yolk and plain flour.'

She got his drift. 'Yes, if it was just a hangover. Useless if you've been jilted.'

Steve twisted around so he could watch her retreat into the kitchen. When she came back, his chin was resting on his hands, his eyes following her all the way. His sexy eyes looked up at her in that certain way making her feel . . . well . . . sexy.

'Your mother needs to get out and about to get over it.'

Honey sat herself down beside him, her arm sprawled languorously along the back of the settee.

'I suggested it. She nearly bit my head off. Told me not to tell her that there were plenty more fish in the sea because men close to her age were almost dead in the water.'

Steve held his hands up in mute surrender. 'What do I know about women? What do I know about men for that matter?'

Honey poured them fresh coffee. 'It's still too early for booze,' she said.

'Has Lothario tried to get in contact?'

She nodded. 'She refused to take the call. Lindsey spoke to him. He told her he was in London.'

'Just as well. It's ended and that's that.'

'No. Not with my mother it isn't. She tried to call him back.'

Sighing he began searching in his right-hand pocket. 'I've got the pathology report on Carmelli.'

Honey sipped and watched him closely as he unfolded a piece of paper torn from a notepad. The way he moved and did things had a masculine sureness about it. Positive. Full thrust on the throttle. Her complexion turned pink. The coffee had nothing to do with it.

Dark-fringed and true-blue, his eyes flickered between her and the scrap of paper.

'Not the official report, of course. I just wrote down what was relevant.'

He smiled a little wearily, as though she'd teased him into being more upbeat.

She put the coffee cup down. 'The coffee's hot,' she said wafting her hand in front of her face. 'It needs to cool down.'

Liar!

That smile again.

Will you please stop that!

His eyes dropped to the paper. 'I think massive contusion to the head is a bit of an understatement, and I won't go into detail on that score. He hadn't long eaten; cooked meat and curry mixture mixed with mayonnaise in a sandwich. The bread was from half a loaf we found on site and the sandwich filling came from a sealed plastic container.'

Honey frowned. 'Sounds like Coronation Chicken. A dish invented at the time of the queen's coronation. Quite standard.'

'Not if the main ingredient is supposed to be chicken. Says here it contained a mixture of ground meat, though there was a plastic box at the scene with that written on the lid.'

'Let me see that.' She grabbed it, her face darkening the more she read. 'Richard had quite a lot of this. He had some in the fridge at his flat and I was in the kitchen at the Beau

Brummell Hotel when he was making a batch. He gave me some. All the plastic containers were labelled Coronation Chicken. Definitely.'

Steve looked thoughtful. At last he said, 'What does it signify?'

Honey gave it some thought too. She shrugged and shook her head. 'Nothing if you're dead. But if that's the case, then Roland Mead is breaking the Trades Description Act besides a host of hygiene and quality-control issues. And I've got the evidence sitting in my freezer.'

'We need to test it.'

She nodded, understanding his implications. 'You can have it.'

Shortly after Steve left, she phoned Mr Westlake referring him to their previous conversation.

'You were talking about the trade in ground meat coming into this country from Europe. Is it illegal?'

'Most definitely! Firstly, there's the Trades Description Act, then there's falsification of country of origin – in some cases it's a case of throwing everything from all over into one big mincer and grinding it up. Not too dangerous if it's all fresh, but the bulk of it is not. A lot of it is past its sell by date, some fit only for pet food, some not even fit for that.'

'Can I ask you if you've ever found any of this stuff in any Bath catering establishment?'

He gave a short cough. 'Ahem! I would be breaching protocol if I told you that.'

'In other words you've never found any suspect meat in Bath.'

'No. Not so far.' He paused. 'Of course, should you ever have information that could help us prosecute, we would treat such information in the strictest confidence . . .'

'I don't think so. Not yet. But I'll keep you informed.'

'Uh . . . yes. By phone. No need for me to come round.'

Honey smiled as she disconnected and couldn't help feeling an overwhelming surge of affection for her mother, so over-whelming that she just had to snatch her from Mary Jane's clutches and offer her tea and sympathy.

Romantic breakdowns are as much torture for friends and rela-tives as they are for the injured party. Honey was at breaking point herself. Her mother was flitting between periods of stony silence and outbursts of red-hot anger.

Lindsey, being young, was used to having friends of her own age sobbing on her shoulder. Having her grandmother doing the same was something different. She tried making useful suggestions – just as she did to her friends.

'How about taking up a hobby?'

Her grandmother had fixed her with a jaundiced eye. 'Like what?'

Lindsey had wracked her brains. Advising friends to take up paragliding or rock climbing was one thing. Advising her grandmother to do that was downright dangerous! Now what hobbies did older people go in for?

'How about something artistic like silk painting or antique restoration?'

The hurt look returned swiftly into the evil eye.

'Are you saying I'm too old for anything physical?'

The implications were obvious. Lindsey back-pedalled on a bicycle of excuses.

'Of course not, Grandma.'

'And don't call me that. Call me Gloria. I want everyone to call me Gloria, not Grandma, not ever again,' she snapped.

Everyone spent the rest of the day treading on eggshells each time they ran into her. A sigh of relief reverberated through the building once she'd departed for her own place.

'I feel so guilty,' Lindsey said to her mother later, after she'd repeated the conversation. They were making the bed in room sixteen. The couple had been on honeymoon and overslept their check-out time. Well, that was what they said though judging by the moans of delight coming from beyond the 'Do Not Disturb' sign, sleeping was not to blame.

Honey shook her head and buried a few punches into the pillow on her side of the bed.

'No need. Just look at it this way, it could have been worse. You could have suggested she took up knitting.'

Lindsey stopped smoothing the sheet down on her side and looked tellingly at her mother.

Honey met her guilty expression with one of shock. 'You didn't!'

'No. I didn't. I only thought about saying that.'

Honey adopted the saintly pose, hands together, eyes raised to the ceiling. 'Thank heaven for small mercies!'

It wouldn't have been difficult not to mention Roland Mead or anything associated with him. Letting bygones be bygones would have worked except for one thing. Gloria Cross would not let sleeping dogs lie. Her dark periods brought her hotfoot from her flat to the hotel. For the fifth, tenth, twentieth time her family, hotel guests, the dishwasher man, the greengrocer and the man who collected the laundry were treated to the details of what had happened and what she would say or do when she saw him again.

Roland Mead was strangely absent; not a phone call, a note or even a message delivered via one of his van drivers.

But he will, thought Honey, depending on his motivation.

Whilst listening to yet another rendition of what a rat he was, Lindsey came rushing into the conservatory where her mother, her grandmother and Mary Jane were trying to enjoy warm scones with clotted cream and strawberry jam.

'It's him,' she said breathlessly. 'He wants to speak to grand-mother – sorry – Gloria,' she added quickly.

'I take it you mean the butcher,' said Honey, sounding offhand and feeling it was OK to be offhand now the romance was over.

The crockery rattled as her mother leapt from her seat.

'I'll take it in the office. A girl has to have some privacy, you know.'

Her gaze swept swiftly over her daughter, granddaughter and Mary Jane.

Mary Jane shook her head dolefully. 'Some women never learn.'

It was some minutes before her mother came back. She was frowning.

Honey dared to ask if anything was wrong. It worried her that her mother was looking strangely calm – like that period before a storm.

'Mother?' Honey's eyes met hers and saw something different about her expression.

'He's rung off. Then I rang and the woman in the red dress told me to stop calling, so I rang his other number, but I couldn't get through. The line made a funny noise, you know, like it does when it's been disconnected.'

Honey waited with baited breath, hardly daring to ask how her mother was feeling. Another try or fry his ass? Which?

'Are you OK?' asked a concerned Mary Jane. 'If you fancy a little pick-me-up, I've got a little of my special tonic left in my room.'

Gloria took only a moment to think about it. 'I'm OK but I do fancy a little something.' A self-satisfied look came to her face. 'I'll take you up on that. I need to pump a little lead into my pencil.'

Honey nearly fell off her chair. 'Medicinal, of course,' she said a little lamely.

'Stuff medicinal,' said her mother. 'This is a celebration. He's toast and I'm single again. Just one thing though,' she said, turning to her daughter. 'Could you just try that number again? If he answers, pass it to me so I can give him a piece of my mind.'

Honey called up 'Roland, London number' on her mother's mobile phone menu. She pressed the name and call selector, her mother hanging over her shoulder. It was like having a vulture perched.

'I thought he was toast,' Honey muttered through gritted teeth.

'He is, but I want to tell him so.'

Honey wasn't entirely sure that was the whole reason. Her mother was a tough old bird, but fragile emotions were at stake here. Forgiveness was only a bouquet and a bottle of champagne away.

The ringing tone was a hesitant buzz rather than the more familiar UK ring. Someone answered. She didn't recognize the accent.

'Who is this please?' said the stranger.

Honey thought on her feet. 'Ministry of Food and Fisheries, London. Do you have a Mr Mead there?'

'He has just left.'

'Do you know where he has gone?'

'London.'

She thanked whoever it was and terminated the connection.

'Well?' demanded her mother.

'It wasn't London.'

Her mother frowned. 'Are you sure it wasn't London?'

'I'm sure.'

Her mother's true feelings were seeping into her expression. She was crestfallen, and she was livid, but she certainly wasn't entirely finished with Roland Mead, especially on one particular count.

'He has such a lovely big, white Rolls Royce.'

The comment came as no surprise. Gloria Cross was covetous when it came to luxury items. What use was a big man with a big bank account balance without a big car? And a white Rolls Royce was numero uno on her 'must have' list.

'A big car isn't everything.'

Smudger came racing in, waving his mobile phone. 'Look at this.' He flicked up the texted photo of a Roland Mead truck with Czech plates. 'Richard sent it before he died.'

Gloria pouted. 'I love men of international standing.'

Honey frowned. 'He doesn't exactly boast about his Eastern European operation.'

'He told me,' said her mother almost indignantly.

Honey heard her, but her thought processes were in overdrive. There was something in that fact. Mead was a braggart and yet he didn't boast about the international side of his business.

She stared off into the distance. 'I wonder why.'

Thirty-Three

Dinner at Steve's place, eight o'clock, come prepared. That was how Honey presented the occasion to her mature but still active hormones.

Dressed to knock Steve Doherty out of his socks, she was poised on the curb like a ballet dancer about to leap into action. The pavements were still wet but the rain had stopped. Cue right a big car going too fast and heading her way. It skirted the red and white cones left by council workmen. The workmen had also left a hole; not just any old hole, but a deep hole, a hole that had filled up with water. The wheels hit the water; the water hit Honey.

'Thanks.'

She stood there draped in water. It trickled from her hair and through her make-up, leaving sooty streaks down her face. Her pressed, fresh clothes were soaked and limp. And why had she brought her 'day' bag? It was big and tan and not at all suitable for an evening out. She undid the zipper and peered inside. She groaned. The big pink brassiere was taking up most of the room. Tomorrow, she determined, tomorrow they were off back to auction.

She rolled her eyes. *What sort of night was this going to be?*

She considered calling the whole thing off. Her body responded, or rather her right foot moved. Her left stayed put. Par for the course. Half of her wanted Steve Doherty, the other half wanted to leave well alone. Her track record with men influenced the latter response but what was left of her hormones were willing and able.

So she stayed. And waited.

Steve drove up carefully avoiding the temporary lake. He peered out of the wound down window, briefly surveying her from top to toe. 'Is the wet look in just now?'

She jerked the car door open and got in. 'Drive.'

'OK.'

She sat silently and sullenly. Seductive was no longer a word anyone could use to describe the way she looked. Steaming might be better; steaming temper, steaming clothes as she began to dry out, *and* she was steaming up the windows.

Steve adjusted the air conditioning so that it blew directly on to the windscreen. He noticed she was annoyed. He did a circuit of the inner city; over Pulteney Bridge, past the old Admiralty Building, now turned into luxury apartments, over the river, back over the river turning back into the city.

Once she had noticed that they were going around in a circle, Honey frowned. 'Where are you going?'

'You tell me. You phoned me. Told me we had to call in on someone before we went to dinner. You didn't say who.'

Honey apologized. 'My mother wants to unburden herself. *Again.*' She said it with a groan. She was so looking forward to an evening with Steve at his place. Her mother's phone call had scuppered that.

Steve made a face.

'In order to get him out of her system, she's going to pick Roland Mead to pieces.'

'Like a vulture?'

Honey grimaced. 'Hell hath no fury like a woman scorned.'

Steve shivered. 'Jesus!'

Her mother's flat had cost around the same as a detached farmhouse with forty acres. Not that her mother would have ever considered living in a farmhouse surrounded by all that grass and mud. She was more a kitten-heel type than green Wellington boots.

They heard her just as they were approaching the front door. She was looking down at them from her balcony. Built in the early nineteenth century, the balcony was constructed of wrought iron. It had a French, Napoleonic look about it, a bit like those found in the French Quarter of New Orleans and it was crammed with flowers.

'About time. I've poured three sherries.'

'I hate sherry,' Steve murmured.

'Humour her,' muttered Honey from the corner of her mouth.

Honey stepped back so she could see better. Her mother's face was framed by pink geraniums and purple petunias.

She did her bit on dishy Doherty's behalf. 'Steve doesn't drink when he's driving, so no sherry for him.'

Her mother's head bobbed in acknowledgement before disappearing.

'Thanks,' said Steve as Honey punched in the security number.

'No great shakes, except that I'll probably end up swilling yours back as well. Not good. I hate the stuff too.'

As usual, her mother was impeccably dressed in a navy and white top trimmed with red buttons on the sleeves and in a diagonal line across her chest. Her trousers were red and matched her toe nails and her lipstick

Eyes outlined with the best liner Estée Lauder could produce, she gave Honey the once over. 'You look terrible.'

Honey didn't dare a smile. It would crack her face. Clothes grim; face glum. 'It wasn't intentional. I looked good when I started out.'

Her mother's look of horror was undiminished. 'Who did it?'

'A car went through a deep puddle.'

Her mother handed her a schooner of sherry. Wanting to get it over with as soon as possible, she downed it in one. Like Steve, she found it too sweet and too rich. Her mother knew this. She'd told her enough times. Cod liver oil came in the same category; her mother considered it good for her. Normally she was totally opposed to alcohol, but for some reason sherry and port wine were exempt or had been. Things had changed recently thanks to Roland Mcad.

'You could do with another.'

Dark liquid glugged like oil into the glass.

'Drink it.'

Holding back a grimace, Honey gave in, this time sipping, making it last in case she got poured a third.

Steve sipped at his orange juice. She envied him.

Her mother turned silent, her eyes downcast and her lips pressed tightly together.

'Aren't you having one?' Honey asked her.

'Certainly!' Snapping out of her reverie, she reached for the decanter.

'Allow me,' said Steve.

Her mother raised her finely plucked eyebrows, looking

surprised that someone who disliked shaving could be such a gentleman.

'Say when,' he said.

'When' didn't happen until the dark red liquid was a hair's breadth from the rim of the glass.

Honey exchanged a surprised look with Steve. She was deeply unsettled when her mother tilted the glass and drank the lot! Roland Mead was responsible for transplanting an alien – a drinking alien – into her mother's body.

'Right!' said Gloria Cross, firmly setting the glass back on the tray. 'Now let's dish the dirt! I'll teach you to cross me, Roland Mead!' She held her daughter's eyes and shook her head. 'I knew I should never have trusted a man with tattoos.' She narrowed her eyes. 'My own mother told me never to trust a man with tattoos, especially when they were hidden from view.'

Honey felt a deep warmth creep up her neck. Was her mother saying what she thought she was saying? Come to think of it, she'd never noticed tattoos on any *exposed* surface of Roland Mead's body.

She and Steve exchanged looks of surprise. They were reaching the same conclusion.

Her mother leaned close – surprisingly close – to Steve, the man who didn't shave enough for her liking. Her eyes narrowed. 'For a start, there are foreigners in and out with their vans and their trucks down at that new frozen place of his in Avonmouth. My, you ought to see that place. It must have cost him a small fortune. He's always on about it. And all those vans he has. He bought twelve new ones this year alone. Can you imagine that?'

Steve frowned. 'I don't quite get the gist of what you're saying.'

'It's obvious,' said Gloria, shooting him an elderly citizen look, 'I know better than you. He's overstretched himself and he's cutting corners to keep the bank manager happy. That's why he's importing from over the water. It's cheap and he can sell it dear. But he keeps pretty hush-hush about it. But I worked it out. I put two and two together.'

'Where do the trucks come from?'

Her mother thought about it. 'All over Europe; a lot from Eastern Europe. He's got a plant there you see, what they call a processing plant. He didn't say much about it, but I took note.' She nodded emphatically and a hard gleam came to her eyes. 'I saw cash change hands. A driver was mouthing off. He was speaking foreign, but I caught the English words. Roland didn't know I overheard. I was supposed to stay in the car.'

Steve rested his elbows on his knees, clasped his hands beneath his chin and fixed his eyes on her mother's face. 'So what was said exactly?'

Steve could do wonders with his eyes. For a start, Honey was overwhelmed with a sudden urge to confess – not that she had anything much to confess – except for a conclusion creeping into her mind. Was it a wild guess, or was she finally on the right track? One person might be able to help her. Whilst Steve and her mother continued to talk, she rang Casper.

Neville answered. She told him that she wanted to speak to Casper.

'He's in the bath.'

What was it with that man?

'He'll wash all his natural oils away.'

'I don't think that will cut much ice,' said Neville. 'He does a lot of thinking in the bath.'

'It can't be helped. I have to interrupt his train of thought. Ask him to put down his loofah and concentrate.'

'Not beyond the bounds of possibility,' he replied in a superior tone. 'Ask me and I'll ask him.' Neville gave the impression of being a bulldog, guarding his master's territory – in this case the bathroom. In reality he was very good at flower arranging and interior design.

'Can you ask him whether he was first choice to head the judges at the competition that Oliver Stafford won, or whether he was called in as second choice?'

Neville coughed nervously. 'I don't think that is *quite* the way to put it.' There was something about the way he said it that made her think she'd hit treble top.

'Was he?'

Neville lowered his voice. 'Well . . . he was . . . in a way. There were some who said he had far too *distinguished* a palate for a commercial venture. You know of course that our chef, Jean Pierre, did not enter?'

She knew of course. Jean Pierre was of the opinion that

any chef who wasn't French was a cook. Entering competitions was not part of his remit.

'So who was supposed to be chairman of the judges?'

Neville's deep sigh of relief reverberated out of the receiver. 'Sylvester Pardoe. He has his own restaurant and hotel in Oxford. At the last minute someone pointed out that he knew too many of the contestants to be impartial, so Casper took charge. Is that all you wanted to know or do you still need to disturb Casper?'

There was no need. The only person who might have warned Sylvester off was Richard Carmelli – or was it Smudger?

'Can you tell me who pointed out the fact?'

'No. No idea. Someone with a vested interest?'

After thanking him, she ended the call. She knew her eyes were shining. She could see the fact just by looking at Steve. His were shining too, reflecting hers because he knew she'd learned something important.

'Sylvester Pardoe was supposed to judge the BITE competition.'

Steve's happy look of impending enlightenment disappeared, replaced by a questioning look. 'We know that already . . .'

'Just a minute.'

She pressed a familiar key on her phone. Smudger answered.

'What sort of dish was Oliver Stafford cooking up at the contest?'

'Something with chicken, same as the rest of us.'

'Cut up or whole chicken breasts?'

'Um.' Smudger thought about it. 'His dish consisted of cutting up the breasts. I think it was some kind of variation on Chicken a La King, though not so mundane as that. Mundane enough, though,' he added with waspish disdain.

Steve was eyeing her expectantly. 'Well?'

Although a bit squiffy, her mother was eyeing her expectantly too, though through a sherry-induced haze. 'Well, Hannah, darling. Spill the beans!'

'The meat. That's what this was all about.' She turned to Steve. 'You found ground mixed meat in Richard Carmelli's stomach. I know for a fact that his last meal was Coronation Chicken. I saw him ladling the portions into cartons, and he told me himself that he was having some for lunch. He said he had loads of it to get rid of and was taking some home with him. And before he shot off to Charmy Down, he cleared his fridge out. There was nothing in it when we checked.'

Steve looked incredulous. 'And someone killed him for taking his work home? I can't see it. Stealing, yes, but nicking a chicken is pretty low in the crime-pecking order.'

He grinned and tugged at the lock of hair falling over his forehead.

Honey fixed him with narrowed eyes that dared him to continue joking. 'Very droll. But that was it. It wasn't chicken; it was a mixture of ground-up chicken and pork. It's cheap and comes in from Eastern Europe. My EHO told me all about it.'

Carried away by this train of thought, Honey failed to control the right hand that reached for the sherry and topped her glass up. She was on a roll.

'The meat comes in from Eastern Europe,' she was saying. 'Mead has a processing plant there. Controls are not as tight as here. To save time and money, some white meats like poultry and pork are shoved in together especially when it comes to ground meats used in pies and curry-type dishes. No one can really tell the difference – which is why Smudger was right in saying that Oliver Stafford had stolen our chicken breasts. Oliver and Stella had found out that Casper had replaced Sylvester Pardoe at the last minute and Casper would taste the difference! Casper St John Gervais is the most fastidious, discerning epicurean I know.'

Steve looked at her blankly.

She explained. 'An epicurean has a very discerning palette. It's of Roman derivation. A god of food or something – I think.'

He nodded good-naturedly. 'I can live with that. And the murderer is?'

Honey didn't answer. Steve followed her sidelong gaze to her mother.

'I wouldn't put anything past that man,' her mother snarled, before sliding back on to the settee, her head sinking into a plush velvet cushion.

There was no point in waking her up. Dinner was still on and gooseberries were not welcome.

Thirty-Four

Tired of living in a city flat, Steve had purchased a small cottage on the Wellsway, the main road connecting Bath with the ancient city of Wells. Both cities vied for trade in the tourist market, Bath boasting its Roman baths and Wells its one-thousand-year-old cathedral.

A continuous stream of traffic passed the front of the property during daylight hours, quelled at around six thirty and happened in spasms for the rest of the night.

It boasted a rear entrance with convenient private parking. Steve drove round the back and parked nose to against his garden wall. A dozen stone steps descended into a small but pretty garden.

Two more steps took them into an octagonal conservatory; two steps more and they were standing in the dining/kitchen area.

Honey eyed her surroundings with interest. She'd expected a muddled, masculine interior with no thought given to design or tidiness; somewhere to sleep and unwind. It wasn't like that. Spotlights had been set into the floor and ceiling, their focused beams the only barrier between the cooking and eating area. The sitting room was forward of that.

He told her it had two bedrooms and a bathroom upstairs. 'You can try them later.'

That cheeky grin again.

This was the point at which a woman of mature years and rounded body got cold feet. Cover of darkness was best before she considered taking a bedroom test.

Perhaps her nervousness showed, or perhaps he was nervous too. She wasn't just one of his colleagues who he took out on a date. They had a relationship going on here – both working and otherwise.

Talking about work formed the breathing space for both of them.

As Honey washed and prepped the lettuce, Steve added olive oil to the pasta and a dash of Valpolicella to the sauce.

'We'll drink the rest,' he said, filling two glasses to the brim.

Honey eyed the generous measures. 'Well, they're certainly more than the advised daily measure.'

Steve handed her a glass. 'You can cope. You can cope with more than you think you can. Cheers.'

Their eyes met as they took the first sip. The wine was warm, full-bodied and rolled around her tongue. They were so close. Too close. Her nerves were in knots. Just a little more time . . . Like a tennis pro at Wimbledon, she took the initiative and batted a safe return

'So! Was there anything on the security tape?'

'From the Beau Brummell?' He looked away. 'No. Mainly because the tapes were not running during the early hours of the morning.'

Honey frowned. The nervousness lessened. 'Are you sure?'

'Definitely.'

'That tape would have shown the murderer! Where is it, I wonder.'

He shook his head as he stirred the sauce. 'You're not listening, Honey. The tapes are run every night and kept for a week. But there were none – none at all for that week – between the hours of one and six in the morning. They were switched off.'

A pillow and a rolled-up sleeping bag popped into her mind. 'The security guard was asleep in the rear bathroom.' She explained about washing her injured cheek on the day he'd interviewed Stella Broadbent and seeing them there.

'But Francis says that when he crept back, there was a security guard on duty.'

Steve offered her a taster of sauce from the wooden stirring spoon.

'Which means that he'd either forgotten to switch it off . . .'

'Or,' said Honey, sucking back the hot sauce, 'there was a second security guard.'

Steve drank more wine. 'Like I said before,' he said thoughtfully, 'there are too many people in fancy dress around here.'

Honey nodded. 'And pork pretending to be chicken.'

'What?'

'And Eastern European truck drivers . . .'

Honey's voice trailed off into nothing. Her thoughts were going full pelt. 'What was that my mother said?'

Steve too was looking thoughtful. Honey guessed that his thoughts were racing along the same track as her own.

'Money changing hands at a meat warehouse,' he said in a low voice. 'And who was SAP?' Steve added.

Honey frowned. 'SAP?'

'It was written in a notebook we found with Richard Carmelli's things.'

Suddenly all thoughts of going to bed with him flew out of the window. Being bedraggled and carrying the wrong bag with her outfit now seemed to fit the occasion. This was all wrong. It should never have happened.

'I thought we were supposed to be sharing information.' She sounded and felt quite hurt.

'We thought it was something to do with Pardoe. Except that he doesn't have a second name.'

'It's not a name. It's a programme!' Honey put down her glass and picked up the phone. Mary Jane answered. Honey made impatient sounds and insisted on speaking to Lindsey.

'What's the name of the programme big companies use on their computers?'

'SAP.'

'Can we get into that programme and find out something about a company's dealings?'

'We don't have SAP on our system. It's for human resources, building maintenance, supplies, tax. We're not big enough. What are you up to?'

'Is there any way we can get into someone else's system and find out their international dealings?'

'You mean is there any way yours truly can do that?'

'You've got it.'

'No.'

'Drat!'

'But I know a man who can. Whose system are we hacking into?'

'Roland Mead and Sons, International Meat Products and Warehousing.'

'I'll get back to you.'

Steve looked puzzled. 'What are you up to?'

'As my beloved daughter has just pointed out, SAP is a computer system used by large companies.'

'You sound very informed.'

Honey made a face. 'I'm only repeating what I've been told.' Her thoughts began having their own Derby Day, racing around her mind. This time Steve's thoughts weren't with her but on a track of their own.

He stroked a lock of hair back from her forehead. 'Look, let's enjoy tonight and get back to work in the morning. What do you say? Hmm?'

His touch made her tingle, but the thought that he'd kept something so vital from her left her feeling annoyed.

'Whilst we're waiting for a result, I think we should take a look at Roland Mead's warehouse in Avonmouth,' she said. She watched closely for his reaction.

'Christ!' He brushed his hand over his eyes. 'Look, Honey . . .'

She pressed on. 'My mother said he has regular deliveries through Harwich and Felixstowe. Once a week and one's due tonight. Don't you think it would be a good idea to get over there and check it out?'

Steve sighed and looked her up and down. 'I could think of other things I'd prefer to check out, but . . .' He shook his head disconsolately. 'I take your point.' Sighing again he turned off the glow beneath the sauce and the pasta and set down his spoon. He then proceeded to make a big show of tidying things up. He was neat, but she guessed he wasn't always *that* neat.

She knew he would question going at all. And why not? After all she was mostly going on gut instinct. He'd have to dig for her Achilles heel to dissuade her. But first he had to find it.

Knowing how much she liked her food, he gave it one more try. 'I take it dinner can wait?'

Honey grimaced. She hadn't expected him to home in that accurately, but prided herself on swift counteraction. 'My waistline can go without.'

Unfortunately, her stomach was not in unison with her waistline and wouldn't stop rumbling on the journey from Bath to the Severnside port of Avonmouth. She considered getting a Mars Bar in a service station on the main road close to the port. Sheer willpower and pride held her off. Steve would say, 'We should have had dinner and let this wait until tomorrow.'

As it was he'd hardly spoken a word since they'd got into the car. Grim-faced, he stared over the steering wheel at the pitch-black night and the dour surroundings.

Transport depots, warehousing and industrial units, some new and some square and flat and dating from the sixties, lined each side of the road. Thinking of Richard Carmelli with his head crushed quickly dispelled all hunger pangs.

The main gates were open.

Steve's gaze searched the perimeter. 'There's bound to be a security guard.'

Just at that moment an articulated truck with foreign number plates rolled in through the gate. The name Roland Mead, International Meat Warehousing, was emblazoned along the side.

They pulled into the same car park next to the same rubbish skips where Richard Carmelli had parked. Like him they crept towards the fence and the gaping entrance to Roland Mead's cold store.

A truck brandishing foreign number plates had just pulled in. The stench of hot diesel fumes fell over them.

Four men stepped forward expectantly, their figures silhouetted against the bright light from within. The driver jumped down from the long-distance sleeping cab and joined them.

Steve crept further forward. Honey followed him to cower behind a dusty bush next to a gap in the railings. As he stepped out of the brightness, she recognized Roland Mead. He was smiling and slapping the men on the back; he shook hands with the driver. Something was said. She couldn't hear what it was.

He wound an arm around the shoulders of a man wearing a black T-shirt and blue jeans. Roland's head was bent close to the other man's, as though he didn't want anyone else hearing what was said.

Honey strained to hear. So did Doherty. Something about 'doing a good job of that one' was all either of them heard.

Honey tried not to make judgement of what was meant. Richard Carmelli sprang to mind.

Roland Mead slapped the man on the back then disappeared behind the truck. An engine fired up. Headlights burst into life. The white Rolls Royce glided slowly out of the compound gates.

The man he'd been speaking to was now making his way back to the other men and facing them.

Honey saw his face. Her heart skipped a beat. She knew him. She felt Steve tensing beside her. He'd recognized him too. It was the security guard from the Beau Brummell Hotel. The *first* security guard, the one who'd lifted the wooden barrier. The second guard they'd come across, the one that should have been on duty, had been asleep. No wonder he'd been flustered.

The men laughed and joked, their voices the only sound on the deserted estate except for the distant hum of heavy traffic on the motorway.

Two of the men did something between the cab of the truck and its trailer where the air and fuel hoses clipped on to the brakes and the diesel tank.

'Two tanks,' whispered Doherty.

Honey said nothing, though she knew from the tone of his voice that two tanks had some significance.

The high-pitched sound of a forklift preceded its appearance. It drove up to the area between the truck and the trailer, to the exact spot where the men had been unclipping hoses and other connections. Accompanied by instructions to be steady, slow and back off now, the forklift edged away from the truck, the large fuel tank resting on its metal prongs.

One of the men raised his hand and called a halt. Honey and Doherty watched in amazement as the top of the supposed fuel tank was lifted like the lid of a suitcase.

Honey looked at Steve and read his expression. Fuel tanks didn't have hinges. They only had a hole where the fuel went in. One tank still remained.

Satisfied by the contents of the tank, the men followed the forklift into the warehouse.

She whispered to Steve. 'That's not a fuel tank is it?'

'Clever. Long-distance trucks travelling all over Europe often have two fuel tanks. That one possibly has one and a half. To avoid suspicion fuel can still be pumped into it but only fills the bottom half. The rest is courier space. And we can guess what that is, can't we?'

Steve dug into his pocket for his phone. 'Damn.' He remembered turning it off, throwing it into a drawer so it wouldn't disturb their night together. Well, that bit was true. It wouldn't, but he could badly do with it.

He was about to ask Honey for loan of hers, but she'd already ducked around the hedge, heading for the gap in the fence.

'I need to call for back-up,' he said once he'd caught up with her. 'Can I borrow your phone?'

'I haven't got it.'

He groaned.

'I left it at home so we wouldn't be disturbed.' She sounded sheepish, felt stupid that she did, but there was nothing to be done. They'd both been of the same mind.

Slinging her big bag more securely behind her, Honey eased her way through the fence. Doherty followed, swearing under his breath. Rules learned on training days specifically stated that he shouldn't be doing hare-brained things like this. Honey hadn't been on the same courses. She just flew by the seat of her pants.

He knew where she was coming from. They should take a look, just to confirm their suspicions. Nailing Mead for food description violations was one thing. Nailing him for drug running was quite another. No wonder he could afford a house in the Royal Crescent.

The light pooling outwards from the wide, truck-size entrance was suddenly dimmed.

Honey paused, narrowing her eyes so she could see better now the glare had subsided.

Steve signalled that they should move to the right.

Honey pointed at the tops of two, perhaps three heads she could see through a glass partition in a brightly lit office. Hopefully all four men were inside. If Doherty was having the same thoughts, he gave no sign of it. They eased away, following rubberized trail markings of the forklift.

A sign just ahead said 'Cold Store'. Without saying a word to each other, they headed in that direction.

Other signs – 'Wash your hands before handling meat products' – proliferated around a set of double doors. There were glass inserts at eye level. On the other side carcass after carcass hung from metal hooks. To their right the hooks and a row of stainless-steel shelving stood empty, no doubt awaiting the delivery standing outside and the morning shift that would unload that particular consignment.

The forklift stood abandoned in front of the shelving, its arms still holding its load.

Carried away by thoughts of glory, Doherty slid up the safety bar that held the door closed.

Honey's breath caught in her throat as the freezing chill hit her.

Steve's face was flushed with excitement. 'Look at this!'

He eased his fingertips beneath what looked like a lip running around the tank.

Even before he heaved it open, Honey guessed what they would see.

Metal scraped against metal as he pushed open the lid.

Silence reigned.

Shivering now, Honey wrapped her arms around herself. 'I take it that's not self-raising flour.'

Doherty shook his head. 'No. That stuff's much more dangerous to your health.'

'Don't you have to taste it like they do on TV cop shows?'

He shook his head.

Something – perhaps a sound or purely a shiver that was due to more than cold – made Honey turn round. A pair of eyes looked back at her through the glass portion of the door.

'Steve!'

The man on the other side had seen them too.

'Hey!'

He sprinted and fell shoulder first against the door. Just as he'd expected it didn't budge. Wrinkles appeared at the sides of the eyes looking in from the other side. He guessed the guy was laughing.

'Let us out,' Steve shouted, beating his fists against the door.

He adjusted a dial to the side of the door. Honey recognized what it was.

'That's a thermal switch.'

The needle was presently pointing at the palest band of blue, but even as they watched, it began to move towards a deeper, more dangerous shade.

Thirty-Five

'We have to keep warm. Keep talking. Tell me about your job with the Probation Service.'

She looked at him. 'Whilst I'm jumping up and down?'

'Keep jumping. You must keep jumping.'

The cold was intense. The fact that they were surrounded by frozen solid sides of cows didn't help.

'So. Go on. Tell me.'

'I worked in IT and I don't mean computers. Perish the thought. I started in Probation typing our Social Enquiry Reports and then I got promoted to Senior Clerical Officer in Intermediate Treatment.'

'What does that mean when it's at home?'

Honey continued to jump up and down and flap her arms. Her breath was still white. Her fingers felt numb. 'Well, we used to take young offenders camping, rock climbing, orienteering, sailing – Duke of Edinburgh Award type stuff. Things to inspire the mind and divert them from their criminal ways.'

'Sounds more . . . like . . . days out on . . . jollies to me,' said Steve, his words expelled between vigorous arm waving and bouts of jumping.

'It's termed therapy,' said Honey, stopping to catch her breath.

Steve stopped too. Usually he'd have made some disbelieving comment. But not here. He shivered.

'Scientists reckon that we lose more heat out of the top of our heads than anywhere else.' He rubbed at his ears and did his best to pull his collar up higher. 'Wish I had a hat. A balaclava would be nice. I hate having cold ears.' He was right to be worried. They were turning blue. He rubbed them again.

Honey thought it through. 'Frostbite can stop the blood supply to extremities.'

'Really.' Steve didn't sound convinced.

But she knew she was right. Her own ears were camouflaged by her hair. Steve's hair was short. He had no protection, and was it true that extremities were prone to gangrene?

She undid the zip of her big brown bag thinking she might have a headscarf. The unmistakable stitching of 'Big Bertha' barely moved at the touch of her fingers.

'Madonna, eat your heart out,' she muttered, grabbed the strap and pulled it out.

Steve was slapping his arms around himself to keep warm. He stopped when he saw the mighty 'J' cups.

'Are they human?'

'Made for a very large woman. And now we're going to wear them. Don't worry,' she said in response to the nervous look in his eyes. 'You don't have to take anything off. You can wear it on your head.'

He looked at her in horror. 'Will I hell!'

'Think of your ears, Steve.'

'I'll risk it.'

'Look,' she said, spreading the brassiere out so he could better understand the possibilities. 'We'll both use it. You have one cup on your head, I'll have the other. And we can cuddle up together to keep warm. Even jump up and down a bit.'

The last bit seemed to sway him. He didn't struggle when she placed one of the super-sized cups on his head and the other on hers. The side panels were left dangling over their ears. Steve had the hooked side, and she had the eyes. She thought about tying them together. Steve had the same thought. 'That's better,' he said.

True. Like Siamese twins, they were closer than close, the bra cups fitting them like caps.

Honey glanced at their blurred reflection in the stainless steel. 'We look like a couple of mushrooms.'

Steve made a shuddering sound with his lips. 'Brrrr. We need to keep moving. How about we pretend that we haven't got our clothes on?'

Honey shivered. 'Are you kidding?'

'I just mean jumping up and down – dancing would be better.'

'OK. Hum something.'

Hugging cheek to cheek was a necessity thanks to 'Big Bertha'.

Steve shivered again. 'This is close to some fantasies I've been having of late, except for the sub-zero temperatures.'

'And the fact that we've got our clothes on?'

'That too.'

'I wanted to speak to your mother before she goes to bed.'

It was one o'clock in the morning and Lindsey had been clearing down when her grandmother phoned.

'She's not home.'

'I was worried she was thinking about spending the night with that Doherty character, the cop who can't afford the price of the razor. But I phoned her and she didn't answer. And then I phoned the police station and asked them to phone that man, but they got no answer either. OK, I know they may have eventually got it together which explains your mother not answering her phone, but a cop would. I'm certain he would.'

It almost choked Lindsey to admit she might have a point. Like a novice trapeze act, her mother and Doherty swung to and fro as though timing the right moment to jump. Up until now they hadn't quite made it, but perhaps Gran was right. It could finally have happened, but Steve Doherty wouldn't want to miss out on any police action.

Grandma went on to relate what had gone on earlier that evening before they'd dashed off. 'Roland Mead is a scumbag. I think they've gone off to prove I'm right.'

'Perhaps you're right.'

'Of course I'm right.'

Lindsey promised she would check and call her grandmother back. The first thing she did was to phone the police and ask for Steve Doherty.

'He's not here. Can you call back later?'

'Do you happen to know where he is?'

The female voice hesitated as though in two minds whether she wanted to know where Doherty was. Good practice won over jealousy. 'I'll check.'

After a few muted mutterings she came back on the line. 'No one's seen him. We've been trying to get hold of him, but he's not answering his home or personal phone.'

That said it all as far as Lindsey was concerned. As she replaced the phone, her eyes caught sight of something on her mother's scribble pad. The 'chicken' in Coronation was under-lined. So was the word 'pork'. Beside it were the initials RC. Her heart skipped a beat. Richard Carmelli. Chicken and pork. Her thoughts did cartwheels as her concern for her mother increased. Everyone had assumed the killing of these chefs was about rivalry and something that had happened three years before. But was it really about butchers and the Trade Descriptions Act, or was she jumping the gun?

Then she picked up her phone and read a text from Warren Slade regarding details from Roland Mead's computer system. She rang her grandmother and explained what was afoot.

'There's big money involved and the sums don't add up. Have you any idea where my mother happens to be?'

Gloria made a shrewd guess.

Thirty-Six

Gloria Cross insisted on accompanying her granddaughter to Avonmouth. Lindsey had tried getting the police to keep a look out for her mother's car, but no one seemed that interested. Obviously Steve Doherty's reputation had a lot to do with it. Shrinking wallflower he was not! And they certainly weren't interested in checking Roland Mead's cold store at Avonmouth. Why should they be?

They checked Doherty's place before leaving. His car was gone and he'd left a table lamp on in the front room, easily seen when Lindsey had peered through a window.

Lindsey floored it to Avonmouth. Perhaps she would have parked next to the rubbish skips too if her grandmother hadn't insisted on being navigator and directed her down the wrong turning.

Gloria Cross narrowed her eyes as she peered into the darkness and commented that there were too many trees. 'I don't remember this many.'

Lindsey pulled into the curb. 'So where is his place?'

Her grandmother pointed towards the trees. 'On the other side of them, I think. There's a lane through there, see?'

Lindsey did see. Normally she didn't like walking down lanes at night, but Avonmouth was like a ghost town during darkness. Rapists and murderers were likely to be thin on the ground. The only criminals around would be more interested in pinching tyres or car parts from one of the many outlets lining the roads around here.

Lindsey looked round as they crossed the road. There was no sign of her mother's car, and surely there should be; unless of course it was hidden, either by her mother or someone else.

The night was warm, but the sudden profusion of worrying thoughts made her shiver. The trees rustled in a warm breeze as they found their way over the soft ground. The lane was a forgotten place, something left behind when the prefabricated warehouses had been built. It led to a mound of earth left by the contractors. Over time it had become covered in grass and foliage. At its summit was a concrete wall.

'I'm going up here,' said Lindsey, her feet slipping on the damp grass.

'Wait for me. I've got my trainers on. They're blue and silver. Designer of course. Do you like them?'

'Not now, Gran.'

She clambered up the slope presuming her grandmother was incapable of following her. She was proved wrong. Red talons grabbed the hem of her jersey and hung on to it.

'Where are we?' asked her grandmother, hardly breathless from her climb.

'There,' said Lindsey. She pointed upwards. Gloria looked up at a huge sign saying Roland Mead Meat Importers and Cold Storage.

She spat into the grass. 'That man is too big for his boots!'

The concrete wall in front of them proved to be a parapet.

Lindsey kept low, kneeling and showing just her head above the wall. She saw a door in the back of the building, but no security cameras. That didn't mean there were none, just that they were hidden from view. 'Should we be creeping around like this?'

Gloria stuck her head up over the parapet. 'Yes.'

Lindsey placed a hand over her head and pressed her back down.

'There could be cameras, though I can't see any.'

Gloria was in no mood to be put off by cameras or criminals. She was worrying about her daughter. 'Are we one hundred per cent sure that Honey is in there?'

'It seems that way.'

Her grandmother tutted. 'I can't believe Roland's taken your mother prisoner. Why would he do that – unless it's for consensual kinky sex?'

Lindsey threw her grandmother a look of pure, jaw-dropping shock. She could accept that due to their years grandmothers should be worldly wise. But they shouldn't shock the pants off the younger generation. And they certainly shouldn't know anything about kinky sex!

'What do you know about stuff like that?'

'I've lived,' Gloria replied with a contemptuous sniff.

Lindsey shook her head and concentrated on what she was here to do. She asked herself why she hadn't gone round to the front door. Because of the evidence, she told herself. Something to do with meat and the mis-selling thereof. Mead wouldn't want anyone snooping around, yet surely her mother had come here. Everything pointed to it. Her grandmother had more or less admitted to seeding their minds with suspicion and sending them here.

Taking big strides, she began edging along the wall, searching for a way down to the rear door she could see. There had to be one, she reasoned. The builders had left a huge mound of earth up against the wall. Someone with good knees could jump down into the yard if they were very brave. She was not that brave and her grandmother's knees might not take the strain.

There had to be another way. If there was a lane through the trees and a mound of earth against the wall, it stood to reason the gap had been left at the very end where the back wall met that belonging to the property next door. Although only narrow she was sure she could get through.

'Stay here,' she hissed to her grandmother.

'Like hell I will!'

Grandma Gloria eased through the wall after her, picking her way down over the tumbled hardcore and slick clay. Nails scratched on the side wall as they felt their way to the flat ground. Lindsey heard her grandmother cursing as a false fingernail popped off into the night.

The two women sprinted across to the door, Gloria remarking on how much she loved trainers and how she was planning to buy more.

'There's bound to be an alarm,' said Lindsey, grateful for her grandmother's casual indifference to the danger they were in. Her heart raced but wasn't quite playing leapfrog. Looking up over the prefabricated wall she saw a door. A door was exactly what she needed, but how to get in without being seen? The sudden sound of voices sent them scurrying behind two huge waste bins, one labelled 'meat waste', the other 'cardboard/recyclable'.

A man emerged, whistling as he lifted the lid of the bin

marked 'meat waste'. A hoard of angry blue bottles rose in a buzzing mass. The lid slammed down and then he was gone.

'No alarm,' whispered Lindsey, greatly relieved. If people were working inside then no alarm would be on.

She tried the door. It didn't budge. Rattling it too much was not an option.

'Locked. Now what?'

'We use a key.' Gloria's whisper bubbled with excitement. She was obviously enjoying this.

Lindsey was taken by surprise as a whole bunch of keys appeared, as likely to rattle as the door. Lindsey grabbed them. 'Where did you get these?'

'He left them behind at my place,' said her grandmother. 'I was going to throw them in the river just to inconvenience him, but I figured they might come in handy. I was right too.'

Pulse racing and hands sweaty with fear, Lindsey studied each key. Some were of the Yale type, made for a slim round lock. The exterior light above the door picked out the most likely in the bunch. One by one she tried the longer, old-fashioned variety. There were four. The first key turning successfully would have been great. But lucky keys they were not. The fourth was the right one. It turned. Her heart racing, Lindsey pulled the door slowly open, praying it wouldn't rattle or that some big galoot wasn't standing on the inside waiting to grab them.

Inside was dimly lit. Offices behind glass partitions clung to the grey walls. A blank wall ran along their left-hand side. Above them banks of compressors hummed in unison, working to keep the cold store down to temperature.

Lindsey was amazed when her grandmother pushed past her, keeping low and padding ahead like a preying panther in pink tracksuit and trainers.

'Grandma! Stop,' Lindsey rasped. This was foolhardy. If she went too far forward without checking, someone was bound to see her.

She stopped dead, turned and loped back. 'You're right. Softly, softly. It's these shoes. They keep running away with me.'

Lindsey had been Miss Calm and Collected up until they'd entered the cold store. Her grandmother's behaviour unsettled her. She tried a few deep breaths before continuing.

Lindsey grabbed her grandmother's arm just in case she felt the urge to sprint across to the other side. She nudged her and put a finger to her lips indicating she remain silent.

'I didn't say a word,' hissed an indignant Gloria.

Lindsey didn't remark that she just had. This was no time to be factious. Her attention was already drawn to the other side of the open space where twin circles of light fell on the squeaky clean floor. Like gold doubloons they held her interest. She could easily be tempted to head for them. The headstrong half of her character screamed at her to do so. The half of her that dealt with self-preservation bid her to duck down behind a stainless-steel wheelie bin.

Her grandmother opened her mouth to speak. Lindsey clapped a hand over her parted lips and pointed to a shadow emerging into the open space.

A man dressed in black T-shirt and jeans went straight to the source of the light pools. For a moment his head intercepted the source of the light. Ash-grey darkness gave objects shape but not outline.

He reached out and fiddled with some kind of dial to the side of a double door and said something, but although she strained to hear what it was, she couldn't. Whatever he said ended in a chuckle; not a jolly chuckle, more a menacing one, the sort mad scientists sport as part of their trade.

As he moved away the pools of light fell out of the portholes in the double doors he'd been standing in front of. He disappeared to their left, his lengthy shadow diminishing with each echoing step.

With the beating of her heart pounding in her ears, Lindsey counted the passing seconds. Thirty, sixty, ninety . . . He had to be gone by now?

'They've got to be over there,' her grandmother said quietly.

Lindsey nodded.

Running fast and low, they gained the other side of the storage area and the big double doors.

Lindsey peered in through the porthole on her door. Her jaw dropped.

Her grandmother was shorter so had to stand on her tiptoes. 'Wish I'd worn heels,' she muttered, before her jaw dropped like an elevator to basement level. She'd spotted the headgear that was binding them together. 'Is that some kind of duo fashion statement they're wearing?' She sounded intrigued rather than surprised.

'It's practical,' said Lindsey. She didn't go into detail. Her thoughts were elsewhere. This was a very special moment. She hadn't told her mother, but she'd felt ashamed about getting involved with Oliver Stafford. She'd always prided herself on being a pretty good judge of character. Obviously she was not. It hurt, it embarrassed, and it also made her feel a great need for feeling good again. Rescuing her mother – and the occupant of the other half of the head-warming gear – would do that.

Using both hands, she struggled to heave up the lever locking the door. Whilst doing so her mind leapt to the next logical step. 'Call for help, but do it outside in case someone hears you.'

'Will do.' Her grandmother grabbed the phone swinging from a chain around her neck and loped back the way they'd come.

Hearing footsteps again, she ducked back behind the waste bin. Her breathing sounded too loud even to her own ears. Could anyone else hear?

She heard the footsteps come towards her hiding place, pause then retreat in another direction. Closing her eyes, she counted the seconds again. Ten, twenty, thirty.

Emerging from behind the bin, she made her way back to the freezer door, peered in and waved. Two faces as pale as frosted icing looked back at her and managed to return a hesitant, chilly wave of their own.

Wrapping both hands around the lever, she pushed it upwards. The lever made a clunking sound. A sliver of escaping air sighed as the seal was broken. Honey and Steve slid out right behind it, teeth chattering and arms flapping in an effort to get warm.

Lindsey jumped with them. She'd done it. Suddenly someone touched her shoulder. If there'd been a high jumping competition, she would have won it.

'I did it,' said Gloria, looking mighty pleased with herself.

'I need to phone for backup,' said Steve, his teeth chattering like castanets.

'Already done,' said Gloria.

'Not that I doubt you, but if you don't mind, a squad car

will get here more quickly if I phone . . .' Shivering, Steve took her phone and went back inside the cold room so as not to be heard.

'That's a good idea,' whispered Gloria, a telling look in her eyes. 'The police should be informed.'

Honey noticed that look and it worried her. 'Who did you ring, Mother?'

The whispering continued. 'Someone good at sorting out crooked butchers.'

On coming out from the cold room, Steve declared they had to lie low until they heard the wail of police sirens. 'Once we know we've got back-up, we can break cover. But not until then, otherwise we might all end up hung on meat hooks.'

He ordered them to go back behind the wheelie bins.

Honey started to go with Lindsey and her mother, but Steve was off in the other direction. 'What about you?'

'I need to tackle them,' he whispered back.

'Alone?' Her eyes widened at the thought. Her fear went rolling like barbed wire through her belly. 'And you're unarmed. Come with us.'

His eyes twinkled when he shook his head. 'I'm going to start the ball rolling. I have to. And I do have a weapon – of sorts.'

He held up the brassiere; the ends were tied round his hands in garrotting mode. The centre stiffness between the cups – flexible steel by the feel of it, would fit neatly against a windpipe. Never mind pillows, the bra cups had smothering potential.

Honey attached herself to his side. 'I'm coming with you.'

'No . . .'

'Yes. I need the action. I need to get my circulation going.'

'So do we,' said Lindsey and her grandmother.

Honey saw the mix of emotions flash through his eyes. Steve Doherty, rough-tough police officer, knew when he was beaten. Criminals were one thing; three generations of related females were something else.

They crept along behind him making for where the security guard had disappeared. They found him and his cohorts in a small office at the end of the corridor. Three of them were sitting around a table drinking beer. The other, identifiable as the driver of the truck, was sound asleep on a scruffy sofa, his snores resonating out into the corridor.

'Do we wait?' whispered Honey.

He was about to shake his head, but Honey's mother had caught a fine long fingernail on the frame surrounding the window.

'Drat! I paid good money for that!'

The men drinking heard her and sprang to their feet. The snoring evaporated.

Doherty looked anxious. He swore under his breath. He had no option but to act.

Kicking open the door, he barged in, his female support crowding in behind him. 'Halt! I'm a police officer.'

He fought to do things properly and get out his warrant card, his 'weapon' still in situ, wound around his fingers. The men stared. For a moment they were dumbstruck.

What would have happened then was anybody's guess, except that the sirens started, screaming like banshees as they hurtled down St Andrews Road and took the route to Roland Mead, Meat Trader and Cold Store. The men at the table and the suddenly roused truck driver ran, but were pursued.

In his haste to escape, the truck driver tripped over a roll of meat muslin and fell headlong into an empty waste drum, trapping him head down, his legs waving in the air.

Uniformed officers spilled through the door, grabbing the would-be escapees as Doherty directed.

'Him,' said Honey softly, her eyes alighting on the man in the black T-shirt and jeans. 'He's the one.'

'Chester,' said her mother. 'He's Roland Mead's chauffeur and does other stuff. Like Odd Job in that James Bond movie. He does everything for Roland, that dirty, stinking . . .'

'Like murder,' Honey said, dragging her mother to one side. 'Leave it to Steve. This is his baby now. He'll have Roland arrested.'

Her mother nodded. 'Quite so. That's why he rang the police.'

'So who did you phone to sort out your ex?'

'Won't tell you. Not until you tell me who got into Roland's computer system and found that secret file.'

'A friend,' said Lindsey. 'Warren Slade, him that was indisposed in room twenty. He did it. He found the secret bills of lading for meat and also the fuel bills and decided it didn't add up. There were journeys not accounted for; and the sizes of the fuel tanks didn't check out with the amount of fuel purchased. Warren Slade has a highly developed mathematical mind. It's all to do with probabilities and possibilities – at least, I think it is.' She looked at her mother and shrugged. 'You can't blame him for wanting some fun and getting tied to the bed. He's a very intense sort of bloke, almost to the point of obsession.'

Her grandmother looked amused. 'So is the friend I rang to sort out Roland. He's got a thing about bad butchers and crap meat.'

Honey burst out laughing.

Thirty-Seven

That morning, Roland Mead heard the hammering at the front door, but did nothing about it.

Rosellia, her of the glorious black hair and swaying hips, stirred beside him, her naked thigh against his. 'Do you hear that?'

He mumbled something incoherent and snuggled down against the cool cotton pillow. He'd only just turned the pillow over and loved the feel of its coldness on his face. He had intended making the most of it, and that is exactly what he would do.

'Chester is off,' said Rosellia, referring to Roland's right-hand man who carried out many tasks for his employer. Chester could be butler, chauffeur and even paid companion when Roland wanted it so.

The vain hope of getting him to go downstairs melted away. Rosellia swore in Italian. There was no other option but to slide her naked arms into a silk kimono. Padding down the stairs, she pondered on her reasons for staying with Roland. He was rich, but ignorant. Why hadn't she found herself a titled man; perhaps a count or a lord? A Swiss banker would have been equally acceptable, his wealth making up for lack of title. She could have stayed in Palermo, she mused, then frowned. Not Palermo. Much too provincial. Perhaps Rome.

The hammering continued. Rosellia's face clouded. The corners of her pouting mouth turned downwards. Whoever was at the door was going to get a tongue lashing. She glanced at her watch. It had to be Chester, though it was still early. Convinced she was right, she released the security chain.

As Smudger swept in, both her and the door swung back and smacked against the wall. She was knocked to the ground. Smudger jerked her to her feet, his big hands holding tightly to her arms.

'Where is he?'

Her big eyes got bigger. 'Who are you?'

'I'm me. Where's the gaffer?'

Shocked to the core, she pointed in a vague way at the stairs.

Smudger grimaced. 'I'll find 'im.'

He took the stairs two at a time. There were many doors along the landing, but only one was showing a gap of some fifteen inches. He crashed that open with as much finesse as he had the front door.

'You,' he said.

If the man had been wearing pyjamas he would have grabbed his jacket collar and dragged him from the bed. As it was Mead was naked; not a pretty sight in Smudger's opinion. Luckily the man had a hairy chest. Clutching great handfuls of chest hair, Smudger dragged Roland Mead from his bed, and literally threw him across the room. His toupee, the glue a little tacky from wearing it in bed, fell off and stuck to the carpet.

'Get dressed,' Smudger said with a ruthless glower. 'The game's up.'

Mead's first reaction was to go on the defence. 'I've eaten little pricks like you for lunch,' he snarled, his hands tightening into fists. 'Come on. Take a poke at me. Go on,' he said, dancing around and grinning as though he were Muhammad Ali when in fact he looked like an overweight dancing bear.

Smudger narrowed his eyes and fixed his thoughts on those Mead had wanted dead. He encountered a problem doing that, his emotions turning to blubber when he thought of what had happened. He needed to focus on something less emotional, but still something he cared about. He thought of rubbish steaks; those with too much fat, those cut too thin, those with too little marbling. It worked. His fingers curled into his palms. His knuckles rose to the challenge. One left hook and it was all over.

The police didn't question Roland Mead's bruised jaw. Smudger told them that Roland had fallen down the stairs.

'She's nothing to do with it,' Smudger added when they attempted to take Rosellia. 'I'll take care of her.'

He smiled at her.

Rosellia smiled right back. She liked the thought of a younger, more virile man taking care of her. OK, he wasn't rich, but until she found another sponsor, Mark Smith would be worth dallying with. She knew she had a role to play first as a witness testifying against her former lover. She'd known of the comings and goings at all hours of the day and night. She could give times and details. And hopefully a large reward was in the offing. A little money to please herself was exactly what she needed. Plus a blue-eyed, younger man. What could be better?

Thirty-Eight

They had a party to celebrate solving the case. Chester had been acting under Mead's orders.

Shattered from the ordeal in the freezer, Honey left Lindsey to make the arrangements. The list of guests pleased her; there they all were enjoying themselves in *her* bar, eating and drinking and laughing together. Even Mr Westlake, the Environmental Health Officer, popped in.

'I don't really have the time,' he said. 'Though I will soon be retired.' His worried eyes swiftly surveyed the room. 'Your mother's not around, is she?'

In response to Honey's 'not yet', he drank the last of his tonic water and bid a dignified though speedy retreat.

Before leaving to take some well-earned sleep, Steve Doherty laid out the whys and wherefores of what had happened. It turned out that Oliver Stafford had been getting a cut from the meat racket, but had stumbled on to Mead's other business. He'd been getting his cut of that too, but had been angling for more. Stella had been in on the cheap meat deal, but got stroppy when Oliver dropped her. She'd threatened to expose the dodgy meat deals and Mead had personally warned her to keep her mouth shut – hence the bruises around her neck.

'And Brodie?' Honey asked Steve.

'He was in financial difficulties, heard what was going on from a drunken Stella and tried to cut himself in. Stella was the loose link in the chain. She had a drink problem and couldn't help sounding off. The meat scam could lead to the drug scam. The gang controlling the deal couldn't chance a big bust. It was through Stella's drinking that Richard Carmelli found out. Once the people Mead worked for heard the bad news, they were all dead meat. Mead had no choice. He was in deep with some very heavy dealers. Chester was one of them, a mover and shaker rather than an odd-job man. Mead was scared of him.'

'And my mother?'

'Two pronged attack. Yes, I suppose he was after your meat order, but he knew of your position between the police and the Hotels' Association. He had orders to keep a tab on things.'

Honey couldn't resist stroking one of his tired-looking eyes. 'Are you going to bed now?'

He smiled. 'Are you?'

Lindsey chose that moment to interrupt. 'What shall I do with these?' She held up the unwanted item Honey had won at auction.

It was on Honey's tongue to tell her to throw the thing away, but somehow she couldn't do that. It had come in useful during the proceedings. Chucking it was like discarding a lucky charm.

'Hide it away somewhere. I'll think on it.'

Steve Doherty made arrangements to see her the following night. There were a lot of things to catch up on that had nothing whatsoever to do with police work, but he needed to rest before expending more energy.

She'd never expected to get rid of the awful underwear, but the phone call from Andrea Andover came from out of the blue.

'I hear you've got something that I could make use of.'

Honey tried to think what on earth she had that the large stunt woman could possibly find a use for. Not a clue!

'I'm doing a Valkyrie type of part for a Hollywood special – stunting for an actress who isn't up to doing anything more energetic than waddling into McDonald's.'

Anyone seeing Honey's expression would have described it as blank. She asked Andrea to elucidate.

Andrea did just that.

'There's a little item I believe you can help me with. I'm willing to pay. Alistair at Bonhams mentioned you bought them by mistake and in his opinion they're exactly what I'm looking for.'

Realization was like a strip of elastic going ping in Honey's brain. Did she mean the mountainous mammary controllers? She asked her.

Yep! Exactly that.

'As I said,' Andrea went on. 'It's a Valkyrie type of part – you know – metal corset and boob defenders the size of pan lids. I could do with a bit of softness to protect my natural padding, if you get my drift.'

'You can have the brazier – brassiere,' she corrected herself.

A price was negotiated. Delivery details were arranged. Honey couldn't help the self-satisfied smile as she ended the call.

'You look pleased with yourself,' said Lindsey, just back from running Grandma home. 'Anything to do with me?'

'I've got rid of something I really had no use for.'

Lindsey slid behind the reception desk and checked the computer over her mother's shoulder. 'You sound like one of my girlfriends referring to a guy she's finished with.'

Honey eyed her daughter's face and felt suddenly guilty. 'I'm sorry about my reaction to the Oliver Stafford thing. I must resolve not to make mountains out of molehills,' she said, stuffing the large bra into an equally large envelope.

'You're making a good start,' said Lindsey, nodding casually at the envelope. 'You were never going to grow into them.'

'Thankfully,' said Honey.

'Are you seeing Steve later?'

Honey smiled. Her thoughts reverted to that slinky black dress with the buttons, fishnet stockings and high-heeled red shoes. They were exactly what was needed.

'Tomorrow night. Once he's had a chance to catch up on his sleep.'